WHISPER DOWN THE COBBLES

WHISPER DOWN THE COBBLES

PRUDENCE JUPE

Cover design and formatting by Flintlock Covers
www.flintlockcovers.com

This book is dedicated to the people of Heptonstall.

Thank you to all the lovely folk we had the privilege to meet during our time living in Heptonstall. The supernatural events that did happen to us appeared spontaneously with no involvement from you! The majority of this story is pure fiction.

You have been a true inspiration and been held in our hearts for the past 25 years. We will never forget your hospitality, friendship and support. And a final thank you to The Cross Inn and Timothy Taylor for the beer!

CHAPTER 1

TAROT READING

It was a cold early January morning in 1998. Diane Fletcher, a barrister and her fiancé Mike Atherton, an RAF pilot, were house hunting in West Yorkshire.

Or perhaps the house was hunting them?

Either way, the loved-up couple had met a year after Di's divorce and had now decided to live deep in the heart of Brontë Country, centring their search on the tourist hotspot of Hebden Bridge. This little corner of the County was bursting with photogenic hamlets around the pretty market town, where cobbled streets rolled between terraces made of mill stone grit from local quarries. Somewhere between austere and beautiful, these terraces had sheer facades, blackened in places by the soot from the chimneys of the old woollen mills, as if an infernal fire had once raged through the streets. Around the town there were steep crags left by the quarries, now filled with deep green woods, and stone pack bridges spanning tumbling streams and canal. Tall mill chimneys still rose over the town, majestic monuments to an abandoned industrial age.

'It says here that Hebden Bridge is the lesbian and hippy capital of the North,' Di read from a local travel guide.

'Well, we won't hold that against it,' Mike retorted, scouring the window of yet another estate agent.

'Hey you, none of that!' Di slapped his arm playfully, mildly irritated by what she knew was his somewhat narrow-minded conditioning in the armed forces, along with the influence of his rather homophobic father. She knew that he was, in truth, a genuinely kind and good hearted man, and now that he was living back in 'civvy' life she was sure she'd soon persuade him to be more open-minded.

Mike was a Southerner. She was a northern girl, born, bred and raised not very far from here in the Calder Valley- in Uppermill; within a group of villages called Saddleworth. This was just over the other side of the moors and the M62.

From way back as a child she had lived a carefree exis-tence, roaming the hills, searching for foxes' lairs, catching frogs and sticklebacks in the ponds, and collecting wild flow-ers, blackberries and horse chestnuts. But her freedom to roam was brought to an abrupt end by the mysterious disap-pearance of a number of children. And then came the awful revelation that the wicked Myra Hindley and Ian Brady had buried the young bodies of their victims on the moors above her home village.

In spite of this, she still loved Saddleworth and felt no other place could be better. She'd been reluctant to move away at first, but she knew it was important to Mike. They were starting new lives together, they should find a place they could both call home, away from the memories of her previous marriage. And both felt this picturesque part of the world would be an easy compromise to make; Mike being fond of the North of England, and Yorkshire in particular, having spent much of his time in the RAF stationed near York.

They were both 44 years old, and still quite youthful, they made an attractive pair. Di was diminutive, slim brunette with large flashing green eyes and a sharp mind. In spite of her height of only 5' 1", she could put anyone in their place in an instant if required. Mike was dark haired, with brooding dark eyes, but more reserved than his ballsy outgoing 'wife to be'. He adored her and was very protective of her, but was nonetheless respectful of her independent and sometimes feisty nature.

Di browsed the little shop windows in the narrow street looking out for estate agents. Today they were in the neighbouring village to Hebden Bridge- Todmorden, and one shop caught her attention. Its sign was painted in gold and black against a purple background in Gothic lettering. 'The Black Cauldron.' Its large picture window was hung with a wispy black net curtain, behind which she could just make out a display of a vast array of bottles of every shape and colour. She felt drawn to the shop, not because she liked shopping; in fact, even going to the supermarket could make her feel positively queasy. But this little place had something compelling about it, and Di had an extremely curious nature, which was a perfect fit for a tenacious advocate.

'Shall we take a break from houses for a bit?' she said, tugging Mike towards the shop door.

'Hold on.' He tapped at a sign attached with Sellotape, just as Di went for the handle. 'BROWSERS NOT WELCOME it says.'

'Who says I'm a browser?' Di teased, a mock show of irritation on her face.

'Oh, are you a witch and you just forgot to tell me?' Mike smiled, indicating the gilded inscription above the door that said- *Spells, herbs, candles, wands, crystals and other artefacts for practising Wiccans and Pagans.*

'Sorry, I should have 'fessed up before you proposed!' Di joked. 'Or perhaps I didn't see the sign,' she winked.

'You can't claim to have missed it. It's huge and it's at head height, assuming you're not a hobbit.'

'Well, that's quite an assumption to make, given where we

are,' Di said, referring not just to the boutique of witchery, but to the street itself which looked as if it were straight out of Middle Earth. 'I'm surprised the place isn't swarming with annoying little students getting kitted out for their first term at Hogwarts.'

Di had just finished 'The Philosopher's Stone' which she'd borrowed from her daughter. She liked to keep an eye on her adored daughter's reading material, and she'd been surprised at how much she had loved it.

'You're mixing up your fantasy worlds.' Mike put a hand on the small of her back. This was both a display of affection and an attempt to lead her back to the house hunt.

But Di wouldn't budge from the door. 'If there was any dispute, it would be an open and shut case.'

'What do you mean?'

'Well, no one can even attempt to buy anything without first browsing. To browse simply means to survey goods for sale in a leisurely way. It implies nothing about an intention not to buy. Anyway, I'm a little chilly and could do with a warm-up'.

Mike looked at her with a delighted resignation and sighed. 'Yes, Your Honour.'

'It's your *learned friend*. I'm a barrister, not a judge.'

'You were a judge this morning, when I wanted to wear my brown corduroys.'

'They were tatty. You looked like a...' she searched for an inoffensive comparison, but couldn't find one. What she was thinking was that he looked like her ex in them, and she had always disliked corduroys along with leather patches on the elbows of jackets.

Mike laughed and kissed her, which meant he was quite happy with the smart designer blue jeans she'd encouraged him to wear instead.

'So come on!' She gently tugged him, not feeling quite as

fearless as she pushed the door and a bell clanged, alerting the shopkeeper to their browsing presence.

The warmth inside, mixed with a cloying cocktail of various types of incense and essential oils was stifling, and Mike had to duck between talismans, dream catchers and trinkets, all dripping from the ceiling. The walls of the shop were invisible behind shelves crammed with bottles of mysterious liquids, altar cloths, tarot cards, beeswax candles of every hue, small statues of pagan goddesses, crystal balls of varying sizes, and crystals of every hue. There were Grimoires and books on ancient rituals, and a pair of large stuffed black crows with glassy eyes in a metal cage which seemed to follow the pair. Their senses were overwhelmed by this cornucopia of pagan and new-age merchandise. Di hadn't seen so much tie-dye and crushed velvet in one place since her student halls in the eighties.

'Were tha born in a barn?' A gruff man's voice barked in a thick local brogue.

'Eh?' Mike said.

Di quickly turned and hissed at Mike to shut the door.

The gruff voice belonged to the shopkeeper who had mysteriously appeared from behind a deep green velvet curtain behind a glass display counter, under which was a beautiful display of rainbow-coloured crystals. He was a gaunt, middle-aged man with bony hunched shoulders, and a large shiny bald forehead trimmed with wispy hair and side burns. He had sunken rheumy eyes, protruding cheekbones, and wore a rather grubby looking white cheesecloth shirt with ill-fitting trousers of an indefinable colour.

'That's better. And what will yer be wantin' then?' the shopkeeper grunted.

'That's a warm welcome,' Mike muttered wryly.

'And a very good day to you,' Di said, emphasising her

own, albeit softer Yorkshire accent with the aim of reassuring the shopkeeper that they were no *mere* tourists.

'Did tha see t'sign ont winder?' the shopkeeper stepped menacingly from behind the counter.

'Yes, but we're not browsers.' Di said, cringing at herself. No point in reading the dictionary definition of browsing to this grump. However, desperate to confound his expectations and not be seen as a browser, Di quickly scanned the shop for something she might have come to buy. Her attention was caught by an inviting sign behind the shopkeeper's balding pate.

TAROT READINGS AVAILABLE HERE.

'A tarot reading please. We'd like a tarot reading,' she said, smiling, before hearing an aggressive clang of Mike's head smacking into some wind chimes as he turned to see what the hell she was doing.

The shopkeeper scowled, just as he'd been scowling since he entered from his curtain hideaway. He seemed to be examining Di's face now for evidence that she was having him on, which, in a way, she was, although the moment she asked for the reading she found herself hoping quite earnestly that he would not refuse. She'd never had a tarot reading before, as she had always taken the whole idea of fortune telling with a huge pinch of salt.

'Right,' the shopkeeper sighed as if it were a great inconvenience. 'That'll be five pounds, ta. If yer'll be both wanting it done, then it'll be a tenner.'

'Are you serious? Do we really have to?' Di heard Mike mumble in her ear, but she paid the money. The shopkeeper then shoved his head round a doorway at the back of the counter and up the stairs and shouted 'Ma! Customers!'

'What? Righto, be down in two shakes of a duck's tail,' came a rather breathy and deep voice from upstairs.

· · ·

Di and Mike watched wide-eyed as the shopkeeper's large rotund wife descended the steep narrow stairs a minute later. She had a lot of long, thick, wavy grey hair which curled over her ample bosom, a large fat hooked nose and a protruding huge brown hairy mole on her chin. Her bright green eyes were kind however, and her voice somehow exactly matched her appearance. She was a magnificent and magisterial sight, dressed in a midnight blue velvet robe embroidered with golden moons and stars. She whipped back a curtain behind the counter exposing an alcove, to give it a generous title, which could barely contain the small trestle table and small stack of green plastic garden chairs. She lifted three of these chairs and set them down around the table.

'Doooo sit down,' she said in an even deeper and huskier voice. 'It's nearly time to make His Majesty's lunch, so we had better begin.'

'Aye, I could eat t'oven door if it were buttered!' her husband added, which somewhat broke the magic of the moment.

'What?' Mike looked askance at this remark, his eyebrows shooting skywards.

'And that's all you'll be getting if you don't stop yer grumbling!' His wife retorted. The shopkeeper harrumphed and closed the curtain behind them, going back to his position in the shop. She then turned to her new customers. 'My name is Roslyn,' she cooed, holding out her chubby hand to her guests and squeezing behind the table, with a great deal more poise than she had, catching her robe on something sticking out of the wall in the process.

Mike and Di shook her hand briefly, then sat across her, making great efforts not to smirk as she took down from a shelf a large pack of gold-edged tarot cards together with a plush deep blue velvet cloth. She spread this out on the table, placing the beautifully illustrated cards in the centre, and began to shuffle the deck while her eyes kept glancing over their shoulders as if looking at others beyond the small space. She asked Di if she wanted to cut the cards. Di did so and handed them back. Roslyn laid the first three cards on the table face down.

'Ahhhh,' Roslyn dramatically breathed in and out several times, tossing her head back so dramatically that she hit it on the wall behind her.

Di sunk her fingers into Mike's thigh to stop them both from laughing then, as invited by Roslyn, she turned the first card of the three: **Justice**. Di unexpectedly drew in a breath as she admired the ornate, colourful medieval drawings.

Mike nudged Di and pointed at the card.

'Ahhhh,' Roslyn said again and nodded, almost smiling, but clearly conscious not to stretch her lips too far, in an effort to retain an air of authority. 'The spirits are with us. There's someone who's connected to law.'

'Yes,' Mike hissed with far too much excitement, causing Di to sink her fingers further into his thigh to tell him he was giving too much away.

'Aye,' Roslyn pounced. 'Someone connected to the law has recently passed over who you are very close to…" Her mouth gaped fish-like and her large green eyes bulged as she urged Di to offer the answer, but Di wasn't giving anything away. 'Your mother…?'

Di shook her head.

'Father…?'

She shook her head again.

'No, no, it's coming clearer now,' Roslyn said, closing her eyes. 'Your uncle…' She prized one eye open ever so slightly to gage Di's reaction.

Di shook her head, trying to look rather anxious than amused.

'Your aunt?'

She pouted apologetically.

Roslyn, eyes wide open again, was looking desperate. '*Any*one?'

Mike couldn't contain himself – 'It's *you*, babe. It's her. She's a lawyer,' he blurted out.

'Ah!' Roslyn exclaimed, whacking her head on the wall again. 'Eee,' she rubbed at where the bump would soon be forming. 'Now it begins to make sense. It was your mother who was telling me *you* were a lawyer. And she's very proud of that, you know.'

Di shook her head yet again.

'What?' Roslyn said irritably.

'My mother's alive.'

'Are you sure?'

Di nodded.

'Your grandfather..?'

'I never met either of my grandfathers, so I doubt it would be either of them.' Then in an effort to help the poor woman, she added, 'Maybe it was my father? He died when I was only seventeen, and I was very close to him.'

'Ah yes, I can see more clearly now. Perhaps if I turn another card, my spirit guide will tell me what the cards are trying to say to you.' She hurriedly looked at her watch. She turned the second card: '**Death!**'

'Jesus,' Mike whispered.

'Do not fear,' said Roslyn in a sage tone. 'Death need not mean death. It might mean…'

'Change?' said Di, not really knowing where this came from - and instantly regretted being such a know-it-all when she saw how crestfallen Roslyn was. So added, 'At least, I think….. Is that right?'

'Aye, it is,' Roslyn said regaining a morsel of authority, and looked as if she was about to speak again when her eyes suddenly rolled back and she inhaled long and hard. 'There is someone from the other side who has joined us,' she wheezed.

Mike and Di gave each other a sarcastic look, eyebrows raised.

Roslyn opened her eyes again, as wide and sparkly as crystal balls. 'The letter D- now what could that mean?'

Di looked at her – 'well my name begins with a D, as you know.'

'But it definitely isn't you this time. D'you know anyone who has passed on, whose name begins with D?' Before Di could rain on her parade, she added, 'Or their name ends with D?' She was floundering now. 'Or perhaps there's a D in the middle of their name… or… *somewhere*…?'

'Another card?' Di offered.

Roslyn nodded and Di turned the last.

'**This suggests the Devil!**' Her eyes were blazing.

'I hope this means good things and not what it says,' Mike shuddered, 'like Death didn't mean death.'

'No,' Roslyn frowned, as if Mike was stupid, her voice deepening even further, 'but it does strongly suggest bad things. Very bad things.' Then she shuddered and lowered her voice to a whisper, 'And I am sorry, but I'm very much afraid they're coming your way.' She stared at Di for a moment before suddenly looking away, theatrically, into the distance.

Against their better judgement, Di and Mike both wanted more, but Roslyn, suddenly and with quiet determination, packed up her tarot deck. Then stood up, knocking over her chair.

'It's getting late. I'm sorry. You will have to go. You can have half your money back. George, give these folks their tenner!' And, as quickly as her small feet and large round body could carry her, she whipped back the curtain and exited the door behind the counter without even saying good-bye, catching her robe on the frame again as she went blundering by.

CHAPTER 2
GRAVESTONES

Di and Mike found themselves on the cold and windy street again, blinking in the relative brightness of the late winter afternoon and searching each other's faces for clues as to what had just happened.

'Well, that was a bit weird,' Mike said quietly, glancing furtively at the people passing by, who were blissfully oblivious of the shop and what had happened there.

'It's actually more than weird. It's bloody irresponsible,' Di said as she marched off down the street, the unease which had gripped her inside the shop now transmuting to anger. 'Crooks like that pray on the grief of others, or their fears. If we were stupid enough to believe what she said, we'd be worrying ourselves sick right now.'

'But she did get some things right,' Mike said, trying to keep up with her.

'Like what?'

'The Justice card?' Mike said weakly.

'Mike!' Di scolded him, but threaded her arm through his lovingly at the same time. 'That's how it works. Say something vague enough so that the client can make a connection to it, however tenuous.'

'I suppose,' Mike sighed, sounding almost disappointed.

'If I wasn't a lawyer, one of us could still make *some* connection to the law. Everyone knows someone who's had a brush with the law, or has a relative or friend who might work in the field. Our brains do all the work and the so-called clairvoyant takes the credit. And our money.'

'Yeah,' Mike said, squeezing her hand. 'You're right, of course. But don't let it spoil the *vibe*.'

As Mike hoped, this made Di smile. 'Vibe, eh? I see you're soaking up the hippy mood of the place.'

When the old mill town was in steep decline in the sixties and seventies, squatters had moved in and then it had become a magnet for hippies and artists. It was soon known as a place of tolerance – hence the high concentration of gay people; and these days, Hebden Bridge and Todmorden were both more bohemian than any other market towns in Yorkshire, with a medley of organic, locally sourced and vegetarian eateries, independent coffee houses, eco-friendly clothing shops and cultural venues. And with that came the tourists. From all corners of the globe they came, to see the inspiration for the Bronte sisters' classics in Haworth just a few miles away, and the home of poets like Sylvia Plath and Ted Hughes who came from the nearby village of Mytholmroyd.

'Shall we drive towards Hebden Bridge up to that little village of Heptonstall?' Mike suggested.

'Which one?' Di asked.

'The one with the lovely looking stone cottages for sale. We saw them in the last estate agent's.'

Something in the back of Di's mind, still riled by Roslyn and her tarot reading had wanted to question why there seemed to be so many cottages for sale in one small village, but she didn't want to spoil the *vibe*. She was so relieved that Mike was happy to be here, a world away from where he was brought up, that she banished the thought from her mind and said, 'Yes. Let's go!'

They went back to the car and drove out of town along the Calder Valley, back towards Hebden. Just prior to the main town they took a left turn up a steep lane.

It was no more than half a mile to the little village of Heptonstall, and the charm of the place impressed them instantly. It looked as though the clock had stopped three hundred years ago and time had stood still.

'Just like in a Hovis advert,' Mike grinned, peering out through the windscreen.

The winding lane had narrowed and become a well-worn cobbled street, with rows of beautiful weaver's cottages flanking either side, each with stone doorsteps worn smooth by so many centuries of clogs and boots tramping over them. Di spotted intriguing narrow 'ginnels' between the houses leading to who knew what, while farmhouses peppered the wide acres of surrounding countryside beyond. As they drove up the steep road towards the village, they spied the steep crags covered in deep deciduous woodland, which gave way to the vast wild moors, stitched together like a huge quilt by hundreds of drystone walls.

When they'd parked the car in Church Lane and pulled up their collars against the cold wind whistling down the lane, they tramped hand in hand through the village, with the excitement of kids at Christmas.

Di noticed a dozen people gathered up ahead. They couldn't be missed. Standing together in a place like this was tantamount to a crowd. And what made them more conspicuous was that they were clearly not from around these parts. Or even this nation for that matter.

'Japanese tourists,' Mike muttered.

'How do you know?' Di said with a degree of mischief.

'Er…' Mike said sarcastically. 'The eyes and the hair and the massive cameras around their necks?'

'They could be Chinese,' Di said. 'Or Korean.'

'Smart arse,' Mike smiled at her as he pulled her close.

As they neared the crowd they saw that the tourists were hanging on to every word of a skinny young man who must have been their guide. He had thick brown hair tied back in a ponytail, and a rather sparse and scraggy goatee beard. His grey eyes loomed large behind thick round wire-rimmed glasses, and he was using a huge golfing umbrella to point out what he thought might be of interest to the group. As she started to listen to what he was explaining, Di thought that the tourists might not be hanging on to his every word, but rather trying desperately to understand what he was saying. His accent was almost as thick as George's from The Black Cauldron, and she knew Mike would struggle to understand some of it, even though he ostensibly spoke the same language.

'Shall we?' Di said, cocking her head at the group.

Mike nodded as if they were doing something naughty by tagging along.

They positioned themselves at the back of the group and listened as the guide continued his spiel.

'These cottages on either side o' th'street were built from local mill stone quarried here just below th' village. The quarrying created the crags yer'll see should ya take paths through woods to valley floor. Some of th' cottages date from twelfth century as did th' first church here, St Thomas a Becket's, but it were ruined which yer'll see in due course.' As he said these last words those magnified eyes of his caught Di's, as if his words were meant only for her. And she immediately felt the hairs on the back of her neck stand up as if a cold breeze had just passed through the street.

'Main industry here were wool weavin'. The wool came from sheep farms which surround th' village," he went on, in the same lecturing tone. "Each small cottage was often inhabited by half a dozen families, oftentimes six members of a family t' each room. Conditions were extremely pooer."

And then, as if an aside- 'The population has decreased tremendously now. Only one family t' each cottage, prob'ly.'

And with that he strode off, the tourists following closely up the cobbled street.

They came to The Cross Inn where he announced, 'There wa' as many as six pubs here in times gone by. Now only two remain, The White Lion and this 'ere...*my* local, The Cross', he added, as if mourning the lack of places he could get a pint these days, though to Di, two pubs seemed like a glut for such a small place.

He continued in a lower tone, almost as an aside, 'Folks say there's a hidden fireplace in Th' Cross where a man was once burned alive. But it's all bin bricked up now. If it wa' ter be uncovered, 'oo can tell what might be discovered or what might be unleashed.'

Di shuddered again and glanced over at 'The Cross' which, contrary to its apparent infamy for violence, looked like a very welcoming establishment. She was beginning to feel this tour guide was enjoying a generous dollop of poetic license.

Next they came to a village square where the guide informed them that Mummers and Morris dancers came regularly to entertain the villagers. To Di it all seemed very quaint, romantic and unspoilt, not unlike a couple of other villages in the area made famous by the Brontë novels and *Last of The Summer Wine*, which were the destinations for many more tourists every day than this little group of camera clickers.

Even the ancient church looked desolate and abandoned. Its walls, arches and tower still stood proudly, the setting winter sun gilding the stone, but its roof was missing and everything inside was gone, leaving a mystical yet romantic shell. What Di found slightly unsettling was the size of the graveyard, which resembled a giant paved patio. It was made up of hundreds of graves, many of them lacking headstones and so tightly packed together that their group had to walk over them as they passed through.

Di's sense of unease, which she was trying to ignore, was exacerbated when the guide said in a low moan:

'Church and chapel now only echo with voices of 'undreds of parishioners long passed away. They are lyin' 'ere beneath our feet. There's so many buried 'ere, they are piled up five er six deep. Can you hear 'em?' The guide went on, as if reciting a rhyme, exaggerating his Yorkshire accent: 'Clogs rattling down the cobbles, hundreds, in yonder year, dawn breaking, clogs would clatter, down the ancient paths through the trees t'mills below. Chillun as young as five, carrying meagre lunches, bread, an' if they were lucky, a scrap o' cheese and half an apple, in an old cloth clutched tightly in theeir little hands, blue wi' th' cawd!'

Di glanced at Mike who was wide-eyed at the images the guide was conjuring.

'Young boys and girls, men and women all, still quiet in th' early mornin', still wipin' sleep from theeir eyes, still weary from yesterdis grind at t'mill, and the long climb up steep hill for theeir meagre evenin' meal.'

And then he went on to tell them about how further back in the past, men and women had worked looms in low rooms in their cottages, before 'new-fangled steam-powered machinery', such as 'spinning Jenny', had taken their independence away and forced them to slave in the mills.

'Aye, spinning machines may 'ave improved the quantity and lowered price o'spun yarn, but did not do so much improving the lives of pooer folks. 'Only on Sundis was theeir any respite from t'dudgery.'

The guide pointed with his umbrella.

'Int' church, th'ole population turned out, in theeir Sundi

best, all clean and shiny for th' preacher, eager for message o'ope, but offentimes only to hear themselves lambasted for theeir sins.'

And on he went to tell them, how before 1847, services had been held at this old church of St Thomas a Becket's. Thomas murdered in 1170. The church built between in the 1250s. And parishioners had worshiped here until-

The guide swung his closed umbrella in a great arch, framing the picture he painted- 'One night with fearful strong winds a'raging, th'ole o'west face fell away.'

'Must have been one *hell* of a storm to do that,' Mike whispered doubtfully to Di.

'Now, these old ruins stand silent,' intoned the guide. 'But when mists and mizzles swirl through this place, as it very often does, it's like a ghostly film. Count Dracula himsel' maybe visits now and then, o' most likely evil David 'Artley er 'is brother visits on dark neyts.'

'Who were the last two?' Mike asked Di, who'd been working hard as his translator throughout the tour. But this time she couldn't help him.

'David Hartley? Not a clue.' But she jumped as the guide's voice suddenly came from over her shoulder, as though he had moved there specially to whisper in her ear:

'There's many a dark secret about this place.'

She turned to see his grey eyes, huge and round behind his thick glasses, boring into her. She didn't know what to do or how to respond. Suddenly a crow cawed loudly and raucously somewhere above her head, and she saw that the sky was now as moody and grey as the gritstone that made the graves beneath their feet.

But then the guide moved away and continued on, loudly so that the whole group could hear, 'If tha knows famous poet, Ted Yews who hails from these parts, he wrote a poem about this 'ere church. It's only a short un and if ya likes, I'll recite it fer yer.'

His enthused audience nodded and mumbled assent, so he recited the Ted Hughes poem *Heptonstall Old Church*, an esoteric piece that didn't make much sense to Di and probably not to anyone else in the group, but the guide's delivery was enough to tell them all that it was laced with sadness, describing a place of light and song that turned into a place of darkness and untethered decay.

He paused and looked around with his eyebrows raised as he finished, waiting for a response. Di gave an involuntary shudder. She didn't feel like clapping but she did so anyway and murmured her appreciation, the others following her lead. The guide took a small bow and, without a word, strode off beyond the graveyard. They all followed like bewildered sheep to a much larger and rather imposing Victorian edifice: another church, this one still functioning; though as their guide put it, 'It's nowt different from all th' other Victorian Churches to look at. I prefer t'other 'un mesel.'

Di had to agree, but the Japanese (or Chinese or Korean) tourists seemed to be getting excited now, as if they were reaching the destination of a pilgrimage and their guide responded accordingly:

'Now then, as many of yer may know, we have another famous poet lying in the new graveyard just beyond. The beyootiful but very fragile American wife of Ted Yews, Sylvia Plath.'

Di's ears pricked up at the mention of Sylvia Plath. She had had no idea Sylvia Plath was buried here. Her suicide was such a tragic end to a passionate love story – she had been such a wonderful poet. Di had studied her in the sixth form at school. At the time she'd been going through a depressingly difficult time herself after losing her father, and had found some solace and affinity with Sylvia's poems. She remembered reciting 'The Mad Girl's Love Song' in her last year at school. She'd even set it to music.

'Di, are you OK? You look pensive darling,' Mike said sounding concerned.

Di snapped herself back to the present.

The tourists were jostling for pole position behind the guide as he led them up to the new grassy graveyard, which was at the top of a crag, beyond the large, imposing and rather sinister Victorian church, where he pointed his umbrella at a surprisingly unprepossessing, pale grey, pitted marble gravestone:

IN MEMORY
SYLVIA PLATH HUGHES
1932 - 1963
EVEN AMIDST FIERCE FLAMES
THE GOLDEN LOTUS CAN BE PLANTED

It looked as though someone had tried to obliterate by scratching out the name 'Hughes' – or had added the name later, badly.

Di would have been only about 9 years old in 1963, the year that Sylvia died.

The small grave in front was planted with various perennial plants – most were dull and dormant now, but a thoughtful person had recently laid a bunch of yellow shop-bought roses on top.

'Aye, she were a beauty if ever there was one, and she wrote bloody good poetry an' all. A tragic case o' suicide cos she were a bit on th' sensitive side and it's said she were wronged by Ted Yews who couldn't keep his hands of other women. He were a bit on t' odd side an all, an' I quote, 'sometimes jubilant, sometimes tormented'. Not really yer typical Yorkshire man, us lot normally being straightforward and useful sort o' chaps'. The guide smiled momentarily. 'Owever, by my notion, there were a bit more to it than that, but maybe that's not fer now'.

Di had found herself nodding in appreciation of his observations, but was bemused by this last comment.

However, the guide went on: 'Sylvia were even mooer tormented. Not as resilient as Ted. She were described as 'avin' a *"stormy luminous senses and a violent, almost demonic spirit."* And atter six years o'marriage, unfaithful Ted left 'er and she tragically took 'er own life.'

Di found herself gripping Mike's arm tightly, a relationship that disastrous was unimaginable to her, in the blissful light of her engagement to her gorgeous, kind and loving fiancé.

The guide gave the group a few minutes to ponder and reflect, while the majority used the time to take photos of themselves hugging the gravestone.

'Who knew Sylvia Plath was so big in Japan!' Mike giggled, watching them.

'Or China,' Di countered.

'Or Korea,' Mike smiled.

Then they all plodded back down to the village.

'I don't know about the likes o' you lot,' said the guide, 'but it's way past openin' time, so I'm off fer a few scoops. If you enjoyed yer tour of the village, yer welcome to donate a bob o' two fer me beer fund.'

He took off his cap and held it out. Di didn't hesitate to put a fiver in it, and so did Mike. They had no doubt it was much better spent than the one they'd parted with in the Black Cauldron shop. As the tourists followed suit, the guide leaned over to Di and muttered.

'Me name's Robert. And there's a lot more I can tell thee about this place which tha need to know if tha wants to live here.'

Di opened her mouth to say, *'How did you know we were planning to live here?'* but he stopped her with:

'I'm off ter wet me whistle. Come find me if tha' really wants to know.' And with his pocket jingling and rustling with cash, he strode off across the cobbles and up the steps into The Cross Inn.

As they watched him go, Mike said, 'Come on love, it's been a long day. I don't know about you, but shall we call it a day and come back next weekend?'

Di readily agreed.

CHAPTER 3
THE VIEWING

That week Di thought of nothing else but Heptonstall, and whenever she called Mike, it seemed he was doing the same. Neither of them remembered the grey skies and gravestones, nor the ghoulish tint Robert the tour guide had painted the place with. He'd just been entertainment for the tourists, Di told herself, recalling his rambles about *many a dark secret* the village held.

Her memories of the place were otherwise more than fond; the low winter sun bathing the old ruined church in gold and the sense of being in a land that time forgot. She imagined the click of weavers' looms coming from the casement windows of the cottages in an era free of machines, free of TVs or phones, free of a daily tsunami of unwanted consumerism and the desperate treadmill of so-called civilisation that the industrial revolution had paved the way for. She somehow felt pulled to that place. She was sure she and Mike and her daughter would be happy there.

And so the next weekend they were back at the estate agent's. It was within spitting distance from the tarot reader's shop, but Di had no compulsion to go back to The Black Cauldron. She made a point of not even looking across the road at it, as the estate agent showed them the details of a charming converted stone property for sale called Goose Barn in the heart of Heptonstall, behind the main street and the Cross Inn.

'It's mid seventeenth century,' said the estate agent. 'It used to be part of a pub complex called The Goose Inn, as were all the cottages in Goose Fold. Large dressed stone, top two courses renewed, we estimate, in the early twentieth century. Stone slate roof. Mullioned windows. And it's all been fully renovated by the current owner with top quality materials.'

'Sounds amazing,' Mike said, nodding enthusiastically. 'What do you think, darling?'

But Di was distracted. Her eyes were now fixed exactly where she had told herself not to look - at the shop across the street. Because Roslyn, the tarot reader, was standing in the doorway, in her robes, looking directly at Di through the window of the estate agent's. For a protracted moment, Roslyn's face was as unmoving, before melting into a warm and kind, but melancholy smile, and Di found herself returning it. Then Mike brought her back into the conversation with his hand on her waist.

'Darling?'

'Oh, yes,' she said, smiling at the two men. 'It sounds perfect. And I love mullioned windows.'

'When can we go and see it?' Mike asked.

'Let me call the owner. Try and get you up there today.'

As the estate agent made the call, Di looked back out across the street, but the tarot reader was gone and the door of the shop was firmly shut again. The sign discouraging browsers was readable even from where Di stood, and she found herself smiling as she remembered the laugh she and Mike had, as they'd debated going in last weekend. She put her arm around him now, and they both watched the estate agent speak to the owner over the phone. He was effecting a seemingly forced, patient tone, only to shake his head as he hung up the phone.

'Everything all right?' Di asked.

'Oh yes, it's OK,' he smiled. 'It's just the owner. Can I say something in confidence?'

They both nodded, 'of course'.

'Be prepared. He's a bit on the blunt side, shall we say.'

'I'm from not a million miles from here,' Di said. 'I'm quite used to that.'

'Oh, good.' The agent grimaced. 'Because this bloke is the embodiment of millstone grit through and through.'

They all exchanged a polite chuckle, then the agent added, 'Though to be fair, he has personally renovated the place beautifully. I know I shouldn't really disclose this, but he's only selling because he and his wife have separated and they are in the middle of getting a divorce. But please don't tell him I told you.'

Di and Mike gave their reassurances to be tactful and discreet.

'So when can we go?' said Mike.

Less than an hour later they were parking the car once again in Heptonstall and strolling hand in hand through the village. They found the tiny lane which led to Goose Yard, which was behind Goose Fold and the main street, and mere meters, as the crow flies, from the abandoned church.

Mike and Di squeezed each other's hand as they entered the cobbled yard and spotted the house, both of them falling in love with it immediately. From the outside, it looked, as the agent had said, beautifully renovated. A large glazed barn door constituted a large part of the front of the house, outside of which stood a cast iron water pump. There was also a polished normal sized wooden door with a large knocker. Outside was a cobbled courtyard in the centre of which was a beautiful stone well. This had a pitched and tiled roof with all the mechanism required to make it authentic, including a chain with an iron bucket. It looked like it was in good working order. Such equipment, so common and necessary in times past, was not so now, but it was very decorative and expertly restored nonetheless. Opposite the well, up a few steps was a small restored double-fronted building, which appeared to have been a piggery or even a place to keep geese for meat, as was the case in days gone by. The couple eagerly went to the wooden door of the house and knocked, grinning at each other with childish enthusiasm and excitement.

The door was opened moments later by a thick set, middle-aged, ginger-haired man in brown corduroy trousers and a thick checked shirt. Di shot a glance at Mike, remembering her objection to his trousers last weekend.

Leonard, or Len as he'd come to be known, sported a dense ginger beard and moustache, above which his piercing blue eyes glared at them without expression, making them both doubt for a moment that they'd knocked on the right door.

'Good afternoon,' Mike said, 'We are here to view your property.'

The man looked them up and down as if they were creatures from another planet.

'If this *is* the right place,' Mike added.

The man continued to glare from one to the other, wordlessly, and looked the both of them up and down.

Mike persevered and stuttered, 'Did the estate agent not inform you?'

Then without so much as an *ey up*, the man said in a voice as gruff as his appearance, 'Nah look here! I spake me mind. I wus not for putting me 'ouse on th' market mesel', but th'owd cow would have none on it. If it were up to me, I would not be selling and I'm afraid, if I don't tek to you, I might not anyways, and that'd gi' 'er summat else to mooan about.'

After a short, stunned pause, Di cut in before Mike could speak again. 'D'you think it's worth us looking round just in case you do take to us? she asked tentatively. 'It's a beautiful house,' she said with honesty, which she hoped would get them across the threshold. 'It looks so very nicely renovated.' She said peering past him into the kitchen-dining room. 'Did you do *all* this work yourself?'

That seemed to do the trick. She saw the man's shoulders relax and then, bristling with pride, he said, 'O' course I did, luv. It's been a bloody labour of luv, tha' knows. Blud, sweat and tears. Ev'ry last stone, beam and lintel, hefted and put up wimme own two hands. Allus working on it fer two years wi'out a break.'

Di glanced at Mike and saw he was straining to understand everything the man said, but she knew now was not the time to translate.

'How wonderful,' Di smiled with genuine admiration. 'We can't imagine how difficult it must be for you to let it go.'

The gruffness seemed to abandon the man for a moment. He sighed heavily. 'Ah weel, I've had me share of happiness o'er th' years. Nowt to moan about really. But I were hopping up and dahn wi' fury th' first few weeks after she upped and scrammed wi' me bricky. Nivver thought she'd be one o' them sorts o' women.'

Mike clearly got the gist of what he was saying now and the man looked so sad that Mike found himself putting an hand on his arm and saying, 'Don't worry. I'm sure you'll make a profit on all your hard work.'

Di cringed. Not just because she had a feeling that touching him like that might well be overstepping a boundary for this dyed-in-the-wool man of the moors, but also because she didn't reckon profit was high on the agenda of this jilted husband. And judging by his reaction, Di was right, but not quite for the reason she expected.

'Eee,' said the man, his shoulders stiffening again, 'there'll be nowt left fer me, atter she's fleeced me.'

Di threw an almost imperceptible glare at Mike. He had set them back, just when she was getting somewhere. To make progress, Di sensed that the man and his lovely property was in need of some appreciation, so she lavished it and him with praise and before long the man's shoulders were softening again.

'My name's Di, by the way,' she said holding out her hand, 'and this is Mike'.

'Oh aye,' the man said, shaking her hand with his huge one, which felt as rough as his manner. 'Leonard. Len.'

And at last, they were over the threshold.

The property inside was even better than outside. It boasted a large lounge with high beamed ceilings, a beautiful country kitchen and a small beamed breakfast area leading off. A wooden staircase led to a spacious landing on the first floor with an arched window. This had a stone window seat that would have looked quite at home in the ruins of Thomas a Becket's over the way. There were two double bedrooms and a huge bathroom with his 'n' hers sinks - and the 'piece de resistance', – the biggest bath Di had ever seen. Di's eyes widened as she imagined the evenings she could spend, wallowing in there with her favourite scented bubble bath, with candles burning and a good book.

Len saw her staring at the bath and explained, 'That there is the best jikoozi bath you'll ever see, is that. I fixed on it t'impress missus. Thought we could both on us gerr in it fer a bit o' fun, if yer get mi meanin, burr it din't work.' Di thought this was too much information.

'Is it broken?' Mike ventured.

'O' course it int,' Len snapped. 'It works well enuff. T'were missus that din't!'

At this, Di quickly pushed back her unwelcome thoughts, and they moved on, ooo-ing and ahhh-ing their way round the house, in part to maintain a reasonable place in Len's good books, but mainly because the house genuinely deserved such plaudits.

Two further bedrooms in the eaves had no doors to them. But there was no need as they had their own separate and private stained and polished pine staircases. They were utterly charming, with exposed beams and skylights for windows, which gave an intriguing view over the roofs of the cottages towards the ruins of the old church and the spire of the new one beyond.

As Di focused her gaze nearer, on the roof top of Goose Barn, she realised that there were three huge crows perched on the chimney. At this proximity she was taken with the quality of their blackness, as though their feathers were covered in fresh shiny tar, tinged with indigo. With their heads on one side, they seemed to be watching her and listening thoughtfully, as if they were weighing up her potential as a resident in the village, assessing her suitability as a buyer for the house, not unlike Len. They suddenly took off with a wild flapping of their pitch wings and a cacophony of cawing, making Di flinch. But she continued watching, mesmerised, as they flew towards the silhouette of the Victorian church tower beyond the ruins of the old church. She couldn't shake the thought that they were carrying their verdict of her and Mike back to some master of theirs, who had their dwelling in that vicinity. She turned away from the skylight and tried to focus on what he was telling Mike - about why the ensuite bathroom adjoining this bedroom was still half-finished.

'When th'owd cow told me she was fed up wi' me, I couldn't be arsed,' he grumbled. 'She had me build this bloody house up, then buggered off wi' me bricky. That's all thanks I get after me purrin up wir 'er nagging for twenty odd bloody years, randy cow.'

Di and Mike, both divorcees themselves, nodded empathetically, but as Len led them back downstairs, all Di wanted to think about was her own imminent wedding to Mike and a future which looked picture perfect to her in this moment, especially if they could live in this house. It was cosy and homely for them as a couple, yet big enough to house all five of their children, should they ever descend upon them at the same time, which they hoped they would, - often. Mike's three were almost grown up, as was Di's son, but her youngest, a daughter, was only eleven. Di and her ex-husband shared custody of Rachel, so it was Rachel who Di had very much in mind while looking around Len's house. She felt sure that Rachel would love it.

The only thing that made Di a little uneasy was a glass panel in the floor at the far end of the living room, just in front of the front window which looked out over Goose Fold. Perhaps it was the thought of Rachel standing on the glass and it breaking that worried her, or just that it seemed a little creepy. The glass covered a hole which was about four feet square – large enough for a body to fall down – and of indeterminate depth. A light had been installed inside, but it only lit the top couple of feet. Whatever was below, that remained in darkness.

'Len, what's down there?' Di asked as she peered into it, feeling a sudden strange, unwelcome sense of slight sickness.

Len hesitated, and it seemed to Di that he swallowed hard before he replied; 'Ah, weel lass, that were the well that were in th' cellar of th'old Goose Pub. I've had it all blocked off now which seemed to do the trick...' Len's voice trailed off and he continued to look hesitant.

Di was worried this was an issue that might affect them buying the house. But she didn't really want to know because, in her mind, she had already moved in.

Mike was more cautious where such a major purchase was concerned, and he asked, 'Was it causing damp?'

'No, it wasn't that. It was a bit deep and I wasn't sure where th' bloody thing ended up....' He muttered something else. Di could have sworn he said, '...or what were down there.'

But Mike was already asking, 'Why didn't you just seal the whole thing over and have done with it?'

Len replied, 'I thought it would be a nice feature fer th'ouse. Looks pretty good when it's all lit up at neyt. And I thought it would please th'old cow, but atter all th'ard work she nivver took to th'ouse, and she nivver took t'mesell atter th'ouse were finished.' He looked downcast again. As they stood at the front door, just as Di was about to say something nice to comfort him, he barked, 'So? D'yer like th'ouse or what?'

Di quickly forgave his directness because to answer him was easy. 'It's lovely, it really is.'

'Yes, it is,' Mike added, 'but we need to think about it for a bit, naturally. It's the first house we've viewed'.

'Well, tek yer time,' Len said kindly, opening the door. 'Be good to make th'old cow sweat a bit.' He then changed tone and added brusquely, 'But if yer come back and it's sold, then it'll be yer own fault.' He turned to look outside. 'By eck, it's cawd. Have yer done? I'm fer shutting t'dooer now.'

Di couldn't help but smile at the less than subtle hint that it was time for them to go, so they thanked Len for the tour and went on their way.

Di looked back over her shoulder more than a few times as they walked slowly out of the yard in the evening gloom. She pictured herself cooking in the cosy farmhouse kitchen of Goose Barn, watching telly in the living room in front of the huge wood-burning stove, her car parked in the cobbled yard. She thought of Rachel having great fun making bubbles in the big jacuzzi bath, and them all exploring the countryside which was right on the doorstep. She imagined a huge, tall Christmas tree, lit up with a myriad of coloured lights in front of the barn door windows, and all the cosy evenings they could have, roasting chestnuts and toasting marshmallows.

She had one more chance to glance over her shoulder as they turned towards the lane and, as she did, she thought she saw the light beaming up from the glass-covered well in the living room, and the silhouette of Len standing over it, looking down into the depths below.

Watching. Waiting.

Di felt the need to shiver, but blamed it on the inclement weather. She shook herself, linking arms with Mike and pulling him close as they went on their way.

CHAPTER 4

THE SURPRISING SUPPER

T hey had told Len that they had to go and think about it, but they both knew they would put an offer in on the house the very next day. What surprised them was how quickly Len accepted without any negotiation, which was great for them, since their offer was a few grand under the asking price, as they had more to spend on finishing that ensuite and getting the place just how they liked it.

It was a Friday, about three months later – and in fact it was Mike's 45th birthday – in mid-April, when they completed the purchase and took possession of the house. They had both taken the day off work and loaded a mattress and some bedding into their 4x4 and took it over to the property so they could sleep over the weekend. It was their intention to get as much decorating done while the place was still empty of furniture. They spent all day painting the considerable expanse of the living room walls, and by 8pm they were ravenous. With no food in the house, and only the means of making a brew of their favourite Earl Grey tea in the morning, they were looking forward to trying out one of the local pubs for supper.

The Cross Inn was almost back to back with their new house. It couldn't be closer, so that's where they headed. This was via another door at the back of the kitchen, leading into Goose Fold. It dark by then, so they took a torch and carefully navigated the tiny cobbled square shared with three or four other cottages, through a wrought iron gate and onto the main thoroughfare. The pub was almost immediately on the left with a flight of six or seven stone steps leading up to the front door.

'Better be careful of these after a skinful?' Mike laughed.

As soon as they ducked inside, Di loved the traditional features: the roaring fire and beams. There was a spacious bow window in the bar lounge, under which was a leather-clad bench seat where Di grabbed a table while Mike ordered the drinks. Not that there was a shortage of space, despite it being the start of the weekend. There were only a few cheery locals propping up the bar, who were no doubt more regular fixtures than the guest bitters, and one or two couples dotted about at other tables.

Mike wolfed down his pint of Landlord bitter, (still his absolute favourite), and a packet of salted peanuts.

'That hardly touched the sides,' Di observed as she sipped on her half pint of Guinness.

'Well, it's great beer and I'm starving,' he said with a contented smile, which told her that, despite being tired and hungry, he was excited about this new world they had chosen for themselves.

Di felt the same and indeed, as she looked out across the street, lit only by a solitary yellow street light, it did seem like another world, or rather another time.

But as the barman came over to take Mike's empty, Di asked for the menu and their little bubble of bliss immediately burst.

33

'No can do, 'fraid no food tonight, folks. The wife's got summat on, and she's gone out.'

'Oh,' Di groaned as politely as she could. 'Do you know if the other pub serves food?'

'They do,' the barman replied.

Mike's face lit up.

'But they stopped serving at eight. Too late fer you, I'm afraid.'

Mike's face dropped again.

Di tried to use her charm, as she had done successfully with Len. 'Oh no, what a shame! We are famished, and it's Mike's birthday. You couldn't just knock up a sandwich for us, could you?'

'Nope, sorry lass. Got no bread indoors till she goes shopping tomorrow. Come back for lunch or dinner tomorrow though. Home-made meat 'n' potato hot pot.'

So much for that, Di thought to herself. There was nothing for it but to order another drink and more peanuts while they figured out what to do.

They we were having a quiet moan about their gastronomic predicament, when a man's voice floated across from a table in the other window.

'Excuse me.'

They turned to see the lean and good-looking features of a bright-eyed man beaming at them.

'We couldn't help overhearing,' he said, gesturing to a cheery chubby woman sitting with him who smiled warmly at them too. 'Do you need to eat?'

'Oh yes we certainly do!' Di said, 'we're starving, and it's Mike's birthday. We really don't know what we are going to do. Do you have any idea where we can go?'

The man took a furtive glance around the pub, as if to make sure no one else was listening then said, 'Come over and join us, we have an idea.'

Di and Mike readily accepted the invitation, taking their

drinks over to the other table. Introductions revealed that this couple were called Terry and Fiona, and they lived in one of the terraced weaver's cottages, just a few doors up the road. To Di, they looked somewhat of a mis-matched pair. Terry was tall and seemed athletic, whilst Fiona was much smaller, and with her walking stick by her side, did not look very well. However, she had sparkling blue eyes, rosy cheeks and a warm smile. She was clearly happy to have Di and Mike join them.

'We've just moved into the village,' Di explained, 'and we've been decorating the new place all day.'

'Oh, good for you - Happy Birthday and welcome to the village,' Fiona said in a welcome tone. 'Which house did you move into?' She asked as she sipped on her pint of lager.

'Goose Barn,' Mike said proudly.

Fiona nearly choked on her drink. As she continued to cough, Terry patted her lovingly on the back.

'You OK?' Mike said a little nervously and Di felt he wasn't just worried about Fiona's health, but also worried that her choking might have been a reaction to the words 'Goose Barn', because she feared the same.

But her inexplicable concern was quickly quashed as Fiona told them, clearing her throat, 'Oh I'm fine. Nothing to worry about. I have a list of ailments as long as your arm. The latest is called myasthenia gravis, and it affects my swallowing sometimes. But I'll be OK. Now, tell them our idea, Terry,' she said changing the subject.

'Well, as it happens, we haven't had supper yet either,' Terry said, 'so you are both more than welcome to join us at home.'

Di couldn't believe her ears. She had never been made such a generous offer by complete strangers before. It simply reaffirmed to her why they had relocated to somewhere so apparently disconnected from the modern world - a world where generosity and community were such rare commodities.

'Really? Are you sure?' Mike gasped with enthusiasm, his stomach growling audibly.

'Yes, it's no trouble at all,' Terry said. 'It's just as easy to cook for four as it is for two. We have plenty in. We were planning to have a good old-fashioned fry-up – will that do for you?'

This was too good an offer to refuse. 'Oh, thank you SO much, that would be *very* welcome!' Di was feeling a little emotional at the selflessness of such an offer – or perhaps it was just the low blood sugar after a day with no food that was affecting her mood.

With that, Terry downed the last drop of his pint and left the pub to get the supper going, saying he would call the pub to let them know when it was ready so they could finish their drinks. Cheerfully anticipating the fry-up, Di and Mike chatted away to Fiona.

'How long have you lived here?' Mike asked.

'Oh, about six years now, so we're still very much incomers to the locals.

'Incomers?' Mike asked.

'Newcomers, I suppose you'd say. Or outsiders even,' Fiona explained.

'Crikey,' Mike laughed, 'what does that make us then?'

Fiona laughed. 'You'll find that the locals are very friendly under their gruff exteriors. But they do call a spade a spade though. No messing.' Mike responded, 'I think we found that out after meeting Len'. Fiona laughed again, knowingly.

Di joined in, 'And where did you come from before?' She could tell that both Fiona and Terry were from the north, but their accents had faded out somewhat, probably through being away at University, like herself.

'Huddersfield,' Fiona said. 'Terry was a lecturer there and I was a secondary school teacher. Until I developed severe rheumatoid arthritis. I used to be as trim as Terry, believe it or not, but the medication they gave made me gain a lot of weight. Now I can barely walk without this thing.' She gestured to her stick.

'Oh, I'm so sorry to hear that,' Di said, feeling a pang of guilt for judging the pair at first sight.

'It's OK. Moving here has helped no end.'

Di was about to ask how it could have helped when there were so many uneven surfaces and inclines to negotiate. The main street in the village alone was a steep hill by anyone's standards. After about 20 minutes chatting away, the landlord interrupted them, the pub phone by his ear.

'Terry says supper's ready,' he called out from behind the bar.

'Ah, thanks, Gary,' Fiona said, downing the rest of her lager and struggling to her feet. 'All set?'

Mike and Di jumped up and helped her out of her chair. As they did, Robert the tour guide was coming in. Although it had been well over a month since the tour, Di recognised him straight away. But he didn't acknowledge her. Instead, he took Fiona aside and whispered in her ear.

Di and Mike stood politely by.

'Isn't that..?' Mike whispered.

Di nodded, straining to listen to what Robert was saying, but his voice was nothing but a mumble. Fiona's, on the other hand, was louder in its indignation.

'I'll invite who I like, thank you!' she said.

Robert mumbled some more.

'He won't harm them,' Fiona said, jamming her stick into the floor irritably.

Robert said something in response, but Fiona huffed, 'Oh go and write a poem about it, Robert!' and shooed him away, turning back to Di and Mike. 'Sorry about that,' she said putting on a smile again. 'Give us a hand down these blasted steps would you?' She held out her hand to Mike, who gladly obliged.

When they were all safely at the bottom, Di looked back to see Robert standing in the doorway of the pub, his thick glasses glinting in the light which spilled onto the steps from inside. Despite the gloom outside, she knew he was looking at her. It reminded her of the way Roslyn looked at her from the witchcraft shop. Perhaps it was just the lot of an *incomer,* she thought. As much as she hated to admit it, however friendly the locals might be, she knew she and Mike would still be foreigners around here for some time to come. But with such a warm welcome from Terry and Fiona, what did that matter?

Their cottage was tiny, but lovely, warm and welcoming.

'Welcome to Terry's Caf, nothing but the best for our new friends,' Terry smiled as they stepped off the lane straight into a cosy living room with a roaring wood burner and a pine dining table in an alcove under the stairs fully laid, complete with all the usual condiments to accompany a fry-up. 'We have bacon, liver, fried eggs, sausages, black-pudding, and baked beans with fried bread. Is that OK for you guys? Shall I dole it all out for everyone?' he said standing by in the kitchen-diner at the rear of the little house.

'OK?' Di grinned as the intoxicating aroma of bacon filled her nose. 'It sounds bloody marvellous, and we are so grateful for this.'

'Could you miss out the black pudding for me please?' Mike piped up.

'No problem, mate. I'll give you extra sausage instead,' Terry said with a wink and a grin, as if he was making an innuendo.

Mike smiled, a little uncomfortable with anything out of his heteronormative world, while Di teased him, 'He's a namby pamby southerner, I'm afraid. He can't yet stomach black pudding.'

'Really?' Fiona said, incredulous. 'We were raised on the stuff. That and tripe.'

'Me too,' Di said. 'Although, to be fair, even as a child, I drew the line at tripe.'

'That's the next course of tripe trifle buggered then,' Terry laughed.

'My grandmother swore by it,' Fiona said.

'Mine too! I remember huge beige and orange slabs of the stuff,' Di said, her eyes glazing with nostalgia, 'hanging from the stalls in Tommy Fields market in Oldham. It had a texture like huge fringes and tentacles. Even the smell of it made me feel sick. I ordered a plate of it by mistake once on holiday in France.'

'I bet that was a gastronomic experience!' Terry commented.

Di nodded, 'All I understood on the menu was *oignons, vin blanc, creme et ail*. That sounded delicious. But I didn't know *tripou* was tripe. When it was placed in front of me, all I could smell was the inside of a sheep's stomach, and it made me heave. I swapped it with my ex-husband's delicious chicken cassoulet.'

Di added, 'Mike wouldn't eat that in a million years. My ex-husband devoured the tripe like the true Yorkshireman he was. He was from Denby Dale, near Barnsley.'

'Ah that explains it,' said Terry nodding his understanding.

As they sat down Di put a reassuring hand on Mike's as she noticed him wilt at the mention of her ex. She knew Mike was feeling enough of an *incomer* already; she didn't need to compound the feeling for him by celebrating the Yorkshire heritage of Rachel's father.

'So are you two married?' Fiona enquired.

'Not quite yet. But we have it all planned for a month's time. Had to get the house all sorted first,' Di said squeezing Mike's hand.

'Were *you* married before, Mike?' Terry asked.

'Yes. Been divorced for a few years now.'

'Ah. We are both, too! We are on our second long term committed relationship, although we never actually tied the knot ourselves, have we, Fi?'

'No,' she sighed. 'Been there, done that.' But just in case Di and Mike felt that her attitude to marriage in some way criticised them, Fi quickly added, 'But I'm sure you two will have a marvellous wedding and be very happy Will it be around here?'

'Not quite. Just up the road in Skipton at the registry office,' Di said looking at Mike. 'I am really looking forward to it. We love the Yorkshire Dales and we're booked in at The Black Horse Inn in Grassington for the night,' she beamed. 'We are going to have a church blessing here in the village sometime later though'.

'But not at Thomas à Becket's,' Mike laughed. 'Far too creepy'.

'But it would be very atmospheric,' Fi said quite seriously, before adding in a more jocular tone, 'you can't rely on the weather though. No roof!'

'You could have a word with the vicar at the main church behind it,' Terry suggested. 'Have you seen it? St Thomas The Apostle. It looks a bit austere, but it's quite beautiful inside.'

Di nodded keenly, despite the image which came to mind just then of the tar black crow watching her through the skylight before soaring back to the Victorian spire.

'Tuck in then!' Terry said.

And they did.

The supper was delightful, as was the company. Afterwards, Terry poured an enormous gin and tonic for himself and Fi, and offered one to Di and Mike. They both accepted gratefully. As they sipped their drinks, Fi told them about filling her early retirement with painting and working in her little pottage garden behind their cottage.

'And we go to the caravan regularly too, don't we, darling,' Terry chipped in.

'Oh yes,' Fi smiled.

'Ooh, where's that?' Di said, expecting some beachside location, as she tried her G'n'T'. 'Halifax,' Fi cocked her head as though looking for a response.

Di coughed on her drink at this surprising revelation – but also, the G'n'T was exceptionally strong.

'You OK, Di?' Terry asked.

'Fine,' Di smiled. 'Just wasn't expecting it to be quite so strong,' she said gesturing to her glass.

'Oh sorry. We like them like that,' Fi remarked.

'Do you need more tonic in that?' Terry asked.

'No, no, it's fine,' Di said quite honestly, the first sip already tickling her brain nicely. 'It just took me by surprise, that's all.'

'Mike?' Terry turned to him.

But Mike was very happy with his too.

'Why Halifax?' Di said, emboldened by the gin coursing through her veins. 'It's so close to here. I'm sure your caravan is lovely but it can't be as lovely as this,' she said admiring the cottage.

'Well, it's a nice change for Fi as she can't get out and about as much as usual.'

It's five miles up the road from Hebden, Di thought to herself. *How much of a change can it be?*

'But I confess that the main reason,' continued Terry, 'is that it's a very well-run and equipped nudist site. You see, we enjoy holidaying in the nude.'

Mike froze with a sausage halfway to his mouth. Terry's double-entendre when he'd refused black pudding suddenly took on a whole new dimension.

Di did all she could to keep a straight face, mainly because she could just imagine the rather prejudiced thoughts racing through Mike's head: *Oh no, they're swingers. We've been lured*

41

here for an orgy. She took a large draught of gin to buy some time, but when she spoke, all she could manage was 'Oh? How interesting.' Mike kicked her surreptitiously. This was not his idea of a suitable conversation with folk -however kindly- who were still virtually strangers, and he did not want to hear any more.

'It's an official naturist's caravan park,' Terry went on. 'In the woods. It's really lovely there. We have been naturists for a number of years now. You should try it. You are welcome to come with us sometime. It's very liberating.'

Di dared to take a peek at Mike's face, which was like a rabbit in the headlights at this revelation. The sense of panic she knew he would be feeling amused her so much that it took the edge off her own mild discomfort. Must be the strength of the G'n'T making even her more mischievous than usual – she couldn't resist. She just came out with it:

'We would certainly be up for giving it a go, wouldn't we?'

No! No, we wouldn't, Mike's eyes screamed at her.

'Oh fabulous,' Terry said with equal mischief, jumping up and pretending to unbutton his shirt. 'I don't usually wear this much round the house.'

Di laughed initially, but as she saw the colour drain from Mike's face, her expression straightened too, and she thought perhaps they'd gone too far.

'Terry, stop teasing!' Fi interjected when she saw the look on Mike's face. 'He's only kidding. Honestly, don't worry!'

Mike got the joke and relaxed. He laughed along with the others.

Terry beamed even more broadly as he buttoned up again.

Fi chimed in, 'I've had Robert trying to ward me off these two, don't make matters worse.'

'When?'

'At the pub on our way here. Don't you frighten them off. It's not for everyone.'

'It's OK,' Di said. 'We're not frightened. It's just the whole naturism thing… Well, I am not sure it's really our cup of tea.'

Mike sighed. But it wasn't just with relief. It was designed as a show of being tired. One which he hoped Di would pick up on. 'Well, thank you, this was an amazing meal. You have been more than kind.'

'Yes it certainly was,' Di agreed. 'But I think Mike's exhausted after all that painting, as I am, to be honest.'

'I am a bit as well, yes,' he said visibly relaxing in the knowledge that Di had gotten the hint.

'But we should have some cake first. It's your birthday after all,' Terry said.

'Let them go!' Fi demanded, then repeated, in a softer but equally tenebrous tone, 'Let them go.' She added as she popped into the kitchen, 'I'll cut you some of my carrot cake that I made this morning, and you can enjoy it tomorrow for your breakfast'.

Di and Mike thanked her for the little package she gave them wrapped in cling film.

'Yes, we really must get some sleep. But we'll see you again soon, I'm sure,' Di smiled.

'You certainly will. You can't escape us in this village,' Terry laughed somewhat mirthlessly.

'When they're ready, they'll come,' Fi muttered to Terry, but Di had a feeling she wasn't talking about naturism, or even another dinner party.

They made their way to the door, thanking them once again for their amazing hospitality, and were soon outside in the safety of the darkness, walking arm in arm towards the lone streetlamp down the cobbled lane beyond The Cross, with its soft yellow light.

Mike flicked on the torch and they ambled companionably and replete, both more than a little tipsy, back to the Barn. 'Do you think those G'n'Ts were designed to get us relaxed enough to strip off?' Mike hissed.

'Well, it didn't work,' Di replied. 'You should have seen your face when he invited us to the nuddie park – and when he started to unbutton his shirt!'

'I couldn't believe my ears!' Mike amiably scolded her. '*We would certainly be up for giving it a go,*' he said mocking her voice, 'what were you thinking?'

Di laughed loudly, before clapping her hand over her mouth, anxious not to wake the village which was now as quiet as the graves in the old churchyard they were passing. 'At least when we arrived,' she whispered as they tottered down the cobbles, 'he wasn't cooking supper dressed in just an apron. That would have spoiled my appetite.'

Mike hummed his agreement and did his impression of Len: 'Any more of that naturist malarky and I would have scarpered back down th'ill as fast as my legs could carry me.'

As they turned off Church Street and crunched their way down the unmade lane to the Barn, their torch light fell on three silhouettes in front of them. They both stopped abruptly and for a moment stared at the six pairs of eyes reflected in the lamplight. Di could have sworn that there were three small children standing there for a split second, before the silhouettes screeched and flew at them. Di smothered a shriek as she and Mike ducked, the creatures taking off over their heads and disappearing into the blackness above.

'What the…?' Mike swore.

'Crows.' Di gasped.

'Bloody big ones,' Mike nodded.

'A bit late for them to be out and about, isn't it?' Di said, shuddering.

'Perhaps they were sleeping down here and we disturbed them.'

'Don't they have nests to go to?' Di said trying to keep the atmosphere light.

They plodded on, Di holding tightly on to Mike's arm until they came to Goose Yard and the light from the well in the living room of their new house shone out like a beacon lighting the way home.

'Ah,' Mike said. 'Thank God you left that light on. I didn't think about it when we left. I would hardly have known the way down to our house otherwise.'

'Mmmm,' was all Di said in reply, puzzled.

She didn't remember leaving that light on. She was almost certain about that.

CHAPTER 5
THE UNEXPECTED GUESTS

T hey slept that night on the mattress on the living room floor.

Mike fell asleep as soon as his head hit the pillow. Di envied his ability to do that. Her mind often kept working for hours after she got into bed, and tonight was no exception. There was so much to think about. The new house, the décor, The Nuddies – as Terry and Fi quickly became known; Fi's strange altercation with Robert, and her cryptic words to Terry before they left; the three crows in the lane. She couldn't help but imagine that they were the same three crows that had examined her through the skylight upstairs all those weeks ago. But that was ridiculous, of course. There must have been hundreds of crows around here. But they were so huge – and why were those three not asleep, wherever crows sleep at this time of night?

And the light. Of course.

She could have sworn that it was off when they left for the pub, but she didn't say anything to Mike. Partly because she wasn't 100% sure. And partly because, the moment she said it out loud, she thought it would become a reality; and she didn't want whatever that reality suggested to blot the blissful landscape she imagined of their first night together in their forever home.

As she lay next to Mike, who was snoring by now, she found herself peering over the top of her sleeping bag towards the other end of the room, at the glass panel in the floor by the opposite window on the far end of the room. Her eyes began to play tricks on her as she strained to see in the dark. She thought she saw the glass, which shimmered in the moonlight seeping through the crack in the curtains, changing, becoming darker here and there as if something was moving around beneath it. But eventually her eyes started to droop under the weight of staring and she fell fast asleep.

Until the chattering.

The voices outside in the yard, unintelligible and excited. Children? Di thought. And the clicking of shoes on the cobbles. Clogs, she whispered with a shiver as she recalled Robert's words on the tour.

'Can you hear 'em? Clogs rattling down cobbles, hundreds of 'em? In yonder year, as dawn breaks, down clogs would clatter, through trees t'mills in town below. Chillun as young as five wud be carrying their meagre lunches o' bread, an' if tha were lucky, a scrap o' cheese and half an apple int old cloth held tightly in their little hands.'

And then she woke.

A dream. It was morning, the early light staining the edges of the curtains. She exhaled long and hard before the sound outside the barn doors made her catch her breath again. There really *were* voices outside. And the sound of shoes on the cobbles. Sounded like dozens of them, chattering and clicking.

Her heart beat raced. She turned over to see Mike was fast asleep. She listened again. She couldn't make out what the voices were saying partly because her ears were so full of the sound of her own blood throbbing through her veins.

'Mike. Mike,' she whispered, shaking him gently.

'Mmm?'

'There are loads of people in the yard outside.'

'What?' he moaned as he squinted over the duvet. 'Don't be daft, there can't be. It's early, go back to sleep.'

'No, there are,' Di insisted. 'Listen!'

Mike listened for a groggy moment then sat up with a start. 'What the hell...?'

They sat there on the mattress for a while, looking at the curtain, then at each other.

'Go and see who it is,' Mike muttered.

'Me?' Di squeaked.

'I've got nothing on sweetie,' Mike said. 'As you know very well!' he added cheekily.

The cheekiness did not work on Di. Her fears were suddenly replaced by mild irritation. Mike's excuse was lame. His trousers were over there on the table. It wouldn't be that great an effort to go and put them on before opening the curtain. She'd been hoping he would come to her rescue like the alpha male he thought he was, but he was either scared, lazy or more like it - a little hungover.

'Perhaps you should go and hang out with the Nuddies then,' Di grumbled.

'Oh sweetie! You go, will you? You've already got something on.'

'Hardly,' Di said indicating her ultra-short and low cut dusky pink silk night dress.

'Just go and see who it is.'

'I daren't. Suppose they're dangerous.'

'Don't be silly. Do they sound dangerous?'

Di listened to the laughter and chatter. She couldn't say whoever was making the noise did sound particularly dangerous, so she reluctantly got up from the mattress and tiptoed towards the barn doors.

Why am I tiptoeing in my own house? She thought to herself as she carefully and slowly peeked out from behind the curtains.

A flash of light blinded her for a moment. She blinked the sensation away and then, as she focused on the yard again, her jaw dropped at the sight of a large group of Japanese tourists in expensive winter coats and puff jackets, holding cameras and milling about, some throwing coins down the well, and some taking photos of it and the house, which included Di in all her morning glory.

She whipped the curtain closed. 'Oh my god, there are loads of Japanese people here photographing our house... and I think one snapped me.'

Mike, emboldened now, wrapped himself in the duvet and stumbled over to the window. He also peered out, with Di looking over his shoulder. The photography continued apace.

'My God. What are they doing here?' Mike said.

And by the looks on the faces of the tourists, they were thinking the same thing about Di and Mike.

Mike made a gesture designed to shoo them away, but this only resulted in the duvet revealing all. As he quickly covered himself again, the only response from the audience was a middle-aged gentleman gesturing to Di and Mike to get out of the way so he could photograph the house.

Di closed the curtain again.

'Bloody cheek!' Mike said staggering back to the bed, bemused.

'What on earth have we let ourselves in for buying this place?' Di said joining him. 'First the Nuddies, now a swarm of Japanese tourists – or whatever!'

'Next week,' Mike said as Di snuggled up to him, 'somewhere in Japan they'll be showing their holiday snaps to relatives. I'll wonder how they'll explain the one featuring an under-dressed brunette and a balding naked man trying to cover his privates with a duvet.'

CHAPTER 6
LOCALS AT THE CROSS

The voices soon faded from the yard. They showered and got dressed, before making a cup of their favourite earl grey tea which they had remembered to pack - along with the kettle, and this was accompanied by a large slice of Fi's carrot cake, which was delicious.

They ventured to open the curtains and began painting more walls.

By lunchtime they were ravenous again. They both of them remembered what the landlord of The Cross Inn had said about potato hot pot being on the menu today, so they hightailed it round to the pub and were not disappointed. It came in two large steaming bowls topped with a big slab of shortcrust pastry with a side of pickled red cabbage. As well as potato, it was packed with slow cooked brisket and vegetables. Mike asked for a bottle of his favourite Lea and Perrins and was presented with the biggest bottle they had ever seen, which he generously sploshed on to his dinner.

'Amazing,' Di said as they tucked in.

'And even better coz we don't have to get naked after,' Mike winked, taking a furtive glance over his shoulder to make sure Fi and Terry weren't in.

50

'Ooo, who's that, getting naked?' asked a rather camp voice over Mike's other shoulder.

Mike jumped and Di looked up to see a stunningly handsome, well dressed and muscular young man of Middle Eastern complexion smiling down at them.

'Ollie, you can't just say that to a complete stranger,' his companion scolded him. 'Do forgive him. I'm Stephen,' he said shaking Mike's hand.

Ollie laughed and sipped on his rosé wine.

'And this is Ollie, my other half, for better or worse.' He was a little older than Ollie, but dressed in a similar style, which made Di think Ollie was the stylist in their relationship.

'Oh, for better, babycakes, most definitely for better,' Ollie grinned at his partner, then took Mike's hand.

Di could see Mike's common courtesy battling with his discomfort of being in such close contact with such obviously gay men. Di offered her hand to Ollie and Stephen too, much to Mike's relief.

'Are you living in the village?' Stephen asked.

'Of course, they've moved into Goose Barn,' Ollie said before Mike or Di could. 'Everyone knows that.'

Stephen glared at Ollie. Clearly Stephen knew that too, but he was trying to be more subtle than him. 'Well,' he said, 'we'd love to have you over for dinner sometime. If you like. As our welcome gift to you.'

'We promise to keep our clothes on,' Ollie sniggered.

Di's face felt as red as Mike's looked. 'Did you hear about..?'

'Terry told us he's teased you about it,' Stephen admitted. 'But you don't need to worry about them. They're lovely. Honestly.'

Just then Di saw Len appear at Ollie's shoulder in a well-worn and aged long black leather coat. He made him jump with a loud, 'Ey up!'

51

'Jesus,' Ollie hissed.

'Sorry, did I surprise yer?' Len said, shaking the rain off his coat.

'No, no,' Ollie lied, taking a comforting glug of his wine.

Di could tell that the atmosphere had changed, and Stephen's words confirmed it for her.

'Come on. We should get going,' he said tugging on Ollie's sleeve. 'It was nice to meet you two. We'll make a date soon, OK?'

Di nodded as Stephen ushered Ollie from the pub.

''Ow yer doing?' Len asked her.

'We're great thanks, Len. And you?'

'Aye, not bad. Fair to middlin.'

There was an awkward pause.

'Hope yer enjoying yer new 'ome,' he said winking knowingly.

Di was about to ask him about the Japanese tourists, but he was already off to the bar and ordering a pint as he perched on one of the stools.

'Do you think he still lives around here?' Di whispered as they carried on devouring their food.

'I guess he must. Or he's just come to catch up with his old mates,' Mike said.

And, as if to corroborate Mike's theory, a few seconds later Di watched as Len was joined by a swarthy looking man who was in his late fifties or early sixties, although he was still trying to pull off the look of a twenty-something-year-old biker. He was wearing a black singlet and jogging pants, and no coat in spite of the weather. He was thick set. Arms like tree trunks and a chest like a gorilla's, with black and white hair sprouting from it which curled above his vest. As he turned to the bar, Di could see his shoulders added to the image of him as a silverback, with black and white hairs meeting his black and white pony tail. Underneath his dark blue jogging bottoms, he wore white trainers and he carried a

52

walking stick. He ordered a pint of Guinness, the black and white of the Irish stout matching his looks perfectly. He started chatting to Len, and Di could make out a Geordie accent.

She tried not to look too often, but the next time she did she caught Len's eye. He nudged his mate and they both came over to the table. To Di it seemed appropriate this time to stand and greet them, as if she were in the presence of an elder statesman, and Mike followed suit.

'These good folks are th'ones who bought me 'ouse.'

'Areet?' said his mate in an unsurprisingly simian register, 'Yous settling in?'

'Very well, thanks, it's lovely,' Di smiled. 'Len did a fabulous job of renovating it.'

'Aye, he did, with a lot of help from his mates, eh, leik?' With that he punched Len playfully in the chest.

The punch nearly knocked Len off his feet, but he managed to keep his balance if not his dignity when he said, 'And some who turned out not to be mates. Least said about that, the better.'

Di cringed in sympathy as she recalled what Len had told them about his wife and the bricky, but thankfully, he changed the subject.

'This 'ere fella is a champion wrestler, very famous, been on telly in times past. 'Is stage name is Big Will Warrior Johnson. Known to 'is friends as Big Will. You may a heard of 'im?'

Big Will smiled, showing several missing teeth and just as many chipped ones. 'Canny ta meet yer leik,' he said.

After much scratching of their heads and blaming of their bad memories to soften the blow to Big Will's ego, they had to admit, they hadn't heard of him.

'Ah well, any trouble wi' anyone, yer let us know, and Big Will will sort 'em out.'

Di and Mike shared a quick glance filled with questions.

One being, - despite packing one hell of a punch, just how useful could Big Will be should *trouble* arise, given he had obviously sustained some injury or developed a disability, judging by the walking stick he needed to get himself about? The other question, Di couldn't help but give voice to:

'Oh. And what sort of trouble should we be expecting?'

Len and Big Will shared a look, as if the question took them by surprise. Then after an awkward moment, Len said, 'Well, I wunt be expectin' any trouble, but... y' know, just in case. You nivver know.'

Di could see that Len had been thrown off a little by her question. As if the question was seriously loaded and he really did not want to answer. But in any event, whatever it was he might have been referring to, he clearly didn't want to spell it out here in front of everyone in the pub.

'Great,' Mike said. 'We might suggest a few Japanese tourists you can warn off.'

'Yer what?' Len frowned.

'Nothing,' Mike waved his comment away. 'Just joking.'

'Oh, aye…Well, we'll leave yer to yer scram,' he said and he walked back to his bar stool.

'Very nice to meet you, pet,' Big Will said to Di. 'And you, laddie,' to Mike. 'Cheerio fo' now.'

He hobbled back to his stool as a much younger, taller and more handsome man, with a ruddy face, wearing a black wax jacket and jack boots against the rain, joined him and Len. The three men sat muttering to each other and looking around the pub and, to Di, they looked just like those three crows perched up on those stools, chewing the fat and putting the world to rights.

CHAPTER 7

MOVING DAY

D i and Rachel spent the next week packing up all their belongings in Saddleworth, ready to move them both to Heptonstall. When the big day came, Rachel was at school and unable to help, though she had tried to wag the day off but her parents would not hear it. However, she had already been to visit the new house and had given it her enthusiastic approval.

Di was supervising the removal men loading all her furniture and years of accumulated possessions into an enormous van. She was thankful that Goose Barn was large enough to house both her stuff as well as Mike's.

Mike was working that day. Between leaving the RAF and joining a commercial airline, he was filling in, teaching would-be pilots that day near York. He would be arriving with his own removal van the next day. Which was just as well, since when Di drove back into the village, she saw what appeared to be a veritable commotion on Church Street at the junction with the lane to Goose Yard.

She stopped her car and hurried to the little crowd that was forming – not of tourists this time, but of locals. Di paled as she took in the object of the entire village's interest. To her horror, the driver of her own removal van had attempted to back down the tiny lane which was almost narrower than the vehicle, and had taken a chunk out of the neighbour's wall, splitting their guttering. Di was mortified.

'Bloody hell, yer pillock!' yelled one of the removal men at the driver from the back of the van. 'Look what yev done!'

The driver was trying to get out of the van to look at what he had done, but there wasn't enough room for him to open the door on either side.

'Why not take the guttering down altogether? We can always shove it back on again,' said one enthusiastic bystander.

'Take the wing mirrors off!"

'Keep going and worry about it afterwards!' helpfully volunteered yet another. All men, of course! Di thought somewhat unfairly, but annoyed and worried.

The van driver, in his infinite wisdom, decided on the latter course, and with a horrible scraping and ripping he continued to back his van impossibly down the lane, with Di barely able to watch.

'Shit,' she thought, 'what a start! The neighbours are going to hate me.'

She stomped up to the scene and accosted the removal man on the ground. 'Don't worry about it, luv,' said he, 'He's insured. 'Appens all t' time. It'll get sorted.'

How reassuring! Di thought sardonically.

'Don't worry. The damage is on a holiday home. The owners are never there,' came a familiar voice behind her.

Di turned to see Fiona leaning on her stick smiling up at her. She felt her face get hotter than it already was.

Oh heavens! As if I need any more awkwardness right now, she thought. Then out loud said, 'Oh, hi, Fi. I'll have to contact them and arrange for the damage to be fixed. Do you have a number by any chance?'

Fi shook her head. 'They left in a bit of a hurry last time. But I have a feeling they won't be back any time soon.'

'What makes you say that?'

Fi shrugged with the look of a naughty schoolgirl. 'Just a feeling.'

Di wondered if Fi and Terry had scared them off with an invitation to get naked, but her wry thoughts were broken by the sound of the removal man:

'Right, let's get this lot inside.'

'Got to go,' Di said. 'Before they break something else.'

She shimmied past the van which had stopped at the entrance to the yard and the men were already lugging her possessions across the cobbles to the Barn. She quickly opened up the house and directed them where to put things.

'Rug?' asked one of the men.

'Ah,' Di said with a sense of relief she couldn't quite understand. 'That goes over there,' she said pointing to the glass panel over the well in the floor.

'Cover it up?' the man asked.

'Absolutely,' Di said. 'And then the glass and marble dining table on top of the rug. But make sure the legs don't rest on top of the glass,' she added for good measure.

She watched as the men followed her instructions and she felt a weight lift off her shoulders as the table was put in place, as if its legs were great nails, pinning the rug to the floor and sealing off what was below.

'Yev nivver enough to fill this place up!' Another familiar voice rang out, but this one startled her.

She turned to see Len standing in the middle of the living room, hands on his hips as he surveyed the move.

'Urgh! You made me jump, Len. What are you doing here? Have you decided to move back in?' she said with a short laugh to cover the passive aggression in her question.

'Sorry to startle thee, lass. Heard 'bout the damage to thon 'ouse. Thought I'd see'd how ye were diddlin' 'ere.

'Yes, I am going to have to apologise for that and pay for it, and goodness knows what damage will be done when they pull out again.'

'Nivver mind that lass, it'll be reight. Did ye need a lift wi' owt? I've got a moment t'elp thee. I can heft and carry fer thee.' Before Di could answer, he added, 'Ee by 'eck, yer nivver going to cover that up, are ye?' He was looking at the floor under the glass table.

Di didn't want to offend Len, but this day had been stressful enough already and she wasn't in the mood to be subtle anymore. 'To be honest, Len, it gives me the creeps. I don't like to look at it. Hope you don't mind.'

Len studied the table for a moment before nodding slowly. Then said, almost to himself, 'Nay, lass, no, no. *I* don't mind.'

Di couldn't help feeling like he was implying that someone else might mind, but a loud crash from upstairs stopped her from asking him.

Di flinched. Len simply looked up at the ceiling and scowled.

'What's going on up there?' she called out. 'Is everything alright?'

'It's a'right, lass, nowt to worry 'bout,' the removal man said as he came gingerly downstairs looking pasty.

'What on earth is wrong?' Di asked – something very valuable must have been destroyed judging by the look on the man's face. 'Did you break something?'

'No, no. it's just…'

'What?'

'Well… argh, it sounds a bit daft, but I could have sworn someone was standing behind me. And it gave me a fright like and I'm sorry, I dropped your nightstand. But it din't break. Things sound loud on that wooden floor.'

'And *was* someone standing behind you?' Di heard herself asking, her voice trembling ever so slightly.

'No. Everyone else were down here. Just me imagination, I s'pose. Sorry about the noise, love.'

The man went back to work, but she could see he was still recovering from the *fright* and it made Di wrap her coat around herself as if the temperature had dropped.

'For goodness sake, pull yourself together, woman!' Di told herself and turned to Len.

But he was gone.

She hadn't noticed him leave, but she was relieved. She didn't need his help, and as friendly as he had been, this was *her* house now – hers and Mike's. She knew he must still be attached to the house, after all his hard work, but he shouldn't be hanging around anymore. He had to let it go.

She went out to the yard to guide the next piece of furniture inside, but just as she crossed the threshold she was struck by the presence of a large black crow with a long sharp beak perched on the roof of the wishing well. It was looking directly at her, as if trying to tell her something. She watched as it moved its head from side to side and performed a peculiar dance. But then one of the removal men came down the yard, carrying Di's writing desk and the crow spread its great black wings, taking off with a soft squawk which sounded like disappointment.

'That were a big 'un,' said the removal man.

'Mmm, it certainly was.' Di agreed.

'Where do yer want this, luv?'

'Oh, over there, please,' Di said distractedly, pointing to an alcove next to the huge chimney.

The writing desk and the rest of her furniture was moved in without any further hitches and luckily, just before the rain started. When it was time for the removal men to go, Di found herself offering them cups of tea as if she didn't want them to leave her alone in the house. But she told herself she was just delaying the inevitable destruction to the neighbours' cottage as the van was driven down the lane again.

When they did finally leave, she didn't watch them go – she couldn't bear to see the carnage. She thought she heard a terrible creaking and snapping as the van went down the lane, but she busied herself, noisily unpacking boxes and unfurling bubble-wrapped ornaments to try and distract herself. She made the bed, hung up some clothes and then made another cup of tea and flopped on the sofa.

Now that all the business of unpacking was done, the house fell silent. As she sipped her tea her eyes kept falling on the dining table. She listened. She didn't know what she was listening for. To make sure she was alone? However, when she was sure she was alone, a feeling of isolation descended on her. So she picked up the phone.

'You're going to need two small vans for tomorrow, not one big one,' she told Mike.

'Why?' He sounded so far away.

'It'll never get down the lane otherwise. Trust me, I know. I'll show you when you get here'

'Oh crikey. What happened?'

'Let's just say I owe the neighbours a new drainpipe. At the very least.'

'OK,' laughed Mike.

'I can't wait for you to come tomorrow,' she blurted out.

'Me too.'

'Come as soon as you can, OK?' she said earnestly.

'Is everything alright?' Mike asked, sensing that it wasn't.

'Yes, yes. I just can't wait for us to start our new life together.'

'Me too,' Mike breathed. 'OK, I'm going to get some sleep. You get some too.'

'OK.'

'Love you.'

'Love you. See y—' She heard the dial tone. '…tomorrow,' she said despondently to no one. He must have hung up too soon.

She slowly hung up too and sat alone in the growing gloom, feeling uneasy. So she got up and went around the house, turning all the lights on. As she closed the curtains she peered up through the rain at the telephone wires, and then immediately asked herself why she did. But she had a sense of being watched. She reprimanded herself out loud. She was a very grounded person, too sensible for her own good sometimes. Her career was built on evidence. Facts. And she had no tangible evidence that there was anything to worry about here. It was just the weirdness that comes with a new home, she told herself. The seventeenth century farmhouse she had left in Saddleworth made all sorts of weird and wonderful noises, and after so many years she knew exactly what each of them were – the boiler turning on, the radiators heating up, the gutter expanding in the sunshine. It would take a while before she knew all the idiosyncrasies of this place too, she thought.

As she went up to bed she decided to leave a lot of the lights on. Her and Mike's bedroom was the larger of the two in the attic space, with the ensuite. She got into bed and looked up at the skylight wishing it had a blind over it. She would go shopping for one as soon as possible.

CHAPTER 8

DOROTHEA

The following day, Di was up before 8am. She immediately made some of her favourite fresh coffee and before long the house smelt like a home. She was keen to get to the shops, not just to buy a blind for the skylight, but some provisions too. However, the weather was drizzly, so for a while, she continued with her unpacking.

As lunchtime approached, the weather had still not improved, so she decided to get going anyway. Mike and his removal vans were not due to arrive until at least 3pm, so there was still time.

She drove down to Hebden Bridge. Despite the drizzle, the place was as bustling and vibrant as ever. She found a decent looking butcher's shop and an organic farm shop selling plump fresh fruit, generously sized vegetables and warm sourdough bread. There were so many tempting cafes and restaurants along her way, so she paused for a brunch of hummus and a roasted Mediterranean vegetable wrap with a large piece of soft, moist carrot cake.

As she stared from the window into the light spring drizzle, washing all those lovely flavours down with a fragrant cup of Earl Grey, she watched the shoppers going about their business with their happy kids skipping beside them, and the feeling of contentment that drew her to move here in the first place came flooding back. The thought of Mike arriving later and them beginning to live together as a couple made her smile, not to mention the thought of all five of the kids coming to visit next week for the wedding.

She looked at her watch. It was time to get back, she told herself, forgetting all about the blind for the skylight.

Back at Goose Barn, as she carried her shopping from the car, she heard a crackly but highly polished woman's voice:

'Hello! Hello there! Are you my new neighbour?'

Di looked about but couldn't see anyone. Then, the same voice came again:

'I am down here, dear, next door.'

Di looked over the small picket fence to the low cottage adjoining Goose Barn at the far side. There in the doorway was a small, bent, and very round elderly woman with dark piercing eyes and bushy unkempt eyebrows. As Di walked closer, she could see that her neighbour had grey wispy hair and whiskers on her chin and upper lip. She wore a grubby looking shawl over her shoulders, an old woollen grey skirt with a torn pocket on one side, and what could have been thick hiking socks rolled down to her ankles. On her feet were old fashioned grubby tartan slippers with what may once have been pink pom poms on top. She was framed in the doorway and was resting herself on a Zimmer frame.

'Oh, hello,' Di smiled. She quickly put down her shopping in her own doorway and went back to the fence. 'I didn't see you at first. I'm Diane, I moved in yesterday.'

'I am aware of that. You made a proper hullaballoo, may I say,' the woman said in her clipped BBC accent. 'I was trying to doze, but there was so much crashing and banging about, that it was impossible, so I completely missed my afternoon nap.'

Di apologised profusely and hoped that Mike's arrival

wouldn't be as upsetting for the neighbour as hers was. 'We're usually very quiet people. Apart from when the kids are here, of course.'

'Oh, bloody Nora, do you have children?' the woman grimaced. 'How many of the blighters do you have?'

Di explained the family tree; that all five kids would only be visiting for the wedding next week and that they were quite grown up. Only her eleven-year-old daughter lived with her, and even then only half the time, she added to appease the woman further. That seemed to do the trick.

'Ah, just as well, small children always give me a bloody awful headache.' She winced as if pre-empting such a headache, but in fact it was another part of her body that was causing her discomfort. 'I am going to have to sit down, it's my poor legs. Would you help me inside please? Perhaps we can become better acquainted over a cup of tea.'

'Of course.' Di thought briefly about her shopping on the doorstep which she needed to put away before Mike arrived, but she decided that prioritising that over this poor woman's legs might incur more of her indignation. So Di awkwardly helped her into her little cottage and was surprised when she directed Di to help her sit onto what was clearly a commode.

Her neighbour groaned painfully as she plonked herself down. 'I habitually sit on this in case I am caught short and need to go to the loo in a hurry,' she explained. 'And hurrying is not within my repertoire these days'. At that she hoisted herself slightly off the commode with the aid of her frame, pulled up her skirt, pulled down her knickers and regally sat down again with a, 'Humph.'

Di tried to hide her astonishment at this flagrant disregard for the kind of decorum she might have expected from such a well-spoken and apparently educated woman. Perhaps, Di told herself, she was not physically able enough to worry about such things as dignity any more, and this made her feel rather sorry for this heretofore rather prickly character.

The small living room was dark and dingy, and it looked as though it hadn't been cleaned for many years. There were ripped net curtains at the windows, and the few sticks of dark furniture she owned were old and tatty. The table by the wall was piled high with books and old newspapers. There were a few faded photographs on the wall: one of Queen Elizabeth in her younger days; the other of Winston Churchill. The room smelt very strongly of alcohol and urine.

Behind the woman's throne, (as Di and Mike always referred to it hereafter), and half hidden under the table, Di noticed a mangy old dog, perhaps a collie, slumped there with its eyes closed. Di thought for more than a moment that it might be dead. In this house, she thought, it might have been left for dead for weeks without being noticed.

'I didn't catch your name,' Di said. She thought it reasonable to ask now, since she had become rather intimately acquainted with the woman already.

'So sorry, I forget my manners. Life has not treated me well. I'm afraid, my brain is now completely addled. My name is Dorothea. Pleased to meet you, Diane.'

Di was surprised that someone whose brain was so *completely addled* could remember her name so well.

'I'm pleased to meet you too, Dorothea.' Di wasn't sure if she sounded sufficiently sincere, so she changed the subject quickly. 'Dorothy…'

'Dorothea.'

'Excuse me?'

'I just told you my name was Dorothea. Do you have amnesia?'

Di stuttered, unsure whether to be offended or apologetic.

'No? So I would thank you to call me by my name.'

'Of course, I'm terribly sorry.' Di said reddening a little. It took her a moment to regain her train of thought. Then: 'Is your dog OK? It hasn't moved or opened its eyes since we came in.'

'Oh, he's definitely alive, but like me, only just. The poor bugger. His name is Brutus.'

And as if to confirm this, the dog lifted one eyebrow to take a lazy peek at Di, then promptly closed it again, resuming his slumber.

'Would you be a darling,' said Dorothea, 'and make us both a nice cup of tea?'

'Yes, of course, I would be happy to make *you* one, but I won't myself. I've just had a brew down in Hebden.'

Di could easily have glugged down another cuppa, but try as she could, it was impossible seeing herself having a drink in that house. She already felt a little queasy and was trying not to breathe in too deeply. The putrid odour in there was overwhelming. Nevertheless, she got up to find the kitchen.

'It's through there my dear.' Dorothea pointed with a walking stick she kept by the side of her commode.

Di walked cautiously into the only other room downstairs, her shoes sticking to the dirty carpet. The cottage's kitchen like the rest of the house had clearly not been modernised or upgraded since the 1960's. There was an old cracked butler sink, filthy green cupboards and Formica surfaces of a faded orange hue crammed with unwashed pots, dirty cutlery and half eaten packets of biscuits, cakes and sweets. Di eventually spotted an old electric kettle among the detritus and a box of Yorkshire breakfast tea bags.

'Strong and three sugars for me, not much milk,' Dorothea called from the other room.

The milk in a small jug by the kettle had already congealed into curds, so Di, almost retching, tipped this away and found a somewhat fresher carton in the grubby fridge. She rinsed out a chipped and stained china cup which clearly had once been part of a very expensive set and made the tea.

'I'll have a biscuit too please.'

At that Di picked up a few of the open packets and smelt them. She fished out a couple of chocolate digestives which didn't smell too musty, and took them to Dorothea with her tea.

Di's host patted a small dark oak table by the commode and she was about to place the tea onto it, when Dorothea said sharply, 'Who brought you up? Use a coaster please!' She handed one to Di, who had to smile secretly at the irony. 'Sit down and talk to me for a while,' Dorothea insisted.

There did not appear to be any discernible place to sit at first, until Dorothea pointed to a chair in the corner upon which were a pile of newspapers and what looked like many utility bills.

'You can dump those on the table over here,' Dorothea said, so Di added them to the piles that were already there. Then, just as she sat down, Dorothea barked, 'I can't see you there. Bring the chair closer to me.'

Di patiently did as she was told, her eyes widening and eyebrows raising as Dorothea reached down and found a bottle of vodka from beside the commode. She poured a huge amount into what was already half a cup of tea, replaced the cap and returned the bottle to the same place.

'My medicine,' she explained. 'I have to partake at least six times a day, or else my health deteriorates significantly.'

Di would have been more than tipsy had she drunk as much as that in one sitting. She watched silently as her neighbour sat back on her throne as she grunted contentedly with her cocktail of vodka and tea in a stained china cup.

After taking a slurp she said, 'Now, my girl, tell me a bit about yourself and I will tell you something about me.'

'Well,' Di smiled, 'I'm a barrister. Grew up in Saddleworth. Actually I've lived there all my life until I met my fiancé'.

'I've lived in this house since 1965,' Dorothea cut in – apparently she'd heard enough about Di already. 'Before that,' she crashed on. 'I was fortunate enough to be one of the few women to enter Cambridge University to study languages. I can speak several languages fluently, including Russian and German and a few more after a fashion, and more likely because of that, I was headhunted to work in Churchill's war rooms, throughout the Second World War.'

Di was impressed - if not a little surprised.

'After that I briefly became an undercover spy for the Home Office.'

Di blinked hard. 'A spy?'

Dorothea nodded quickly as if she was a little irritated at being interrupted, 'And then I was pensioned off at the ripe old age of fifty, put out to pasture here in Heptonstall where I lived with my long-time companion, Alice. Unfortunately, she passed on to the other side in 1985. Liver complications,' she said, her eyes misting over. Di wondered whether the liver complications was down to the frequent partaking of vodka.

There was a moment of silence and Di watched with sympathy as Dorothea seemed to reflect upon the memory of Alice. 'I miss her terribly,' she sighed. 'She was the life and soul of any party. Since she left me, I have been trying to contact her, alas to no avail.'

It took a while for the implication of her words to sink in. 'Contact her?' Di said.

'Yes.'

'What do you mean?' Di asked, a sense of unease staining her mood again.

'I have been summoning her spirit of course,' Dorothea said as if Di was a complete fool to not have surmised that. 'Or at least trying to. I am a practicing Spiritualist you see', she said as if this explained it.' She looked at Di slyly, as if gauging her reaction.

Di felt her heart sink. She was not only disappointed at this well-educated, erudite woman believing in such mumbo-jumbo, but she was also unsettled that this woman lived right next door to her. However, right at that moment, she was saved by the sound of a horn tooting in the lane. She looked at her watch.

'Goodness, is that the time already? This has been a really fascinating conversation, and we must carry this on another time, but I think that's probably my fiancé with his removal men so I really should dash.'

'Yes, yes, off you go. Don't mind me. Come and see me again when you find a minute in your busy life', Dorothea said shooing her off, her dark eyes boring into Di as she hurried out.

It was indeed Mike and the removal vans – two smaller ones thankfully. Di grabbed her shopping from the doorstep and saw that some had fallen out of the bag. But just as she went to return it she realised it wasn't part of her shopping at all. It was a small piece of bread, half an apple going brown and a round lump of cheese. All three items were half eaten and the bite marks were small, like those of a child. The sight made her stop dead. Her head began throbbing, but she didn't know why.

'Hey, sweetie!' Mike's voice snapped her out of her petri-fied state, and she immediately scooped up the scraps and threw them into the dustbin, near to what was the pigsty which she intended to make into an office at some stage.

'Hey,' she said hugging him so tightly he stumbled a little.

'Woah!' he laughed. 'You OK?'

'I am - now you're here.'

'Hey Charlie,' she said bending down to welcome Mike's scruffy little brown and white Jack Russell terrier to her new home. Charlie wagged her tail, jumping up to greet her. She was always so pleased to see Di, and never jealous of the new lady in her master's life.

After the vans were unloaded and sent on their way, Di and Mike spent the evening exchanging news, cuddled up with Charlie in front of the large cast iron log burner with a couple of beers. Di told Mike all about her trip into Hebden Bridge and meeting Dorothea.

'You had better keep on the right side of her in case she makes a wax doll of you and sticks pins in it,'

Di slapped Mike playfully. 'It's not funny. Dabbling in the occult.'

'But if you already believe it's all a load of rubbish, why are you so worried about her living next door?'

'Because…' Di had to think for a moment. 'We don't need to live next door to a nutter.'

'It doesn't sound like she can get off her potty unaided, let alone come and stab you in the night,' Mike said screeching like the *Psycho* soundtrack.

Di slapped him again and wrapped herself in his arms, enjoying the sense of protection they gave her. She started to doze there in front of the fire, and in her reverie images of the half-eaten food on the doorstep came back to her. And then Robert's voice from that day they first toured the village accompanied the images:

'Chillun as young as five wud be carrying their meagre lunches o' bread, an' if tha were lucky, a scrap o' cheese and half an apple int old cloth held tightly in their little hands.'

Her eyes snapped open. How weird was that!

CHAPTER 9

A LOCAL SHOP FOR LOCAL PEOPLE

The next morning, it was still grey outside.

Before they carried on with the unpacking, Mike made a breakfast of toast, marmalade and tea.

'That's the last of the butter,' he called out.

'Oh no!' Di said. 'We need a few other things too. I'll pop down to the post office on Church Street. See what they have.'

When she arrived at the little shop it was closed.

'Sunday,' Di growled at the door with its opening times written on it. 'I forgot it was Sunday. No Tesco Express around these parts,' she sighed looking around the empty street before plodding back up the hill.

On her way she noticed several large crows among the old church ruins, and she heard more of them arguing noisily in the tall trees in the new church yard. It occurred to her then that she had not seen nor heard any other bird in Heptonstall. She recalled that somewhere she had read how crows scare away or even eat other birds, so it wasn't surprising that they quite literally ruled the roost here. She was just pondering on this as she came back into Goose Yard, when she noticed an elderly gentleman pottering amongst his plants outside the cottage which adjoined Dorothea's on the far side.

'Hello,' she called out.

He looked up and Di could see he was very slim, quite dapper, with a pale, pointed, sad-looking face, but with well-groomed silver-grey hair.

'Hello,' he said. 'You must be our new neighbour. I also have the unfortunate honour to live next door to that silly old lush,' he said nodding over to Dorothea's house between them.

Perhaps that's why he looks so sad, Di smirked to herself.

'Have you met her yet?'

'Yes, I met her yesterday. Made her a cup of tea.'

The gentleman looked surprised. 'You went *in there*? Well, you *are* a brave woman! I went in there once, fifteen years ago when it was Alice's funeral. Never again.'

Di made a face to suggest that Dorothea might be listening.

To that he replied, 'Oh, you've no need to worry about her, she doesn't stir until at least midday, and sometimes, if she has had a really busy night, if you get my drift, it could be four in the afternoon.'

Di hoped a busy night meant drinking vodka and not communing with spirits.

'Anyway, I forget my manners. I'm Jeffrey, by the way. And your name is?'

Di introduced herself and Mike in absentia. She mentioned, rather proudly, that they were getting married next week.

'Congratulations my dear, I wish you a wonderful wedding. I hope you both will be very happy together.'

Di thanked Jeffrey, relieved to meet such a lovely, genteel man, who was lacking, she hoped, the *quirks* of other villagers she had met so far.

'Do you know if there are any shops open in Hebden Bridge today where I might buy some basic provisions?' she asked him.

'You've no need to go so far,' Jeffrey said. 'There's a very good shop which serves the locals just up at Slack Top. It's run by a woman called Jenny. She always seemed rather an odd ball. Not seen her for a while as I no longer drive'.

'Where's Slack Top?' she enquired, amusing herself by wondering if there was a Slack Bottom nearby too.

'Just up at the top of the village, there's a farm track leading up to a farmhouse, you can't miss it. It takes ten minutes to walk, two minutes if you drive. It sells everything. The locals have bets on what they might not sell, but they've always got it in, whatever it is you need.'

'Sounds amazing,' Di smiled. 'Thank you very much. I will try it. Is there anything I can get for you whilst I'm there?'

Suddenly Dorothea's door opened a crack. 'I *am* awake and I heard every word you said, Jeffrey Davis. You are a bloody nasty little poofter, and if I were you Diane, I would steer well clear of him. He's a sodding nuisance, and a very boring uneducated man to boot.'

Jeffrey just shrugged his shoulders and said to Di, 'Well, that's a first, nosey old busybody.'

'Wait there! *I* need something,' commanded Dorothea. 'I'll get some money.'

Whilst she was gone Jeffrey said quickly. 'Don't let her put you off moving here. She's hard work, but her heart is in the right place really. We have been bantering away like this for a few years now, but that's because she kept falling over in the yard blind drunk, and I got tired of picking her up. Eventually, I couldn't anyway because she got too heavy, and I'm not strong enough, so I called in social services. She's never forgiven me for that. She's a proud woman, hates social workers, she thinks they're just silly ignorant nosey parkers. Thankfully, she stays inside now. Neither of us can go out unless someone is able to give us a lift. I haven't the strength to walk up and down these hills.'

Di felt sorry for the little man. He looked so forlorn as he spoke and it was obvious that, like Dorothea, he was lonely.

Dorothea's door cracked open again. 'I'll have the cheapest vodka they've got and a packet of Mr Kipling's fondant fancies if you don't mind, my dear.' She thrust her arm out of the door, and as Di reached for the banknotes, she noticed Dorothea's long dirty fingernails and the very tatty nightdress she wore under her shawl. 'And, whatever you do, don't believe a word that silly old poofter says to you!'

Di didn't know how to respond to her slight, and simply said she would be back as soon as she could.

'Sharpish then, I am dying of thirst here.'

Di wanted to suggest that water might quench her thirst better, but she assumed this would antagonise her neighbour, who withdrew her scraggy arm and firmly closed the door. She asked Jeffrey again if he wanted anything. He thanked her, but said no, that he had everything he needed for now, and his sister would be bringing him some supplies later that day.

Mike and Di decided to walk together to the local shop at Slack Top, donning on their anoraks before heading off. After the cobbles of the main street of Heptonstall ran out, the road became tarmacadam. It took them into the open moorland, which was crisscrossed as far as the eye could see with the millstone grit drystone walls. The sheep had lambed, and both mothers and offspring were taking shelter from the resuming rain, leaning close against the walls as the drizzle turned to a more significant precipitation.

Eventually, they arrived at the farm. It was a low, black and forbidding place, and Di felt as if it, or its inhabitants, were watching them approach. It didn't look much like a shop to them, but Jeffrey had assured Di that it was in the building in the farmyard behind the main house.

As they rounded the corner they saw a light in a little

latticed window. A sign of life. So they entered through a stable door and a brass bell announced their arrival.

As Jeffrey had promised, the shop was well stocked. In fact, they had never seen such a cornucopia of stuff. It was in no particular order as far as Di could see. However, she was pleased to see a fridge at the far end containing dairy products, so she headed for that, while Mike looked around for the bread, cakes and biscuits. There didn't seem to be anyone around and after five or so minutes, Mike and Di had found everything they needed, apart from Dorothea's vodka which, like all the spirits usually are, was on a shelf behind the till.

They turned to the counter and, startled, suddenly came face to face with a tall scrawny woman of ruddy complexion and indeterminate age. Everything about her face was large: her nose, atop which was perched a pair of red-rimmed cat-eye-shaped glasses, and her eyes, red-rimmed too which protruded from her skull. She wore her hair in a red headscarf and was draped in a pink housecoat, which may have been red too once upon a time. Her hands were half covered in fingerless, red woollen gloves. She stood behind a large pair of brass scales and an old-fashioned cash register. Di and Mike had no idea how long she'd been standing there – despite her size, she must have arrived with feline stealth.

Di put her shopping on the counter and asked for a bottle of vodka. 'How much is that please? she asked.

The woman said nothing at first, but simply stared at Di then shifted her gaze to Mike, who shifted about, disconcerted. Then, after what seemed like a very long pause, she spoke. 'It depends 'ooz askin.'

Di was puzzled by the reply. 'Well… I am, I suppose.' She did not know what else to say.

She stared at Mike; 'Is it for yerself?' Her voice reminded Di of a cat meowing.

'I am over forty, so I am allowed to buy alcohol, am I not?' Mike said wryly.

'No need to be cheeky wi' me, young man,' she said. 'Do yer live in these parts?'

'We've just moved into Heptonstall,' Di smiled - before Mike could wind her up even more.

'Oh yes? Whereabouts in Eppenstall?'

'Goose Barn to be precise.'

'Goose Barn, issssss it?' the shopkeeper meowed.

'Yes,' Mike said impatiently. 'Please may we pay you for the stuff? We've got to—'

'Yev moved next door to dotty Dorothea then?'

'Yes,' Di said finding herself defending her neighbour. 'We've moved next door to a lady called Dorothea.'

'A lady is she? And this'll be fer 'er, am I right or am I wrong?'

'How do you know that?' Mike laughed.

'Because I have been 'ere a very long time, which you 'ave not. An' another thing, she will have yer buying this every day fer 'er if yer not careful. 'Ow much did she gi' yer?'

'Fifteen pounds,' Di said somewhat fazed.

'And am I guessing right that them fondant fancies are fer 'er an' all?'

'How did…' Mike shook his head in disbelief.

'I teld yer a minute ago, I knows, an' you poor buggers 'ave a lot to learn.'

Di was irritated now. 'Look, how much do we owe you? Can we just buy our goods and go?'

'Ye can, but the vodka and fancies come to seventeen quid so yer need another two quid fer 'er stuff.'

'That's fine, I'll cover it and ask her for it when I get back.'

'You do that luv, but good luck w'that, ye'll be lucky to gerrit off 'er.' At last, she reached for the vodka and placed it on the counter. 'There yer go. Don't drop it! I saw yer walking up, struggling up th'path. She'll have yer guts fer garters if yer drop it. Len did that once and…' She paused for dramatic effect, no doubt, '…ee paid fer it in other ways,' she said darkly.

Di shuddered. *My God, another weirdo,* she thought.

'Don't you worry, we'll be really careful," said Mike sarcastically, paying the woman and packing the stuff into his rucksack.

'Aye, it'll be nice and safe in there,' she said admiring Mike's bag. 'And welcome t'Eppenstall. Good luck wit' neighbours…… 'uman or t'otherwise,' she added with a sneer.

Di couldn't get out of the shop fast enough. She tramped back down the track much quicker than she climbed it, pulling Mike along, back to the sanctity of their home through the incessant rain.

'Slow down!' Mike protested.

'Why has she got such a 'downer' on poor Dorothea - and what the hell did she mean by that parting shot?' Di grumbled.

'She's obviously heard about Dotty Dorothea trying to commune with the spirits. She's taking the piss,' Mike reassured her.

Di allowed herself to be reassured, but when she delivered the vodka and cakes to her neighbour she couldn't help but feel unnerved.

'Why don't you come in and we can continue our conversation from yesterday?' Dorothea said.

'I'm sorry,' Di said, 'still loads of unpacking to do.' She was telling the truth, but she would have said it even if it were not. 'Another time,' she called out as she hurried back to the safety of her home and her husband to-be. She didn't bother to ask for the two quid she was short, and it wasn't offered - though Di had given her the receipt.

CHAPTER 10

THE UNEXPECTED VISITORS

There was an air of celebration about the place now that all their five offspring had arrived. Four of their brood were now young adults, and the two boys and Mike's two girls had come home from University, especially to enjoy this precious family time. The house smelt of roasting meat and vegetables, and the large marble and glass dining table was laid with festive splendour for this, their first family meal together in Goose Barn. Di had been running around yesterday making sure everything looked as close to a photo shoot from *Hello* magazine as she could, and that Rachel's bedroom had all her favourite things in, so she could feel at home straight away. Di seemed to have succeeded because Rachel had been up there for ages showing it off to her big step-sister, Chloe.

As she fussed over the lunch preparations, Di took a moment to appreciate how well their blended family got on. Both Di and Mike had started their respective families at a young age, which they like to think kept them youthful, as well as on their toes!

Chloe, a small, pretty and chatty 'mummsy' 19 year old,

was a very capable and sensible student nurse. She was the eldest of the girls and she had instantly taken Rachel under her maternal wing. Di's 24 year old son, Joshua was a tall, handsome and gifted mathematician who already had two first class degrees under his belt. He was likely to remain a perpetual student and had no interest in making any money. He was just curious and hungry for knowledge. He was obsessive about Chess and Bridge and was an expert player in both - as well as being a brilliant juggler. He favoured buying his clothes from charity shops, in spite of his mother's vain attempts to smarten him up when he came to stay. Mike's 22 year old son, Andrew, was slightly shorter than Joshua. He was also very handsome, but unlike Joshua, he was more fashionable and very ambitious. He had designs on becoming a millionaire by the time he reached the age of 30. In spite of their obvious differences, the two young men got on as well as any young blokes in their early twenties might – bonding through beer and video games.

Mike's youngest, Isabella, was a brown eyed beauty - which she did her best to hide behind heavy black make-up and long blue/black hair which hung like rats-tails around her face. She was just 19 and studying to be a school teacher. She was also a talented musician in a semi-famous rock band. She favoured the 'goth' look, listening to and playing music which her parents found incomprehensible. She lived in student digs with her flatmates in London, working hard and playing hard by all accounts. She always seemed to become a moody tween when she was in her parents' presence, as if she was counting the minutes until she could be free of her 'boring old parents' again. In spite of this, Di adored her and was thus completely tolerant of her mood swings.

As Di glanced over at her younger child, Rachel - once again, as it often happened, her heart gave a sudden leap of pure love. Rachel was an ethereal creature, formed from air and spirit, like a little angel. She was diminutive in size like her mother, but was much fairer and had blue eyes. Even as a toddler, she had always seemed older than her years and had an almost permanent enigmatic Mona Lisa smile on her lips - as if she had been on this earth in a previous life. She was also a clever girl and excelled in all her subjects at school. She was adored by everyone.

'Rachel!' Di called up the stairs. 'Chloe! Dinner's ready.'

Isabella, known to them as Bella, was already slumped at the table, checking her gothic make-up in the reflection from her cutlery with her ear pods firmly in place, no doubt listening to 'Long Fingernails' or some other such music. Andy and Josh dumped their joysticks at the mention of food and raced to join her. Mike brought the joint of roast beef to the table, and when Chloe arrived she helped bring all the trimmings: the Yorkshire puddings, the roast potatoes, the peas and parsnips.

'You've gone all out,' Chloe said.

'Well, it's so exciting to have you all here,' Di smiled as she put the gravy in the microwave to reheat it.

'What's wrong with this, Mike?' Di asked, realising that the microwave had stopped buzzing.

'Nothing,' Mike frowned. 'Well, it was all fine when I set it up.' He said coming over to check the plug.

'Chloe, please take out your ear phones at the table', Di asked somewhat irritably, but it was more the malfunctioning microwave than Chloe's earphones that was at the root of her annoyance. She wanted everything to be perfect when the children were here – this lunch, the wedding, everything – and the slightest thing going wrong was stressing her.

'It's OK,' Mike said. 'It's working again. Must have been… Well, I don't know what it was, but I'll check the wiring later.'

Di sighed with relief as she watched the gravy spin slowly in the microwave. It was hypnotising, but before the timer pinged she was snapped out of her trance by a huge clunk on the floor above.

'What on earth was that?' she called out, looking up at the ceiling. 'Who's upstairs?'

Di stared at the ceiling perplexed.

'No-one. We are all here, doh!' Josh mocked. 'Why are you looking up there?'

'It sounded like one of you had a fall or something.'

'Why?' Rachel said.

'That bloody great thud.'

'What bloody great thud?' Mike said. 'Come and eat before it gets cold.'

Di took one last glance at the ceiling and shook the concern from her head, fully intending to enjoy every minute of this family lunch.

'Does it ever stop raining around here?' Andy said looking out of the window.

It was a rhetorical and slightly petulant question, yet Di and Mike found themselves looking at each other and mulling it over. They looked at each other across the table, telepathically acknowledging that they couldn't remember a day without at least a drizzle since they'd got here.

Chloe said, 'When it stops later we'll all go out for a stroll in the countryside.'

'Urgh, do we *have* to?' Bella moaned.

'We've got a tomb raider match to finish,' Andy protested.

'You need some fresh air,' Di cajoled them.

'Well, Rachel and I are going, aren't we,' Chloe smiled at her little step-sister, who nodded enthusiastically. 'Dad? Di?'

'We'll come, for sure,' Mike said. 'The countryside round here is so beauti—'

'Shhh!' Rachel hissed at something below the table and stamped a foot on the floor.

Everyone stopped to look at her.

'What's up? What are you doing sweetheart?' Di asked.

Rachel looked up and said with a smile. 'Nothing. It's fine now,' and carried on with chomping on her meal in a way that brooked no further discussion on the matter. So everyone else went back to their food and the conversation too.

'As I was saying,' Mike said with a shrug, 'you have to *see* the countryside. It's gorgeous, even in the rain.'

Di couldn't engage fully in the conviviality straight away. She studied her daughter, as she always did if she ever thought something was wrong with her baby, and her eyes fell to the floor where Rachel appeared to have directed some displeasure. She had almost forgotten what was under the rug until that moment. Now she felt herself shiver and she slowly dragged her feet back away from the hidden well and underneath her chair as far as she could, as if she thought something might grab at them otherwise.

'…and the moors are just beyond the top of the village,' Mike was saying, still extolling the virtues of the local environment, 'and they're absolutely unbel—'

Suddenly, the handle on the front door clicked and everyone looked towards it, their eyes widening and mouths open, as what appeared to be six or seven Japanese tourists trooped into the room.

'—ievable,' Mike finished.

The uninvited tourists didn't say hello, nor did they acknowledge the family around the table in any way. It was as if they couldn't see them there - eating a Sunday lunch in their own home. They were so utterly surprised, no-one said a thing.

They proceeded to walk around the living room and the kitchen, stopping now and then and chattering to one another, presumably to remark on the furniture and décor. They walked around the dining table and to the incumbent families' disbelief, completely ignoring the seven of them who sat in astonished silence, forks half raised to their mouths agape. Even when they each stepped over Charlie, she didn't move or bark, as if she was just as stunned as her owners were; she just raised one then the other eyebrow as each tourist passed over her.

Incredibly, when they had seen everything downstairs, they tramped upstairs. The astonished family listened to them walking above, chattering away, floorboards creaking. Mike stood up slowly, his instinct to protect his home and family kicking in, but still battling with his utter disbelief.

Presently they came downstairs again, round the table once more, as if the residents were mere items in an exhibition for their pleasure, and waltzed back out of the front door.

'What. The. Fuck, just. Happened?' Josh said with shoulders raised, both hands flat on the table.

Di would usually admonish him for swearing, but now wasn't the time, and anyway she felt exactly the same sentiment. 'What… What, what, what utter audacity!' she stammered.

'They didn't even leave us an admission fee,' Mike laughed despite the shock.

'Were they a load of tourists then?' Andy asked.

'Probably, - but whoever they were, they have a damned cheek!' Di retorted.

Everyone laughed at this, but Di wasn't laughing, although she did later when recounting this episode in the local.

'Why didn't you say something?' Chloe asked her father.

'I'm not entirely sure,' Mike said shaking his head, 'but I reckon they wouldn't have understood anything I said anyway. And I didn't want any unnecessary confrontation. Last time, we saw them in the yard by the well outside, and they clearly felt that they had more right to be here than we did'.

'Do they think this is a museum?' Andy said.

'A museum of what?' Chloe added.

Di got up and hurried to door. She locked it firmly. 'Well, this museum is closed. For good,' she said, making a mental note to keep all doors locked in the future even if they were inside.

CHAPTER II
A WALK IN THE WOODS

'Dad, the TV's on the blink now,' Andy pouted throwing his controller on the sofa.

'Are you sure you didn't turn it off because you were losing?' Mike teased.

'No, there really does seem to be something wrong with it,' Josh confirmed.

'Well, hang on!' Mike said putting the plug back on the microwave. 'I have to sort this out first.'

'Do you think maybe some things got bashed in the move?' Di said. 'I mean, why else would all our electrical stuff be going wrong?'

'Well, it's not everything,' Mike grumbled as he squinted at the little screws he was refitting. 'Just this and the dishwasher.'

'And the microwave, remember,' piped up Di.

'And now the TV,' Andy said pulling cables in and out of the back of it. 'And the music system was playing up in the week, you said.'

'Wouldn't surprise me, the way those removal men handled the driving,' Di said.

'It's probably the wiring in these old houses,' Mike said

with authority. 'This village is so stuck in a time warp the electricity supply probably isn't even three phase.'

'What does that mean?' Di frowned. 'Anyway, that's not very likely, it's newly renovated, remember?'

'Oh, it's working now,' Andy called as the TV flickered to life again.

'Oh, it's not,' Josh laughed, as it flickered off again.

'No, it is, look,' Di said looking at the image glowing on the screen.

There was an image of an old man staring out grimly at her. His balding pate was framed by a cloud of white hair. His lipless mouth was turned down at the corners, and his grey monobrow sat heavily atop his black deep-set eyes. He seemed to be wearing a heavy coat the colour of millstone grit, and the dirty looking shirt beneath it was topped off with some kind of limp black cravat. It was difficult to tell as the image flickered so much.

'No it's not,' Josh tutted.

'It is,' Di insisted. 'What's that then? The old bloke in the old-fashioned outfit.'

'Er, the screen is blank, Mum. And anyway, we were playing *Tomb Raider*. I can assure you Lara Croft never wears anything like that.'

'Thank God,' Andy leered.

'But…' Di couldn't tear her eyes from the old man. His gaze seemed to fix her, pinning her to the floor, until…

'There!' Andy shouted and Di jumped.

Lara Croft, in far fewer clothes than the old man bounced athletically around the screen.

'We're back on,' Josh said and grabbed his controller.

The microwave buzzed into life, and the heretofore inert dishwasher hummed as it began doing its job at last, too.

'Well, that's sorted,' Mike said trying to sound in control but clearly not knowing exactly what the problem had been. 'What about that walk then?'

Di was rooted to the spot still staring at the TV, but she was not seeing the platform game the boys were enjoying. She couldn't get the image of the old man out of her head, and yet, she didn't know if it had ever really been there – no one else seemed to think so. She shuddered involuntarily.

'DARLING?' Mike said more forcefully than he intended.

Di snapped out of her trance and looked at Mike.

'Shall we go for that walk? Look! Charlie can't wait, she's getting impatient.'

The dog had heard the word *walk* and was already running around frantically looking for her lead.

'Yes, yes,' Di said, the sight of Charlie innocently bowling about the room soothing her and making her smile. 'Come on, boys,' she said, knowing that the answer would be:

'No! We have to finish this game.'

'Chloe! Rachel!' she called out. 'We're going for a walk.'

The girls quickly came bounding down the stairs with almost as much excitement as Charlie.

'What about you, Bella? Coming?' Di asked gently.

Bella looked up from her Goth Rock magazine, as if that was the dumbest question she'd ever heard.

'She's coming,' Mike said grabbing the magazine and chucking it on the table.

'Dad!' Bella moaned. 'I'm not a kid.'

'Then stop acting like one and come for a walk like a grown-up,' he grinned.

She pantomimed a grin back at him and lolloped to the door. 'It's still raining,' she grumbled.

'It's just a light drizzle now,' Mike said, hurrying her along and taking his stick from the umbrella stand. He said his knees had become a little creaky now that he was older, after all the military exercises he had done as a young soldier before he joined the RAF. Not that Di had noticed. She wasn't convinced that he needed a walking aid, he just liked the idea of having one on countryside walks.

Di and Mike walked hand in hand down the hill through the village directing Rachel, who, with Charlie, tugged Chloe along in front. They were encouraging Bella to keep up as she slouched, day dreaming at the rear of the group.

'Are we going the right way?' Chloe called back.

'Yes, yes,' Di said. 'Keep going straight on for now', as she watched her own footing along the uneven footpath.

'What's that?' Rachel asked pointing at the door of one of the cottages on which hung a five-pointed star. 'It looks like the star they put on the Jews in the war. We learnt about it in history.'

'This one's not about Jews,' Chloe said, 'but I'm not entirely sure what it's for. Dad? Di? What do you think? Look, they're here too!'

Di and Mike looked about them at the doors of the cottages they passed, and indeed they noticed for the first time that a few of them had five-pointed pentagrams hanging from them, some festooned with dried flowers as if to make them into pretty wreaths.

'I'm not sure,' Di said. Although she knew exactly what they meant. She just didn't want to say in front of Rachel. Di squeezed Mike's hand in order to stop him from blurting it out too. Many 5-pointed stars had hung from every corner of George and Roslyn's witchcraft shop in town, and were even printed in gold on black table cloths. Di knew they were a symbol used in Pagan rituals - turning away evil influences, although it had gained a more nefarious reputation in horror books and movies. Of course, she thought it was a load of rubbish, but it made her feel slightly nauseous to wonder what evil influences everyone thought they needed to protect themselves from. 'I think it might be for a sort of festival. Like Halloween,' Di said out loud, but to convince herself as much as everyone else.

'But it's nowhere near October,' Rachel said with the directness of youth.

'No,' Chloe joined in, helping Di out. 'It's *like* Halloween. But there are quite a number of pagan festivals throughout the year.'

'Pagan?' Rachel asked.

'Yes,' Chloe said. 'It's a sort of ancient religion, like Christianity or Islam.'

'And what's this pagan religion called then?' Rachel frowned pointing at yet another door with a pentagram. 'I guess it's called Paganism', Di mused.

Bella began to take an interest. 'That is so cool,' she remarked.

'Bloody Bonkers,' Mike whispered in Di's ear.

Di was grateful to him for cutting through the conversation, and she laughed loudly.

'What was that you said, Mike? – louder please!'

'Nothing, darling. Now turn into the woods there,' he changed the subject, pointing grandly with his stick.

They did just that, and were grateful for the shelter under cover of the trees. They all found themselves looking around, admiring the beauty of this fairyland forest. The woods certainly had an ethereal quality, as a misty light from an invisible sun lit the ground through the spring time canopy. It revealed a carpet of creamy-white lily of the valley, and the bluebells were also beginning to bloom. The perfume was intoxicating. They then followed a narrow path towards the sound of babbling water, and soon came across a small tumbling river that sparkled as if making its own light. Chloe and Rachel tried out the stepping stones across the water while Mike stopped momentarily, transfixed on a couple on the bridge ahead.

'Goodness,' he gasped quietly to Di.

'What?' Di said, her heart skipping a beat at Mike's tone of voice.

'Look at that!' he said nodding at the two women kissing passionately on the bridge.

'Oh,' Di replied with relief. 'What about it?'

'Well, that's a bit much isn't? In public and all.'

'They're just kissing, Mike, and they're clearly in love. Wouldn't you kiss me here?'

'Of course I would, but we're--'

'Yes?' Di said goading him.

'Well… we're not a couple of girls.'

'Yes, they are indeed lesbians,' Di said with a glint in her eye.

'Indeed,' Mike replied, realising how much Di was enjoying his unreasonable discomfort.

'Fancy that! A couple of lesbians in the lesbian capital of the north. Who would have thought it?'

'Oh shush!' Mike said as Charlie sped past them and headed for the bridge. 'I'll get used it. Give *me* a kiss then!' So she did.

'Charlie!' called Di. 'Come here!'

But Charlie wasn't listening. Di assumed she was racing to greet the couple on the bridge, so she and Mike hurried after her to make sure she wasn't being a nuisance. However, before the bridge, Charlie had ducked down by the bank. Di followed him down as the couple above strolled away.

'What have you found?' Di said hoping Charlie wasn't terrorising a rabbit or a fox. She was a terrier - and she just couldn't help herself.

She found Charlie sniffing around the damp black remains of a fire which had been made in front of a less than rudimentary table. It was made from a warped piece of wood lain across two upright logs. On the table top were the stubs of a number of black candles, a few white shells, and, disconcertingly for Di, the jaw bone and femurs of a long-dead animal big enough to be a small sheep. Or a dog. There were also three or four pretty dream catchers hanging from the trees.

'What is it?' Mike asked as he caught up with her.

'Looks like an altar,' came Bella's voice, sounding more enthusiastic than she had been in a long time. 'Cool.'

Di wanted to usher them all away, but she watched with a strange fascination as Bella knelt in front of the altar and examined all the things left there.

'Don't touch it!' Mike yelled as Bella picked up the jaw bone.

'Why not?' Bella said, her eyes still fixed on it.

'You don't know where it's been,' Mike said lamely.

'I do. Inside the face of an animal. Just like your jaw bone. And anyone else's for that matter.'

'Come on, let's go,' Mike said sounding uneasy.

'Why?' Bella grumbled.

'Whoever made it might come back soon.'

'Good,' Bella smirked.

'Come on,' Di said. 'Your dad's probably right. We don't want to mess with someone else's… stuff.

She turned to lead them back up the bank, and on the outskirts of the clearing she stopped suddenly as she came face to face with a 12 inch or so effigy, of a what was clearly meant to be a human form figure hanging by the neck from a tree. She gasped. It was quite well made from an old pair of tights, as far as she could discern. The face was drawn in a childlike manner on a little oval of white cloth stitched to the head. Red lips, arched eyebrows and a little rouge on each cheek, told Di this was meant to be a woman. Its hair was represented by a few strands of brown wool stitched over the top of the head to resemble a short bob. And the clothes it was dressed in were reminiscent of……

'Hey, Di, it looks a bit like you!' Bella observed.

'What?' Di gasped, knowing exactly what she meant.

The effigy was dressed in tiny blue jeans, and a floral top over which was pulled a small well-knit mustard coloured cardigan. Di couldn't bring herself to look down at her own attire. She knew exactly what she would see: blue jeans, with a floral top over which she wore a mustardy yellow cardigan. She had worn this last time she and Mike had been in The Cross.

'Don't be daft,' she said uncertainly, and then more playfully than she felt, she shoved Bella up the bank to hide the fact her blood was running cold.

'Is it part of a ritual?' Rachel said trying to pull Chloe down the bank, as the rest of them came up.

'Probably,' Mike said. 'Come on!'

'I want to see,' Rachel insisted.

'Tell her, Chloe!' Mike said quietly.

'Come on,' Chloe said dutifully, but Rachel was already down by the altar.

Di felt a sudden sense of panic and hurried back down to the bank to get Rachel, but she stopped in her tracks as she heard Rachel whisper to Chloe:

'I think there's someone in that hole in the floor under the table, and he hates this.'

'Who hates this?' Chloe asked distractedly as she looked above the altar from where other bones and talismans hung.

'The man in the basement.'

'The man in the basement?' Chloe asked fingering a brightly coloured rag tied around one of the branches above.

'Yes. I feel it makes him very angry. That's why he sometimes makes noises.'

'The man in the basement,' Chloe said as if trying to work out a cryptic crossword clue. 'What basement? I thought it was all blocked up. Does someone live down there?'

'I don't think so. But I can hear him under our feet.'

'Under our…Oh!' she exclaimed suddenly. 'You mean, like hell? The devil? Down there below the earth. The basement!' Chloe laughed. 'What have you been up to? It's not good to mess with the occult. You never know who or what you might conjure up.'

Rachel sighed and went up the bank saying, 'I don't think it's the Devil. I just don't know his name.'

Charlie barked as if in agreement and ran up the bank too.

'Who?' Chloe frowned.

'I don't think his name is The Devil,' Rachel repeated, chasing Charlie up the bank and off into the woods, leaving Chloe looking at Di and wondering why her future step-mum looked so pale.

CHAPTER 12

CROWS!

Di was already feeling uneasy, but she had gone very pale after overhearing the girl's conversation. She made an excuse to the resident family's student nurse, Chloe, to explain her pallor; she told her she'd eaten too much apple pie and custard at lunch. It was quite plausible. She loved apple pie and the whole family knew it. She had just needed to walk it off, she told Chloe.

And yet at the same time she couldn't wait for the walk to be over – at least in the woods. She was spooked, which wasn't like her, but she couldn't bear the idea of seeing another effigy hanging from the trees. She had an irrational fear that if she did, it would resemble other members of the family. *Irrational*, she repeated, but she couldn't shake the sight of her likeness hanging from the tree by the bank. And she was starting to become worried about Rachel.

She directed her fellow ramblers out of the wood, and along the paths by the drystone walls so that they could marvel at the endless moors and stare adoringly at the little lambs playing tag and bouncing on and off a hay rick. She was aching to take Rachel aside and ask her what she meant about the man in the basement, but at the same time she feared Rachel's answer. *Irrational*, she repeated, watching Rachel's innocent joy at the sight of the pretty lambs and telling herself that Rachel's words to Chloe had been equally innocent, the typical workings of a child's imagination.

When they got home, damp and muddy, Di ushered Rachel up to the bath. Her daughter needed very little persuasion. She couldn't wait to try out the jacuzzi. Bella grabbed her magazine from the dining table to pick up where she left off before being interrupted again. Chloe helped Mike with the clearing up.

'Where are the boys?' Di asked on her way up the stairs.

'They left a note,' Chloe called from the kitchen. 'They've gone to the pub.'

'Mmm, not a bad idea,' Di said feeling frazzled. A stiff drink could steady her nerves right now.

She made sure Rachel had everything she needed before going up to her bed to lie down for a moment. She took with her a glass of her favourite white wine. She just wanted to be alone, recharge, recalibrate, calm down her mind, and think logically as she did about every case she had ever taken on. But before she had even begun to sort out the jumble of thoughts and emotions this new home had stirred up in her, she started to doze.

It was the tapping that woke her. Her eyes snapped open, but evening had arrived since she lay down, so she had no idea where the tapping was coming from at first. The room was just a collection of grey shadows, and so her eyes focused on the crepuscular glow which loitered in the skylight. The tapping was coming from there. She could make out a shape, darker than the dusk around it. The shape of a large bird. And its beak was tapping on the glass, as if trying to get her attention.

'Bugger off, bird,' Di said groggily, feeling inexplicably

hung over though she hadn't had enough wine for that, but she never liked sleeping in the afternoon, and it never made her feel better. 'Must buy that blind and get it fixed up there.'

She waved her hand at the skylight, but the crow kept tapping. In fact it tapped harder and faster than before. Tap, tap. Tap, tap. Tap tap tap tap. TAP TAP TAP TAP.

'Stop it!' Di called out. 'Get lost!'

But the bird now struck the glass again and again so hard that Di thought it would bash its own brains out. Then the glass cracked just a little, but the beak was unable to penetrate the window. Di thought the bird's eyes flashed red, or perhaps it was blood from its beak. She wasn't sure, because a piercing scream from downstairs suddenly grabbed her attention.

It was Rachel.

'Agh! Help!' she shrieked.

Di found the bedroom light, flicked it on and flew down the stairs. She was halfway down, when the lights went out again and she nearly fell head over heels in her haste to get to Rachel. Regaining her balance, she fumbled down the remaining stairs and along the landing. She hit the light switch there. Nothing. So she groped her way through the darkness to the bathroom and towards the noise, Rachel's screams and sobbing guiding her along the way. Di's heart was in her mouth, barely breathing as she threw the door open, desperate to get to her child. As she entered the bathroom, all the lights suddenly came on revealing something lurching and lunging at her from the edge of the bath. It wailed and waved around its arms like a banshee. To Di, as her eyes tried to adjust to the light, it looked like some kind of yeti; a strange white bubbly fluffy creature.

'Mum!' Rachel yelled.

'Rachel!' Di called out about to strike out at the entity coming at her when she realised Rachel's voice was coming from inside it.

'Help! I can't stop it.'

Rachel fell into her mother's arms, and the bubbles which enveloped her puffed up into the air revealing her terrified face. Meanwhile over Rachel's shoulder, Di saw the jacuzzi spewing up mountains of more and more bubbles until the bath itself was invisible and the bubbles were piling towards the ceiling.

'What the hell?' Di heard Mike say from somewhere behind her as she fought her way through the fog of foam looking for the 'off' switch.

The other girls had come out of their rooms to see what the commotion was all about. The two girls shouted their concern;

'Is Rach Ok?'

'What's happening? Why did all the lights go out?'

'Sorry, Mum,' Rachel whined as her mother wrapped her in a towel. 'Sorry. I couldn't turn it off, and the lights went out.'

'It's OK, it's OK,' Di said opening the window and wafting some of the bubbles out. 'I think you could have used a little less of this though.' She held up a near empty large bottle of bubble bath which certainly wasn't anywhere near empty before Rachel got in the bath.

'Sorry,' Rachel said again, sheepishly.

Di was so relieved that there was no catastrophe and it was nothing more than her daughter getting overexcited with the jacuzzi and bubble bath, that she burst out laughing.

'Mum! It's not funny, I was really scared!' Rachel pouted.

Mike and her step sisters hugged her close and grinned at Di.

'Sorry, darling,' Di snorted. 'I'm just glad you're OK.'

Mike and his girls cleaned up the bathroom and the image of her Rachel, covered head to toe in bath foam kept them all laughing and giggling as they did so.

Everyone was so giddy that Di totally forgot about the

lights failing on her way downstairs, as if someone was deliberately trying to trip her, and the crow smashing its beak into the skylight in the bedroom.

But when her and Mike went up to bed that night the small crack in the window brought it all flooding back.

'What happened here?' Mike said looking up at the glass.

'I thought I dreamt it,' Di whispered.

'Dreamt what?'

'The crow. One of those bloody crows cracked it. When I was having a lie down. Just before Rachel… as if…'

Mike was huffing and puffing at the breakage. 'We'll have to get that crack fixed first thing. With all the rain we get here, it'll no doubt widen in time and the rain will drip into our bed. We will get a blind fixed as soon as possible too.'

Di held Mike tight as he fell asleep, but her eyes wouldn't close. They were fixed on the skylight and the crack which just somehow felt like a warning. She thought of the crow and the blood; of the bones in the wood, of the Pentagrams and the effigy hanging from the tree.

She found herself tossing and turning, she simply could not sleep for ruminating about what she had experienced so far in this place, and eventually she gave up trying. Although she couldn't quite believe what she was doing, she found herself swinging her legs gently out of bed and slipping on some warm clothes. She tip-toed downstairs, slipped into her wellies and coat and, pocketing the torch, she quietly let herself out of the house.

CHAPTER 13
THE COVEN

S he stopped in the courtyard and listened, her heart thumping. She thought she heard a snigger coming from somewhere. She listened again. Nothing, must have been the breeze fanning her hair. She made her way down the path out onto Church Street and down the cobbles through the village. At this time of night, it seemed as long-abandoned as the old church. She retraced her steps from earlier today, and into the woods, looking for the altar again. She seemed to know somehow, that whoever worshipped at that altar would be doing so at this time of night. If so, she might get some answers as to why there was an effigy that had been dressed almost exactly like her hanging in the tree there.

She followed the sound of the eternally flowing water to the river and snapped off the torch, when she heard voices downstream. The river glowed in the dim moonlight which helped to mark the path for her to follow. She smelt wood smoke and saw a warm flickering. Someone had reignited the fire by the bank. Her heart beat faster. The sound of drums being beaten reached her, and there were voices chanting something she couldn't quite hear. She crept closer and closer, until her foot slipped on the muddy bank. She didn't fall, but she let out a gasp. She clamped her hand over her mouth and waited.

The drumming and chanting continued. No-one heard or saw her.

She stepped carefully onwards, until she could make out the fire clearly by the river bank and several figures dancing about it. Someone was sitting outside the circle, drumming out a rhythm on some sort of percussion instrument. From here the figures were just silhouettes. She needed to move around and up to the bridge to see more clearly. So she sidled into the trees and staying in the shadows, moved around to where the couple had been kissing earlier. As she turned towards the bridge something brushed her shoulder.

She froze.

She slowly turned and made out a dreamcatcher hanging from the branch near her shoulder. She let out the breath she had been holding and stepped onto the bridge using the drystone wall to hide behind.

As she peered over the top, down towards the dancers she saw with surprise that the figures were all near or completely naked. The firelight illuminated their faces, and then she realised that she knew at least five of them. She slapped her hand over her mouth again to stop the inevitable gasp at the sight of Len, Big Will and the young man they had both shared a pint with at the bar, prancing around more or less in the buff. Less surprising perhaps, was that two others were Terry and Fi, totally naked. What shocked Di most of all was that Fi appeared to dance around without the aid of her stick. And so did Big Will for that matter.

Were they lying about their ailments, Di thought, or had they suddenly been healed by whatever was going on here?

Just then Terry hissed, 'Shh!'

The drumming and chanting ceased abruptly.

Di heard someone say, 'All quiet. Someone's watching!'

Then louder: 'Who's there? Come out, show yourself, stranger!'

As the dancers looked about, Di threw herself back from the wall out of sight. She fell back and hit her head on the other side of the bridge, but she quickly scrambled to her feet and ran. She tried to turn on the torch, but she was running too fast to steady her hand. This was no time to stop, so she stumbled on through the trees, their branches scratching her from all sides. She heard someone's footsteps crashing up the path behind her.

'STOP!' someone shouted.

She ran even faster.

Someone or something howled behind her and her breathing became loud and asthmatic. Her head ached from the knock and she couldn't think straight. Everywhere she turned just looked the same: an oily swirl of shadows. She felt faint from lack of breath, panicky as if she were in a maze, and that she might never find her way out.

'STOP!' the voice called out again. This time it was closer, as was the howl that followed it.

'Shit, shit, shit,' Di said almost hyperventilating. She heard running water and her heart sank as she realised she was back by the river.

'*Stop*,' someone hissed in her ear and the blood drained from her body. 'This way.'

It was Bella! Oh, thank God! Her stepdaughter grabbed her hand and ran with Di the short distance to the edge of the wood where they hurtled up the street, Di struggling in her wellies. The hill seemed steeper than ever. As if in a horrid nightmare, Di's legs grew heavy as the ground felt as if it had turned to mud beneath her feet. Bella dragged her on, both expecting to be apprehended by Big Will and Len at any moment. After what seemed to be an eternity, they found themselves ducking off the main street into the lane leading to Goose Yard.

Thank God, she thought as they stumbled towards the door. 'Where in hell's name did you come from Bella?'

'I heard you go out and followed you,' Bella explained.

'Well, well, well. Where do you think you're going?' a man's voice demanded.

Bella and Di skidded to a halt, arrested by two large figures blocking their way.

CHAPTER 14
A HIDDEN MESSAGE?

D i raised her torch to use as a weapon, then the penny dropped.

'Josh!' Di panted as she recognised her son's voice.

Andy laughed. 'The look on your faces! Where have you been at this time of night?'

'More to the point, where have you two been? All of you, get inside, quick,' Di said trying to sound like a responsible mother again and not in fear for her life.

With them all wide-eyed in the kitchen light and the door locked firmly behind them, Josh said, 'Where were you two coming from and why the hurry?'

Di wasn't sure how to answer so she thought it best to deflect the question with one of her own. 'Never mind us, what were you doing out there at this hour?'

'We came back from the pub. There was a bit of a lock in, so we stayed to play a game of poker'.

'You'll get the landlord in trouble if the police catch you at it,' Di said gesturing at the kitchen clock which said 12.45. 'It's way past closing time.'

'The police don't bother coming up here. Anyway, we were invited in to your neighbour's for a night cap.'

'Jeffrey?' Di was astonished.

'No. Dorothy,' Andy said.

'Doro*thea*,' Josh laughed. 'Get it right or she'll have your guts for garters again.'

'Oh yeah. Bloody hell,' Andy giggled. 'She's a card, isn't she?'

'Drinks like a fish.'

'We loved her. Her house is a bit smelly though….and that dog farts constantly!'

'Oh, well,' Di said smoothing down her dishevelled hair and checking the growing lump to her head. 'Don't know about you, but we're knackered, aren't we Bella.'

Bella nodded, eyeing Di with a mixture of amusement and suspicion.

'We're off to bed.' And Di hurried with Bella upstairs.

'Kick your arse on *Tomb Raider* before bed?' Andy poked Josh.

'Like hell you will,' Josh said diving onto the sofa to grab the best controller.

'For goodness sake, haven't you had enough entertainment for tonight? It's really late, don't stay up much longer,' Di suggested.

'No, Mother, we won't!' the boys assured her cheekily. Di was not convinced, but was too tired to argue.

On the first floor landing, Di bundled Bella into the bedroom opposite Rachel's. Since Rachel had insisted that Chloe sleep with her, Bella had the other bedroom all to herself, as the boys were sharing the room in the attic space next to Di's.

Bella flopped onto the bed and reached for her magazine, but Di stopped her.

'Bella,' she hissed. 'What were you thinking? Why did you follow me?'

'Errrr,' Bella said looking at Di with a disapproving glare. 'Don't you need to explain what *you* were doing?'

Di felt herself shrink. She sat on the edge of the bed and they both remained in silence for a moment. Then:

'Wasn't it cool?' Bella grinned.

'Cool?' Di said, incredulous.

'Well, not all those bits and tits flapping around, which was *gross*, but the whole ritual thing. I knew there would be something going down around midnight. It was getting really interesting until you blew it.'

'Me?' Di snapped.

'Well, I would have been there for ages to watch, if they hadn't noticed *you*.'

'You could have got yourself hurt,' Di said, but she had a feeling she was in more danger than Bella.

'A load of middle-aged overweight people naked in the woods?' Bella smiled. 'I wasn't worried about being able to outrun *them*.'

'They're not all old. And Terry certainly looks like he could shift,' Di said with great certainty.

'You know them?' Bella sat up.

'Erm, well……,' Di stuttered, wondering how much information to give Bella. But she had a feeling she needed Bella to give her some information too, so in the spirit of sharing she said, 'I've met some of them. We bought this house from one of them; the ginger bearded guy. His friend was the old stocky hairy bloke. And another two are a couple who live in a cottage up the main street. I knew *they* were a bit odd, but I had no idea Len would go in for stuff like that. He doesn't seem the type. If they had seen us, Bella, God knows what they might have done.'

'Tied us to the altar and added us to their collection of bones?' Bella whispered mischievously, relishing the image.

'Don't joke!' Di hissed. 'If they're bonkers enough to

prance around the woods naked or semi-naked in the middle of the night…'

'Why did *you* go?' Bella probed, brooking no evasive answers this time. 'Was it the effigy on the tree? It was meant to be you, wasn't it?'

Di shook her head, but she wasn't disagreeing with Bella. 'I… It… it was weird that it had the same clothes on and… some strange things have happened in the house since we moved in.'

'Like Japanese tourists invading at dinner?'

Di smiled wryly. 'Well, yes, that was bloody weird, but some less explicable things, shall we say. And I wondered if someone was messing with us. Trying to scare us off. And now this…' her voice trailed off as she wondered if Len was the common denominator here. He never seemed truly happy about selling the house. He had let slip how much he was losing financially to his wife. Perhaps he now regretted selling for the price he did, - and that maybe it was his intention to scare off any new buyers so he could swoop back in and get the house for a song. She'd exposed more dastardly plots than that in court, before now. Surely, it wasn't that unlikely.

Bella reached for her magazine again.

'Bella,' Di huffed. 'Please just put that down for one minute, will you?'

'No Di, listen to me a minute, I'm not reading it. I want to show you something.' She flicked to the centre of the magazine. 'Strange things happening in this house you said. Like this?'

The centre pages of the magazine appeared to have been burnt, but not completely. Holes here and there, some bigger than others, some joining others, and the articles on the pages beneath showing through.

'Who did this?' Di asked.

Bella shrugged. 'It was fine before we went out for the walk this afternoon. Dad took it off me and chucked it on the dining table, and it was all in one piece. It was still there when we got back, but as soon as we got in, I opened it again and saw this. I didn't see any bits of ash around either. It's SO weird'.

'Did you ask the boys?' Di said, already sure they would never be so stupid as to do something as destructive or dangerous as this in the house.

'No, but look,' Bella said, folding back the pages beneath and holding the burnt ones up to the light.

The holes were not haphazard; they formed the shape of a face. An old man's face. Just like the one Di had seen in the TV. She froze. Her skin crawled, and her scalp tightened. She stared silently at the pages for so long, until Bella eventually whispered, 'Di?'

Di blinked and saw Bella looking anxious for the first time in as long as she could remember. She snatched the magazine from her and Bella flinched.

'Not a word about this to your brothers and sisters, especially Rachel. OK? We don't need to scare her.'

Bella nodded, her eyes pooling.

'It's OK,' Di said softly, seeing she'd upset Bella. 'I'll have a word with Len and get to the bottom of this. Until then, not a word to anyone. We don't want him to get wind we're on to him.'

She kissed Bella's forehead.

'Get some sleep now sweetheart. For now, can we keep this to ourselves?'

Bella nodded and gave her a weak smile.

She went back downstairs where the boys were still playing video games and threw the magazine in the kitchen bin.

'Night, boys! Not too loud now.'

She marched back across the living room and put one foot on the bottom stair. Stopped. Turned and marched back across the room to the kitchen, where she fished the magazine from the bin and took it outside in the courtyard.

She looked at the dustbin.

No.

She thought about burning it.

That might draw unwanted attention.

She marched outside to the wishing well and tossed it in. She heard it flap and slap its way far down to the water where in the darkness she imagined it becoming sodden and sinking to the bottom where it could rot for all she cared.

'Make a wish,' she suggested to herself with a healthy dollop of sarcasm.

But she did wish, despite her cynicism. She wished that whoever was messing with her would get their comeuppance soon enough. And if she had to get the police involved, she would. She was no stranger to the law. Len bloody Greenwood didn't know who he was messing with.

CHAPTER 15
THE WEDDING

The main wedding event went ahead in Skipton with great excitement without a hitch. It was a lovely day, and was thoroughly enjoyed by all. They had planned their church blessing a few weeks later, which was arranged to take place in the Victorian church in Heptonstall. Mike's parents had divorced many moons ago. The split had been acrimonious and sadly, and they still didn't speak to each other, hence the two wedding ceremonies. Di could not bear the idea of any awkwardness on what was meant to be the happiest of days. Mike's mother attended the registry office in Skipton, and Mike's father was coming up from the south to attend the church blessing. The children all came up for it and Di invited some close friends from Saddleworth and from work, as well as a few new ones from the village.

'Well, of course I won't be able to attend, silly girl,' Dorothea said, smacking her crumb-laden lips together as she indulged in a chocolate Hobnob. 'I can't leave my commode for any length of time, whatever the circumstances.' She looked over her shoulder from where she leaned on her Zimmer frame in the doorway, as if to make sure her throne was still inside, in the likely event that she would need it again soon.

'Oh, that's a shame,' Di spoke a half-truth, leaning against the fence that separated her property from Dorothea's. 'The boys really enjoyed your company when they visited you last time they were here. .'

'I'm sure they did,' Dorothea munched. 'They seem like good boys, and they probably haven't had such intelligent and interesting conversation in a long time.'

Di smiled politely, ignoring the possibility that there was a swipe at her in that comment and looked across to the next garden. 'What about you, Jeffrey?' She raised her voice to catch his attention.

He was tending to his beautiful flower bed. 'Well, I would be honoured to come. Thank you very much for the invitation.'

'Oh well,' Dorothea interrupted, 'that's another good reason not to attend. Glad I'm bound to my piss pot after all.'

'So am I,' Jeffrey countered. 'You'd probably turn to dust the moment you stepped over the threshold of the church anyway,' he said making a cross with his fingers and wielding it in her direction.

'Oh do get back to your roses, you big pansy,' Dorothea spat.

'They're begonias actually, ignoramus,' Jeffrey huffed.

Dorothea winked at Di. She knew exactly what the flowers were, and she also knew exactly what buttons to press in her neighbour. Di felt that both of them actually enjoyed winding each other up, although they would never admit it.

'Well,' Di said feeling rather awkward, 'we're going to have a little party here in the yard after the church blessing, so please join in the fun if you can. There will be plenty of people here to help.'

'Will there be food?' Dorothea asked through a mouthful of biscuit.

'Absolutely. We're planning a barbecue, weather permitting,' Di said looking up at the sky which was as grey as ever.'

'Well, then yes, I'd love to come, irritating old poofters permitting,' she said with a sideways glance at Jeffrey.

'Jeffrey, you are very welcome to come for the food too, of course,' Di said firmly as a means of gently chastising Dorothea.

'You are very kind. Thank you, my dear,' he said all but sticking out his tongue at his neighbour.

Di had popped down the village to the Post Office a couple of days later to buy some envelopes and stamps and to post a letter.

'We hear you're getting married here in the village soon?'

Di felt her shoulders tense when she heard Fi's voice behind her. She hadn't seen Fi since she was dancing naked around a fire in the woods.

'Oh...' Di said, noticing immediately that Fi was back leaning on her walking stick. 'Yes, we are. Well, not getting married as such. We're actually legally married already. It's a church blessing. So not a big affair, you know.' Di hoped Fiona would interpret that as: *only close friends and family are invited*. But then, she reasoned, if Fi had heard about the blessing, then she might have also heard that a few others from the village had been invited.

'Well, sounds delightful, nonetheless,' Fi beamed.

There was an awkward moment as Di fiddled with the letter in her hand and Fiona continued to smile at her.

Then Di cringed inwardly as she heard herself say, 'Haven't seen you for a while.'

'Really?' Fi said with a twinkle in her eye. 'I feel like I've seen you.'

Di blanched.

'But,' Fi went on, 'it was probably at a distance as we both went on with our business around the village, you know.'

'Ah… er… yes, probably.'

'In fact, now that I think about it,' Fi frowned, 'we haven't got together properly since that night you came to ours for dinner. It's a shame. We should remedy that.'

Di, fearing another dinner invitation, or worse, that she was vying for a reciprocal invitation, reasoned that having Terry and Fi among a crowd of their nearest and dearest would be a much safer option, so she said, 'Well, you are most welcome to attend the blessing. And we're having a barbecue at ours afterwards.'

'Weather permitting,' Fiona said like an echo of Di earlier to her neighbours.

'Of course.'

'Well, that sounds divine. Terry will be so pleased too. Thank you so much. We'll see you then,' she said hobbling out of the shop.

Di looked down at her hand. The letter she held was quivering as if a breeze was rushing through the place. But it was just her hand trembling.

CHAPTER 16
THE BLESSING

On the day of the Church Blessing, the sky was still grey, but the rain held off as Di in her cream and mauve Chinese-style silk shift dress walked arm in arm with Mike through the churchyard of Thomas à Becket towards the new church. She looked proudly on as her blended brood of five, all scrubbed up nicely for the day, led the way; Rachel looking back at her mum with her usual enthusiasm, hand in hand with Chloe of course; Andy and Josh looking dashing in their suits; and Bella looking interestingly stunning in her own individual gothic kind of way, as she posed for a photograph in the churchyard amongst the graves. Very appropriate, Di thought to herself, wryly! The girls had been allowed to choose their own dresses, and all held summer flowers in natural style poseys, as did Di. However, the flowers in Chloe's posey were almost entirely monochrome and matched her outfit perfectly.

Di carefully picked her way over the paving of large gravestones that filled the churchyard, hoping her heels wouldn't get caught between any of them. As she looked down the name on one of the graves caught her eye:

David Hartley
1770

She'd heard the name somewhere before. It sparked a memory in her. The memory was strong and clear, because she realised she had heard the name spoken for the first time in this very place, on the first day her and Mike had come to visit the village. It was Robert the tour guide who had said:

'When all mists and mizzles swirl through this place, as it does very often, it favours a ghostly film. Mebbi Count Dracula himself o' most likely evil David 'Artley visits on dark neyts.'

She noticed that a number of members of his family were also buried in the same grave, their names etched underneath his. She resolved to find out more about this mysterious man and whether he was connected in some way to Goose Barn.

But now wasn't the time to muse on such dark matters. This was going to be a fabulous and very happy day, as was their 'first' wedding in Skipton. She glanced over her shoulder and smiled at Ralph, Mike's father, who had donned his military officer's uniform, proudly wearing his medals for the occasion. Mike's stepmother, Anna, was dressed to the nines as well, with a hat fit for Ascot. All five of their children looked amazing, and even Joshua wore a navy suit and matching tie. She was pleased to see Ollie and Stephen there too, and they looked simply splendid, like catwalk models in their bright tailored suits.

Di's face dropped somewhat, as she saw ambling behind Ralph and Anna was Len, Big Will and their young friend. They were processing side by side down the path through the gravestones, chests puffed out as if it were they who were giving away the bride. Notwithstanding Di's misgivings, they were a sight to behold. They had made a genuine attempt to look smart in their Sunday best, which, she thought sardonically, was a huge improvement on their birthday suits!

Di stumbled in her expensive highest heels, which caught

in a crack in the ancient path, and as Mike gripped her tightly, she thought it best to concentrate on the path ahead until she got safely inside the church.

Once by the altar, waiting for the vicar to commence the service, Di and Mike looked behind them, greeting the congregation. Di spotted the three men again, who she referred to as 'The Three Musketeers', standing near the back and, although she pretended not to, she examined them as thoroughly as she could from this distance.

The youngest was a good head and a half taller than the other two, and at least fifteen years their junior. He was by far the smartest, with his short moussed spikey hair do, but his dark blue off-the-peg suit was probably last worn at his own wedding, when he was a slimmer version of himself. He would have looked fine and handsome, had it not been for the tight fit and the cuffs of his jacket, which were rolled up to show his sinewy hairy wrists. The collar of his off-white shirt was turned up, leaving his tie loose around his protruding clavicles, and his enormous feet shod in black leather shoes that had long lost their shine. Len, stood beside him, hands in pockets. He was looking surprisingly dapper. His wiry ginger hair, usually a little on the wild side, was slicked down firmly to the sides of his head. He was wearing a pair of mid-brown corduroy trousers, a beige shirt, brown tie and a checked sports jacket with brown suede shoes. Both he and his younger friend wore checked brown and grey wool peaked caps, which they removed when Big Will gave them a nudge and a sign to remove them. Will's black and grey hair was also plastered to his head. He wore a black jacket, a little short at the arms, a white shirt and tie of opalescent hue. If it wasn't for his beetle black eyes and his incongruous jogging pants and trainers, Di might not have recognised him.

'Ey up, you two,' called Len loudly across the church as he caught Di's eye. 'Ow yer doin'? Fine day fer t'nuptools.' He raised his thumb. 'Sadly, I think it meight rain latter.' His voice echoed around the stone church. 'N'er mind, we'll have a good do anyways.'

Di wanted the ground to swallow her up, but not from embarrassment. It seemed Len had invited himself to the barbecue too. A large contingency of the witches' coven, or whatever it was that she had seen in the woods would be coming then!

Mike, on the other hand, still blissfully ignorant of the coven, sniggered at Len's contribution to the ceremony.

And when Big Will added loudly, 'Ee lass, ye's look as pretty as a picture,' Mike's son joined in, joking laughingly. 'Yes, haha, yes, our wicked step mother looks divine!'

Josh, standing on the other side of his mother from Mike retorted, 'Hey that's my mother you're calling wicked!' He turned to his mum and melted her heart when he said, 'You look lovely Mum,' and then kissed her on the cheek. Di's eyes welled with tears.

An impatient clearing of the throat made Di jump. She turned back to see the vicar right in front of her, ready to start. He was an austere, tall, slim vicar who towered above her. He peered down his bony nose at her and Mike as he bestowed blessings from heaven upon the happy couple. Despite the fact that the vicar resembled a skeleton, and despite the fact that Di wasn't particularly religious, she felt a strong need to take all the blessings she could from him.

Di was pleased that although divorcees were still not legally allowed to marry in church, the ceremony was very much akin to a proper wedding service. They even had the church choir, thankfully turning the usual tuneless drone of the congregation into a rousing ethereal swell as the hymns were sung.

During the first hymn Di could hear one voice rising above the rest, and she soon realised it was Len crowing like a cock. When the hymn was done she – and everyone else – heard him say to his two friends, 'Ee by gum, there's nowt better than a good old fashioned 'ymn ter raise the roof and t'spirits.'

Di had become overly cynical by now, and in her increasing paranoia, she imagined the comment was designed to agitate her.

When they got back to Goose Barn for the BBQ, the heavens opened and rain poured down, just as Len had predicted and as Di suspected it might. But she was not to be put off. Mike and the boys erected two enormous parasols in the yard under which everyone crowded, determined to remain in the open air in the spirit of all British barbis, while Di strategically placed a few retro polaroid cameras about the tables so that everyone could take snaps whenever they wanted.

Dorothea's commode was placed in her doorway under-cover so she could sit there safe from any mishaps and still feel part of the action.

'Fresh out today, isn't it?' Di commented.

'Fresh my arse. It's bloody cold,' Dorothea spat.

'Well, I'll fetch you a warm shawl, and you can get this down you. That'll soon warm you up,' Di said boldly handing her a large glass of vodka and tonic, before popping into the house for a warm blanket to cover her knees Nothing was going to ruin the day for Di, not even Dorothea's little snipes. She clinked her glass with Dorothea's and downed her own drink, fully intending to get 'merry'.

'Lovely ceremony,' Terry said as Di returned to the shelter of the parasols. He was helping himself to a particularly large glass of gin.

'Thanks. Yes I thought so,' retorted Di curtly, and with the alcohol already loosening her tongue, she added, 'You and Fi like a good ceremony, eh?'

Terry examined her for a moment as if trying to work out the subtext in her comment, then simply said, 'Yes of course, that we do.'

She turned away from him and found Mike, who looked like he was on a mission to get legless.

'Having a good time, my wifey?' he asked, kissing her warmly.

'I am, my husband' she smiled. 'You?'

'Oh yeah', he said enthusiastically.

'And your dad and Anna?' she asked as she poured herself another drink.

Mike and Di looked around and saw Ralph and Anna chatting animatedly to Ollie and Stephen, while Jeffrey made sure their drinks were topped up and sorted them out with food.

'Oh my God,' Mike laughed.

'What?'

'Wait till Dad finds out they're all gay. He won't be so pally with him then.'

Di scolded Mike, 'What does that matter? If they get on, they get on.' But Di knew in Ralph and Mike's military world, being gay was still very much frowned upon. The beginning of the twenty-first century was in sight and yet, amazingly, such draconian, bigoted laws still applied. No wonder Mike had such trouble looking at two women kissing on a bridge in the woods. However, he was beginning to change, she noted, and for the better.

The thought of the bridge in the woods suddenly sent the image of the effigy hanging from the tree beneath it racing to the forefront of Di's mind. And, as if he could read her thoughts, Len was suddenly upon her, hand on her shoulder, saying, 'Ow yer doin', lass?'

Di drew in her breath sharply at his touch. Len must have felt her recoil and drew his hand away as one would from a hot pan.

'Len,' was all she could say. So she took a large draught of her drink to fill the gap, as she considered whether or not now was the perfect time to confront him about his nocturnal games.

'Lovely church do - and lovely scram. This 'ere is Rick.' He presented the youngest and tallest of his little gang.

Di put out her hand automatically and shook Rick's. It was strange meeting someone for the first time when you already knew what they looked like almost naked.

'Congratulations. Nice do. Thanks fer invitin' me,' he said coyly. She hadn't, but let this pass.

'Rick is a bloody good builder. He helped with all the renovations on my… your… on this place,' Len said gesturing to the house.

My place, Di thought to herself, a little rattled. Then she said, 'It's hard to let a place go when you've put so much into it, isn't it?'

Len shrugged. 'Needs must….'

Di finished the idiom for him, '…when the devil drives?'

'Aye, too true,' he agreed.

'So, Rick, did you have anything to do with the electrics?'

'Mmm?' Rick hummed with a mouthful of burger and ale.

'Because we seem to be having a lot of trouble with things turning off and on by themselves.'

Rick swallowed and opened his mouth to speak, but Len cut in:

'No, Rick and me are not electricians. We 'ad someone else ter come in and do most of that. But 'ee were a proper professional, so it should be workin' fine, it's all new.'

'Then perhaps someone's just messing about from outside the house somehow. Trying to spook us.'

''Oh aye, an' 'ow could they do that?' Rick asked, perplexed.

Di shrugged. 'I suppose you'd have to have a good knowledge of the house already,' she said pointedly at Len. 'But I'm not an electrician. So what would I know? But my husband,' she said, 'trained as an electrical in the army before he joined the RAF. Electrics are no problem to him. He'll get to the bottom of it, and if he finds out someone's been messing with us then…' she let the threat hang in the air, mainly because she didn't know how to end it.

'Di!' her mother-in-law called out, saving her from having to know how to finish.

'Excuse me,' she said with a parting meaningful glare at Len and went over to Anna.

'You OK, Anna?'

'Your little one's been telling me about the jacuzzi,' she laughed nodding at Rachel who was filling her face with cake nearby.

'It went crazy, didn't it Mum,' Rachel said. 'The bathroom was full of bubbles to the ceiling.'

Di chuckled. 'I really shouldn't laugh. You were very frightened at the time, weren't you darling?'

'She said I looked like a yeti or something,' Rachel pantomimed a sulk.

Anna clapped her hands with delight at the image.

'It was just like the Magic Porridge Pot,' Rachel added.

'The what?' Anna frowned. She was Swedish and maybe hadn't heard of it before.

Rachel explained, 'It's a fairy tale about a little girl and her mum who were very poor and had nothing to eat. One day an old witch gave the girl a special magic porridge pot and gave her the magic words to say, so that the pot would start making porridge - as much as they wanted, out of thin air. And then she told her the magic words to say to make it stop. The girl's mum was *so* happy that they wouldn't have to go hungry anymore. When the little girl had gone out, the mother asked the pot to start cooking, but she hadn't been told the magic words to stop it. So the pot kept cooking porridge, on and on and on, so the pot overflowed and filled the kitchen, the house and then the whole town up with porridge!'

'Oh. How awful. What's the moral of *that* fairy story?' Anna said over the top of her glass.

Rachel shrugged. She looked to her mother for an answer. Di was about to offer a suggestion when Len's voice cut in over her shoulder:

'Don't start somethin' you can't finish,' he growled.

'Excuse me?' Di raised an eyebrow.

'The moral of that story,' he said suddenly cheerily. 'Don't start somethin' you can't finish.' He winked at Di and then went over to chat with Fiona and Terry.

'Not a bad bit of advice,' Anna said. 'Eh, Di?'

But Di wasn't listening. She was watching as Len muttered something to Terry and Fi, and they looked over their shoulders at Di, raising their glasses and putting on the briefest of smiles before going back to their huddle.

'Say cheese, Di!'

Di turned to see Anna wielding one of the polaroid cameras. She put on a smile, determined that no evidence of the shadow these uninvited guests had cast over her party would be forever documented. Click! Another moment captured for posterity.

CHAPTER 17

CREEPING ANXIETY

Di woke with a heavy head. She wasn't surprised. She had put away more than a few gins and tonics last night. It had been her intention to make sure she had a good time, but after her run in with Len, she found herself drinking more than she should, to numb the feeling of anxiety that he and his four weird friends had planted in her.

She turned to Mike and saw that he was still sound asleep after drinking copious amounts too. The entire wedding party had eventually been defeated by the weather and was moved to The Cross Inn. All except Dorothea, of course, who, when Len, Terry, Mike and Big Will offered to carry her to the pub, commode and all, told them:

'Do fuck off, don't be ridiculous. I have a date anyway this evening.'

'A date?' Mike had whistled bravely. 'Who with?'

'Jeffrey?' Len had laughed.

Both Jeffrey and Dorothea had then replied perfectly in sync, 'No bloody way.'

'Well, who then?' Terry had asked.

'I have a date,' Dorothea had said, 'with this large bottle of vodka and…'

Her voice had trailed off then, but Di knew that Dorothea was hoping Alice would be joining her and her vodka, and it moved her enormously. If only she could enjoy the company of the living more, surely she would be less lonely?

Di was quite exhausted after a hilarious attempt at midnight tucking her inebriated husband into bed, amidst his protests. The bittersweet memory of yesterday made Di put her arms around her gently snoring husband and she held on tight. She smiled at the memory of Mike at the pub falling from his bar stool more than once, and Chloe finding it hilarious to help him back up. Not a very good example for the children, Di thought with a wry smile. Mustn't make a habit of it! But Di's reverie was interrupted then by the sound of voices downstairs. The sound of furniture moving. Glass, pans and crockery crashing about.

She slid out of bed and tiptoed to the boys' room. They were still snoring. She crept downstairs and past the girls' rooms, the doors still firmly shut and no sign of movement. She looked around for something to brandish as a weapon. Nothing. She listened. It was the unmistakeable sound of the large dining table being pulled along the floor. The voices hissed at each other. Di felt herself trembling, her head throbbing with more than just a hangover, and her heart thumping. She told herself maybe she should just rush downstairs and catch them off guard. So she took a deep breath and went for it.

Still in bare feet her descent down the stairs had cat-like stealth, so when she arrived in the living room it took a moment for the intruders to even realise she was there. And in that same moment Di saw, with a huge sigh of relief, the handsome faces of Ollie and Stephen, as they buzzed around the place, putting the furniture straight, carrying dirty glasses and crockery to the sink and generally making a huge effort to clean up.

'Here she is. Sleeping Beauty!' Ollie winked.

'Oh my! We didn't wake you, did we? I told you to be quieter, Oliver. He can't do anything quietly, Di, I'm so sorry.'

'No, no, it's fine,' Di said blinking through the pounding behind her eyes. 'I don't feel so much of a beauty this morning, I can tell you. But thank you so much for this. I really appreciate it'.

'You should be having a lie in on your...' Stephen searched for the word. 'What do they call this, the morning after the wedding?'

'The start of purgatory?' Ollie grinned at Di.

Stephen slapped Ollie's arm as he minced past him, clutching as many glasses as he could manage in one go. 'Be serious for a moment! What is it? The honeymoon? Or is that only the holiday part?'

'I really don't know. Owe, my head hurts!' Di said putting her hand to the side of her head, but nevertheless enjoying the sight of her two new friends flitting about the place. Even more enjoyable now that she knew they were not the intruders she thought they might be. 'Here,' said Ollie holding a glass of something fizzy. 'That will sort you out, my lovey ducks.'

Di took it gratefully, and drank it straight down without asking what it was. It was lemony and very refreshing. 'You guys think of everything. Thank you SO much. You should be having a lie in too,' she added, walking to the sink to help wash up. 'Not cleaning up after us.'

'We told you we would. Our wedding gift to you,' Ollie said.

'Only coz he's too tight to buy you anything,' Stephen said from the corner of his mouth.

'I heard that, Stephen,' Ollie hissed.

'You were meant to,' Stephen countered.

'Did you tell me you were coming over this morning?' Di asked.

'She was too sloshed to remember,' Ollie said to Stephen, before turning to Di and adding, 'Yes darling, we did tell you. Said we'd crash on the couch, but you wouldn't hear of it. So we went to Mike and persuaded him to give us a spare key so we could let ourselves in and have it all done before you even woke.'

'Or we would have done, if motormouth here hadn't been so noisy,' Stephen scolded.

'Mike shouldn't have let you, but thank you again,' Di whined giving them both a hug to show how grateful she was nonetheless.

'Oh, he seemed very happy with the idea.'

'I bet he did,' Di scowled.

'But then he was even more sloshed than you. It wasn't hard to persuade him,' Ollie said. Di giggled, loving the double act of these lovely people and feeling safer than she'd felt in a while.

But now the wedding and the blessing and the holidays were all over. The kids were going back to their lives, and it was time to get back to reality. Mike had given notice at the airfield where he was working in the interregnum between careers, and he had accepted a job with a major airline as a pilot. However, the downside was that his retraining would take place in Stockholm. He was excited and Di was excited for him, but it coming so soon after the wedding wasn't quite the honeymoon period Di was hoping for. When she saw him off at the airport the following day, she promised to visit him as soon as she could, and they would enjoy a little honeymoon in Sweden.

She returned to Heptonstall that evening alone with a

heavy heart. Rachel was staying at her father's that week, and as Di rumbled up the steep cobbled street in her 4x4 red Subaru, the village was as deserted as her house would be after a couple of weeks of so much life. The only thing that seemed to be alive was the white and grey mists swirling off the road as she drove through it and danced around the old church yard.

When she pulled into Goose Yard, the windows of her house were black. Beetle black. Like Big Will's eyes. The association made her shiver and she hated herself for even making the link. Now the very windows, or something behind them, seemed to be watching her coldly.

'Shake yourself out of it, woman!' she whispered. 'Don't be such a wuss, there's nothing there. How can there be?'

She slid out of the car wearily and walked slowly down the yard towards the door. No light shone from the neighbours' windows; Dorothea and Jeffrey must both be asleep. There were no streetlights to light the way, save for a faint glow over the roof of her house from an old gas lamp on the main street. She could make out the outline of the stone wishing well which loomed eerily in front of her. And then the front door. She heard a deep moan as she approached, followed by a scratching. She felt her skin tighten over her scalp.

Her rational mind quickly dissected the atmosphere and concluded it was only a cow from the nearby cattle shed lowing, and probably mice in the well scratching about.

Just remember to bring a torch next time if you're likely to be out after dark, silly woman, she berated herself.

She walked towards the door over the cobbled yard and almost lost her balance, twisting her ankle badly as she did so. She was not yet used to negotiating the cobbles in the dark.

'Ouch, shit!' she hissed, instantly regretting not wearing her trainers instead of the heels she had worn today in order to make herself as attractive as possible for Mike on his last day in the UK for a while.

She felt tears in her eyes, and an unfathomable sense of sadness. What on earth was wrong with her?

She limped tearily with the pain the rest of the way, fumbled for her keys and opened the door. There was no Charlie to greet her with her welcoming barks. Rachel had persuaded her mum and Mike to allow her to take her father's for that week, so there was dead silence. The door felt strangely heavier than usual, and Di had to push really hard with her shoulder to enter. As she did so, she felt a rush of cold wind and a feeling of dread wash over her. She froze, eyes widened. There was a heavy silence. She continued to stand stock still. From where she was on the threshold, she could see almost all the open plan ground floor. She warily looked around, holding her breath. The far corner of the room, near the well in the floor under the rug seemed to be darker than the rest of the room, as though indigo ink was flowing down the wall. Di felt that there were resentful eyes glaring at her from that corner. After a protracted petrified moment, she found the strength to shake herself to her senses and quickly turned on the light. She gasped as the light flickered on and off, then thankfully stayed on and the atmosphere in the house seemed to return to normal. Almost. Di couldn't shake the feeling that someone had just left the room, and had left a residual presence behind them. She looked around, her heart beating fast. What was happening here? Was it all in her imagination? Of course, it had to be. She flicked on all the other lights downstairs and listened intently. Nothing. She could feel her heart thumping at her chest as she shakily entered the kitchen and opened the fridge to pour some milk into a pan to warm.

She made herself a hot milky drink, cupping it in her hands for comfort as she sat down on the sofa. Reluctantly, she looked again into the corner of the room, eyeing the rug and the dining table that concealed the well. She could not tear her eyes away from it. She felt compelled to shove the table aside, peel back the rug, open the glass panel and explore down there to see what was really down there.

'But I'm not totally bonkers,' she managed to laugh at herself. 'I'll do it in the morning.'

Later that night, she was tossing and turning, inviting sleep, counting sheep. Eventually she was just managing to doze off, when she had the distinct sense that someone had entered the room. She sat bolt upright, looking wildly around in the pitch dark. As she did so, something caught her attention in the far corner of the room. And then her blood ran cold. A faint blue shimmering orb of light about 9 inches in diameter hovered silently in the shadows. It appeared to Di like it was observing her. As she stared at it, motionless with fear, her hair pricking at the back of her neck, the orb started to move around the walls of the room towards her. Her heart pounded through her ears. She sensed that she had seen this somewhere before – many years ago, and she was petrified. And she knew what it might be trying to tell her.

CHAPTER 18

A MEMORY

She was a young teenager when it happened. It was a Sunday evening, and the swinging sixties were giving way to the struggles of the early seventies.

Di lived with her parents and siblings in a large imposing stone four storey Victorian house on the main street in Uppermill. It happened to be next door to the Spiritualist Church. She and her best friend at that time, Susan, had visited the church out of curiosity on two or three occasions.

One Sunday evening after one such visit, they were in her attic bedroom, when they decided to try to communicate with someone who had 'passed over to the Spirit World,' as death had been described by the Spiritualists.

'Whose spirit shall we call up?' Susan asked poking her fingernail into the brown threadbare carpet upon which she sat, cross-legged.

'Can't we just see who's around?' Di said, hanging over the edge of the little bed she lay on.

'No,' Susan suggested, 'It has to be someone one of us know and who might have a message for us.'

'Hmm.' Di thought for a while then said, 'What about my great grandparents?'

'Yeah!' Susan said, 'but it might help if we had something of theirs, something they touched, to help us make contact with them.'

Di frowned. 'How do you know?'

'Well, I don't, not for sure, I just think it's more likely to work that way.'

Di thought for a moment. She had her parents' old bureau in the far corner of her room which opened out as a desk, upon which she would do her homework. She knew it contained some old letters, postcards, photos and knick-knacks from her mother's youth. Whenever she rummaged into it, she felt like she was opening a portal to times past. She'd spent many a rainy day reading the sepia postcards and examining old photos of her great grandmother, and some of her great grandfather overseas in a war she didn't really understand. She fished out the bayonet that her mother had told her had been attached to his rifle during that war and the pince-nez he used to wear to help him to read.

'My great granddad definitely touched these a lot,' Di said. 'Careful!' she growled as Susan took the delicate looking pince-nez and balanced them on her nose.

'How did anyone ever use glasses like these?' Susie giggled.

'And this was my great grandma's,' Di said pulling out a pretty silk handkerchief, ivory in colour with a beautiful hand-laced scalloped edge.

'Alright,' Susan said. 'Now we put them on the floor here with a few of the photos.'

She sat back down on the carpet and arranged the items between her legs and Di's.

'Let's hold hands,' Susan said.

Di had no idea if this was likely to be an instruction from the medium at the Spiritualist church, but it made her feel safer – and she had a feeling Susan felt the same.

'What are their names?' Susan asked.

'William and Emily.'

Susan closed her eyes so Di followed suit.

'William. Emily,' Susan called out in a suitably spiritual voice, emulating the medium they had heard in the church that afternoon. 'Are you there? Please show us a sign that you're here!'

Di gripped Susan's hand tightly and waited.

And waited.

'Please come and visit us from the spiritual plane, or wherever you are,' Di pleaded.

She opened one eye and saw that Susie was looking disappointingly at the items, then at the ceiling, then all around her. Di felt her shoulders relax, somewhat relieved that nothing had happened. Suddenly:

'What's that?' Susan whispered, tightening her grip on Di's hand and staring towards the window.

Di followed her gaze to where a pale blue globe of light shimmered in front of the glass. Both girls were quietly fearful, but unwilling to show it to the other. Gaining strength from each other, and not letting go of their friend's hand, the two girls stood up and moved closer to see whether something from outside the window was creating it. But they could see nothing that could have possibly caused this phenomenon. The light was a globe about the size of a netball hanging impossibly in the air. As they approached it, a strong, sweet smell of lily of the valley was emanating from it. The luminous blue sphere began to float gently across the back wall, and the gobsmacked girls, now feeling somewhat braver, followed it. The perfume was clearly coming from the globe. It paused above the old bureau, then seemed to sink into it. Susan looked at Di, as if asking for permission to do what they both desperately wanted to do. Di nodded and opened the desk to see if the globe was now inside it. The heavy, sickly scent of the woodland flowers burst from the bureau now, and was so strong that it almost knocked the girls off balance, unnerving them and causing the fear to return. Since the globe was nowhere to be seen, the frightened girls grabbed the items from the carpet and tossed them back into the bureau, closing it firmly and running down the three flights of stairs to the lounge to tell Di's parents what had happened.

'What the hell do you think you're doing, meddling with such things? It could be dangerous!' her father had shouted. The fierce, uncompromising stare he gave her was far less unambiguous. She loved her father so dearly that whenever he was angry with her it felt like a knife to her stomach. She wished she had never let Susan talk her into such a silly thing.

CHAPTER 19
UNWELCOME VOICES

Back in the present, Di shook herself out of her reverie as she stared at the blue globe. It had come within a few feet of her face when she was suddenly overwhelmed by the sickly cloying perfume of those woodland flowers – lily of the valley! She could never forget that smell. She had remained frozen to the spot bolt upright in bed for what would have been only several minutes, but which had seemed liked hours. Then with trepidation, but resolute determination she got up onto her knees and reached out to touch it. As soon as her hand reached the spot where the globe hovered, it simply disappeared, and the perfume also vanished.

It was then she heard the voices. What now? Maybe it was Ollie and Stephen back. But why would it be? There was nothing else to clear up. The blessing and the BBQ was a week ago. But they did still have a spare key – they and their children were the only people who did. Maybe it was a couple of the kids. But why tonight? They were not due to visit for a few weeks. She lay there listening for a while looking up at the skylight. The glass was now replaced and a blind had been fitted over the window. However, she could tell from the pale dawn glow around it that it was still very early in the morning. She glanced at her alarm clock. It was just after 5.10am. There were more than two male voices and the accents did not have the crystalline sibilance of her favourite couple in the village - and she could tell clearly now that it was certainly not their boys, - she would recognise their voices immediately.

'It's probably those damn tourists again,' she huffed, getting up and quickly donning on her dressing gown and indoor trainers before they came upstairs. 'But I would have locked the door. I always lock the door since the last…'

Her ankle hurt, and it brought back memories of the scare she had given herself last night. She now doubted whether she had actually locked the door. She had been too busy allowing her eyes to play tricks on her, and she was so focused on that well in the living room that she had probably neglected to lock the front door. And now the tourists were back. But at this time? A sliver of doubt crept into the back of her mind. She shook her head.

That's what you get for being such an idiot, she scolded herself, as she limped down the stairs. 'There must be some kind of town council that deals with tourists,' she grumbled to herself. 'Someone who can put up a sign or something to stop this ridiculousness.'

She paused on the landing to rest her foot. She stretched it, cursing herself again as she looked out of the arched window at the silhouette of the old church just becoming visible against an ultramarine sky. Then she steeled herself and descended the final flight of stairs into the living room and said loudly, authoritatively:

'Excuse me!'

But there was no one there.

No tourists, no kids, no helpful neighbours. Not even any weird, occultist scheming neighbours.

And yet the voices persisted. The voices clearly did not belong to Japanese tourists. It was an accent much nearer to home, and whoever it was did not sound very friendly to say the least.

She checked that the door was locked. It was. She looked out of the window and saw that the yard was devoid of tourists. Devoid of anyone. But the voices weren't coming from outside. They were coming from…

She slowly turned around, hoping it wasn't true. The voices were coming from under the floor, under her very feet! All her senses immediately were on high alert. The hairs on the back of her neck prickled. So she took a deep breath and then held it so nothing, not even her own breathing, could impede her ability to hear what was going on below.

She recognised the voices were definitely local. The Yorkshire accents were thick. She tried to identify Len's voice, or Rick's. But she couldn't be sure. They sounded too rough and old fashioned.

How the hell did they get down there? She thought. *There must be another entrance to the cellar that Len never told me about. It can't be blocked up, after all.'*

Then, as quietly as she could, she dragged the dining table with considerable difficulty across the floor, and rolled the rug back to reveal the glass panel. There was no light coming from below, and the voices had stopped. '*They must have heard me. I bet the light Len had installed was never just for decoration. He's still using our cellar, the bloody cheek of it,'* she said to herself and flicked on the switch on the wall to the light in the well.

The panel had a metal handle on the frame. She gripped it and pulled the panel up. It opened easily on its hinges, like a trap door. She peered down into the gloom, and thought she could just about see a floor, so she lowered herself gently down. It was obvious to her that the hole in the floor had not been filled in, as Len had told them. Why had he lied? What the hell was he up to down there?

'No you don't!' Di growled. Fearing that they would escape before she had a chance to catch them, when there was nothing but her head and shoulders above the living room floor, somewhat unwisely, she let herself drop. She was desperate to see who was down there.

The pain that shot through her already weakened ankle as she hit the damp stone floor was excruciating. Thankfully, the drop was only about seven feet, but far enough for her diminutive height and sore ankle to cause her problems. She winced, both with the sensation of acute pain and with anger at having given the intruders even more time to escape. So as she nursed her ankle she shouted:

'Who's there?'

The lights from the hole above her head only bleached the edges of the darkness around her. She squinted around the room, waiting for her eyes to adjust.

'I know you're there,' Di called out trying to keep her voice from trembling as she got to her feet again, adrenaline numbing the pain for now.

She shuffled around the basement which was nowhere near as big as the living room above it, probably about half the size, maybe only ten feet square, and she soon found her hands pressed up against a wall. She moved around like a mime artist, patting down all four walls of the place until she was sure, much to her bewilderment that there was no obvious exit in any of them. She could discern there may have been a doorway on one wall, but it was well and truly bricked up.

Her eyes had almost adjusted to the gloom by now so, on her hands and knees, she smoothed the floor for signs of some other trap door which might lead to somewhere even deeper than this basement. She had just about covered the full expanse of the floor, when her fingers hit something hard and metallic sticking up from it. She squinted at it, and in the gloom she made out an iron ring nailed into the floor attached to what was a chain with thick iron handcuffs. Her fingers recoiled from the shackles, and she found her hand touching something sticky and warm. She held her hand up to her face to get a better look. It was dark and viscous, but she still wasn't sure. She held up her hand to her nose to smell it, as she was concerned there may be a leak of oil or other liquid in the room. She froze once again as she could clearly discern the cloying smell of blood in her fingers. Every muscle, every pore in her body clenched with fear. 'Oh my God, what the…..!' she croaked into the gloom whilst looking wildly around her. She managed to stand up with the intention of taking herself to the light in the well shaft above when she slipped on three iron rods lying on the floor, which made a condemning clang as they rolled to one side. She put a hand on them to silence them and found that not only were they very hot to the touch, but they too were covered on one end with the same substance that was on her hand. She tried again, more carefully this time, to get to the light and see whether her worst fear was correct.

She stood under the shaft and held up her fingers to the light. This confirmed her fears - that her fingers were indeed covered in deep red blood!

She darted a look back at the ironworks behind her, and realised as her eyes had adjusted a little, that she'd been looking at instruments of torture. Instruments that had clearly recently been used. She thought she could now smell burning flesh. She wanted to vomit, but her will to get out of this basement was greater. But how? She looked up. The base of the well was only inches above her head, but the exit to the living room floor was another two or three feet up, she guessed, with nothing but sheer walls on all sides.

'Help!' she called out. Then recalling the house was locked from the inside she shouted louder, 'HELP!'

'No one's coming t' help thee,' the evil, cracked voice of an uncouth man croaked into her left ear. She could feel his hot breath on her neck, and a putrid indescribable smell hit her senses. Di spun around to see who spoke.

CHAPTER 20
THE ESCAPE

There was no one there.

Just the sound of metal rods being dragged along the floor in the darkness. Then the smell of burning coals. The sound of something fizzing as it was plunged into the fire. But she could not see what was happening.

Di was hyperventilating now. Her head was spinning. She looked up and jumped as high as she could, ignoring the searing pain in her ankle as she did so. She grabbed at the walls of the well but her hands, still slick with blood just slid down them.

'Fuck fuck fuck!' she panted as a scream filled her ears. She thought for a moment that it was her own wailing, but as it came again, she realised it was not her voice but that of a man.

He screamed a piercing scream of pain again and again, followed by sobbing. And worse, a strong smell of burning flesh.

'No one's coming t' help thee,' said his torturer. 'Thass what tha gets for messing with the 'Artley's.'

Another agonising scream propelled Di upwards and this time, as her hands slid inevitably down, she felt an iron handle in the wall of the well she hadn't noticed before, which gave her the impetus to try once more, as the screams became unbearable. She jumped and found the handle, grasping it tightly in her now very sticky hand. Hanging there for a moment she felt around for another, and found one above it on the opposite side of the well. She dragged herself up on them until she could wedge her feet against the walls of the shaft and then, with a wail almost matching the intensity of that emanating below her, she hauled herself out and onto the living room floor.

She wanted to slam the glass panel shut but feared she would break it and leave whoever – or whatever – was down there an easy escape route, so she lowered it with weak and shaking arms and quickly rolled the rug over it, pushing the table back into position.

It was only then that she noticed with complete astonishment, that her hands had no trace of blood on them, and they were not sticky at all, although they were very grubby from scrabbling about in the cellar. How strange!

She listened. There wasn't a sound coming from the basement.

Perhaps she had dreamt it all. She waited for herself to wake up. She pinched the skin on the back of her hand. She slapped her own face. Her heart sank. She was definitely wide awake.

She felt bruised and battered. Her ankle throbbed. And her mind was filled with the image of her father's fierce stare when she was young.

'What do you think you're doing, meddling with such things?' he had said.

Against every rational fibre in her body, it was a question that she felt compelled to put to Len and his little gang now. Cross examination was her forte.

So, brooking neither doubt or delay, and, unlike her, not stopping to change from her dressing gown, change her shoes or wash her filthy hands, she hobbled breathlessly out of the house and up the lane lit by a pink dawn, and rapped on the door of Terry and Fiona's house. But no one answered. She had no idea where Big Will or Rick lived, nor where Len lived after moving from Goose Barn. She had to find them, but her ankle throbbed so badly now that she found herself returning to the house and delving into the umbrella stand for Mike's walking stick; the one he loved to stroll around the woods with. And it was the woods where Di was returning to now. But before she left the house again she grabbed one of the polaroid cameras which had seen so much action on the day of their blessing.

Leaning on the stick to take the pressure from her ankle, she made her way with some difficulty down to the river. As she headed for the altar, the familiar smell of the lily in the valley which now covered the part of the woodland floor filled her senses and made her stop. She knew that cloying perfume so well. It spurred her on to the altar, which stood abandoned again, though it was obvious that someone had recently lit a fire there. As she sat on a tree stump, she tried to reflect and think clearly. The sun was just coming up, and the dawn chorus was so beautiful. She was now glad no one was there; glad the Nuddies hadn't been at home – or at least hadn't answered the door, because she didn't know what she would have said in her angry state of mind. But she desperately needed to find out more; she needed to arm herself with more information about this hocus pocus the five were peddling, before she confronted them. So Di took some photos of the altar and took them to the one person she thought might understand something of this craziness.

A view of Heptonstall village

Sylvia Plath's grave

The ruined church of St Thomas a' Becket

Up the main street towards The Cross

A further perspective of the Old Church

CHAPTER 21

SEEKING SPIRITUAL ADVICE

I'm a spiritualist, dear, not a bloody witch,' Dorothea grumbled, annoyed at being woken at such a fucking *ungodly hour,* as she had put it.

'Sorry, what?' Di said.

She was helping Dorothea onto her commode, where the old lady promptly urinated in horse-like quantities while saying, 'the least you can do is make me a cup of tea when you come knocking down my door at the crack of dawn.'

It wasn't exactly the crack of dawn. It was now 8am. Di had returned home after coming back from the woods, and knowing it was unreasonable to wake Dorothea that early, she had got herself showered and dressed, made herself some coffee and put a bag of frozen peas on her ankle, all the while staying as far away as she could from the dining table and what lay beneath. Of course time went far too slowly! When it got to 8 am, she just couldn't bear it any longer. She was still very sore, so she grabbed the walking stick to support her ankle as she went through the picket gate to her neighbour's house, rapping on her door until she heard Dorothea turn the air blue as she hauled herself out of bed.

Di didn't argue with Dorothea about the definition of

dawn, she knew she had to keep her sweet if she was going to get any information out of her, so she dutifully went into the filthy kitchen and put the kettle on. Even the kettle seemed to take forever to boil this morning, so while it heated up, Di went back into the living room and showed Dorothea the photo again.

'This is from the woods nearby?' Dorothea framed it as a question, although Di had a feeling she already knew it was.

'Yes. And they dance around it naked in the middle of the night.'

'Oh, who do?' Dorothea's interest was now piqued, and her eyes sparked with excitement and enthusiasm.

'Len your old neighbour, his mates Big Will and Rick, Terry and Fiona from Church Street, and a few others I didn't recognise.'

'You saw them all dancing naked around this fire?' she said poking with her dirty fingernail at the ashes in the photo.

'Yes, most of them anyway. Someone else was sitting on a log banging away on a hand-held percussion instrument.'

'I bet that was a sight for sore eyes!' Dorothea beamed sarcastically.

'What?' Di said impatiently.

'Well, the thought of it - Len and the, no doubt, inaccurately named Big Willy, naked. How awful,' she grimaced, 'but Terry and Rick might have been quite easy on the eye, as they say. Not that I am interested in that sort of thing in the slightest at my age, or at all as a matter of fact. How's that tea coming on, dear?'

Di contained her frustration and went to make the brew. Between sniffing several part-full cartons of milk in the fridge she called out, 'Did you know Len got up to this kind of stuff? I mean, he was your neighbour for some time. Did you ever hear anything?'

'You mean did they dance naked in the yard and chant in

the house? No, dear. They go out into the woods to do that. They commune with nature. It's part of their religion.'

'What sort of religion is it?' Di probed bringing in the tea – only half a cup – and a packet of stale custard creams.

'Didn't I tell you already?' Dorothea tutted, filling the rest of the cup with vodka from the bottle next to her commode. 'Pay attention, girl!'

'Did you? I don't remember, I'm sorry. Is it Witchcraft?' Di said, feeling her face flush as it used to when she was being told off by a teacher.

'Yes, yes, but it's modern witchcraft, not like you read about in fairy stories. Wicca to be more accurate', her neighbour said tucking into the custard creams.

'And what is that exactly?'

Dorothea was too busy munching to answer immediately. But eventually, she washed down a mouthful of biscuit with her vodka-tea cocktail and said with a smack of the lips, 'What is it exactly? Well, my dear, it's a load of codswallop as far as I'm concerned, but if you want someone who actually takes this seriously to explain it to you, you should talk to Roslyn,' she said stabbing again at the photo on her lap.

'Roslyn?' Di asked, feeling stupider by the second.

'She and her husband have the witchcraft shop in Todmorden.'

'Oh,' Di said as the memory of the tarot reader came upon her like a cold ocean wave. 'I never thought of that, yes, I know the shop. The Black Cauldron, I've been there.'

'Well, you better go back there - if you really want to know what this is all about.'

Di was already standing up and finding her stick, which she had left by the front door, when Dorothea stopped her.

'Is that it?' she asked stuffing another biscuit into her mouth, her eyes seemingly twinkling with the knowledge that that wasn't all Di had come for.

Di stopped for a moment, leaning on the walking cane.

Dorothea picked up her own walking stick, which leaned on the commode, and waved it at Di.

'Snap!' she said with a wink.

Di's empirical brain told her Dorothea was referring simply to the fact that they both had walking sticks, but her newly discombobulated mind reminded her that Dorothea hadn't once asked about why Di was using a stick since she'd arrived.

That's because she's a self-centred old woman, Di told herself. Then she thought, it's because she doesn't have to ask. She already knows.

And suddenly *snap* took on a whole new meaning. Not just *snap,* that they both had walking sticks, but *snap* that they both possibly acquired their injury in the same way.

'It's a bit of a drop down to that basement isn't it?' Dorothea said, as if reading Di's mind and confirming her conjectures.

'How do you know?' Di said.

Dorothea wet her whistle before she began. 'There was a time when I was a little lighter on my feet. I was round Len's one evening, so. He was out. I was keeping his wife company. Glenda, her name was. She ran out of wine, and so had I, so she popped out to the pub to buy some more. She hadn't been gone a moment when I heard voices of men, and screams. I went over to the window on the far side of the living room and could clearly hear the voices were coming from under the floor there. There was no glass panel in the floor then. Just an old wooden trap door as they were still renovating the place. I thought that someone was in pain and distress, so I tried to get down there to help. And as I was struggling to lower myself in, I just dropped and fell into the cellar, and that how *my* ankle went snap!'

The words came tumbling from Di's mouth now, 'There were rods with blood and chains and…'

'I saw nothing of that sort, or anything for that matter. The place was almost pitch black,' Dorothea cut in. 'There was no fancy light at the opening at the time, and I'd barely hit the floor when Len's big old hands grabbed me and hauled me out. God knows where he sprang from, but he told me to say nothing to Glenda about it.' She took a long draught of her tea and topped it up with more vodka.

'When I managed to get out of the basement,' Di said urgently, 'the blood on my hands had gone. So I must have imagined it. The voices, the chains, all of it.'

'We both imagined voices in the same place?' Dorothea frowned.

Di nodded pathetically. 'Don't you think so?'

'You're asking me what I think?'

Di nodded again.

'You're asking me whether *you* should believe what happened to *you*?' Dorothea smiled.

Di wilted. It all seemed so ridiculous, and yet utterly serious at the same time.

'The day Len pulled me out of that basement, I came home and after some reflection, I knew for sure that I had heard the voice of someone who had passed away down there. Len told me nothing about them, and I really didn't care a jot about who they were at that time. All I could think about was Alice. If I could hear *them*,' she jabbed a thumb towards Goose Barn, 'then surely I should be able to hear Alice, who passed away right here. I joined the Spiritualist Church in the valley the very next day and I spent every night asking her to speak to me, just waiting to hear her.' Dorothea chuckled wryly at herself. 'Every bloody night. Drove me daft,' she sneered at her cup and took a gulp on her tea.

'So… you don't believe you really heard anything in the first place,' Di said clutching at the rational straws of her neighbour's story.

Dorothea studied Di for moment. Then she shouted, biscuit crumbs flying like missiles from her angry lips, 'Of course I heard something, you silly girl. And I still do. Hear them all the bloody time. Even in here, in my little cottage, which should be my sanctuary. So why oh why,' she cried, 'do I not hear my beautiful Alice?!' A deep sigh and a sob escaped from her crumby bloodless lips.

It brought Di back to her senses. She went to put a comforting arm around the old lady who looked so tragic on her commode in her grubby nightie, her knickers still around her knees and thick 40 denier stockings round her ankles.

But Dorothea shooed her off. 'Leave me alone! Coming in here and upsetting me at this hour. You have no idea. No fucking idea at all what I've suffered. Leave me be, will you! Take your bloody pictures to Roslyn.'

Di backed off. 'I'm sorry, I'm so sorry'.

Dorothea slung the photograph of the altar at her. Di picked it up from where it landed on the sticky, dirty carpet and hurried out, her ankle burning as much as her face.

CHAPTER 22
THE WICCANS

'Well, I'll go t'foot of our stairs!' George said as Di entered the shop. 'I din't expect to see you in 'ere again so soon.'

Di smiled sheepishly at him as she approached the counter.

'Husband not with yer today? Or was he yer boyfriend?'

'Husband. Well, he was my fiancé when we were last here. Now he's my husband. Anyway, no. He's away, working.'

'Mmm,' George nodded knowingly. 'Handy. Worried he'll think tha a nutter if you brought him back 'ere? Although, I reckoned he were a bit more open-minded than you.'

'What do you mean?' Di asked indignantly.

'To things of a spiritual nature, let's say,' George attempted a grin that favoured a grimace.

'Well,' Di said defensively, 'I'm only here on the advice of my neighbour. She thought your wife would be able to help with something, that's all.'

'Oh, aye, you mean Dorothea?'

Di wanted to ask how the hell he knew where she lived and who her neighbours were, but she told herself not to be surprised. She was already painfully aware that this was the kind of place where you couldn't sneeze without the whole of the Calder Valley hearing about it. So she nodded and asked, 'Is she around? Roslyn?'

'Two ticks,' Len said, leaning back on his heels. 'Ma!' he called out without taking his eyes off Di. 'She's 'ere again, just as you predicted,' he said as if they were expecting her.

'Ooh, good. About time,' came the response from upstairs. 'Thought we were going to have to send out a search party.'

'Did Dorothea tell you I was coming?' Di asked, bemused.

'No, why?' George said busying himself behind the counter.

'Because I went to see her and she suggested I come here. Did she or did she not tell you I was coming?'

'Nope. Never spoken to the woman in me life. Bit of a grumpy 'ole lush, be all accounts.'

Di had no time to respond, even if she could have found something to say, because Roslyn then swept in, already be-gowned in her tarot reader's robes. She took her place in the little alcove behind the curtain which George had deftly whipped back.

'Come dear,' she said grandly - but softly and kindly to Di.

'I didn't come for another reading,' Di began, already pulling the polaroids from her pocket.

'I know. Please. Take a seat, my dear,' Roslyn repeated firmly.

Di sized up the woman for a moment, then did as she was asked and put the photo on the little trestle table between them.

'Let's have a look then,' she said, as if she had expected Di to show her the pictures. 'Hmmmm, I see, mmmm', she cooed for many a moment.

'It's in the woods near Heptonstall. I've seen people dancing round it naked in the middle of the night. They had an effigy too…' Di stuttered.

'Of you?' Roslyn said.

'How do you--?'

'Was it?'

'Well, it had similar clothes to what I was wearing that weekend, but that doesn't mean…..'

'And yet here you are?' Roslyn's eyes were blinking at her.

'I have experienced some strange and inexplicable goings on …and I just wondered…' Di faltered, then continued, 'My neighbour said it had something to do with Wicca? I don't know if they're messing with things they shouldn't be.'

'Oh yes, it's Wicca all right,' Roslyn nodded sagely.

'Can you explain to me what that is?'

'Well, it's just a modern and benign form of witchcraft. A Pagan religion,' Roslyn said gently.

'The kind of thing you do here?' Di said rather dismissively.

'Exactly the sort of thing we cater for here, as well as other forms of New Age and Pagan religions,' Roslyn smiled, her eyes ablaze. 'Look, my dear,' She suddenly became quite lyrical and started to speak dreamily, as though she was speaking through a higher being, enunciating her words beautifully. 'As Pagans, we understand deity to be manifest within all nature, the whole universe in fact.' She waved her arm in an arch to represent the universe. 'We believe that nature is sacred, and that the natural cycles of birth, growth and death observed in the world around us carry profoundly spiritual meanings. Human beings are seen as part of nature, along with other animals, trees, stones, plants and everything else that is of this earth and in fact the whole cosmos. It's all energy, part of the Divine'. She pointed to the photo. 'This is why their rituals, as well as their spells, or prayers are always better delivered outdoors.'

Di listened with genuine interest and fascination. Roslyn continued, 'We Pagans believe in infinite reincarnation. There is no such thing as death, it's just a transition, - part of a continuing process of learning towards perfection. Our Gods and Goddesses take many forms. Goddess worship is especially central to paganism. We believe that women are strong, creative forces of nature. But I don't need to tell you that, now do I?' Roslyn looked at Di kindly with her large green eyes and a small smile, 'you also being a mother?'

Di managed a smile in response before she wondered how Roslyn knew she was a mother.

'Woman is the creative link and force behind many wonderful things in the universe,' Roslyn continued. 'That's why it chose you and not your husband.'

'What?'

'I said…'

'I heard what you said. But *what* is it? What chose me?' Di demanded.

'I told you when you first came. Someone with the letter D was trying to reach you.' Roslyn's voice reverted to normal.

'When we first…?' Di was incredulous. 'You mean during your tarot…' She searched for a polite word. '…performance?'

Roslyn cocked her head and looked at Di kindly, but somewhat patronisingly, refusing to be offended.

Di went on derisively, 'You didn't know anything about me, or who might be trying to contact me.'

'I do admit, I was a little distracted that day of the Reading. But that would be His Majesty worrying me about his grumbling stomach.'

'Don't blame me, lass,' came the disembodied voice of George from the other side of the curtain. He'd obviously been listening to every word.

Roslyn rolled her eyes, 'But when you left the shop, I knew something wasn't right. Something is trying to communicate with you, coming at you, for you. I told you there was a D involved in the name.'

Di muttered, 'But you didn't know if it began with a D or

ended with D, just like you didn't know if my grandmother was still alive. Were you just winging it?'

'No dear. I know now that it was because the name began *and* ended with D. I worked it out in the end. The spirits' messages are not always as clear as they should be. It's not their fault, it's ours. It's a bit like watching telly with a dodgy aerial, you know before this new digital TV thing came along. Our minds are not always as open as would like, to what they are trying to tell us.

'What DO you mean?' Di said becoming increasingly frustrated. .

'David.'

Di shrugged.

'Begins and ends with a D. *David.* That's the name of the unhappy spirit that's messing with your life. Or one of them anyway. I sense that your daughter knows he's there too. Youngsters, especially girls can often hear and see them more clearly than adults.'

'I beg your pardon?' Di said, upset by Roslyn dragging her daughter into this.

'Your little one. She knows, doesn't she?'

This was too much for Di. Her heart started racing. She suddenly had an urge to slap the old witch, but not just because she felt protective of Rachel, but mainly because of the memory her words conjured in Di. The memory of their first family lunch at Goose Barn:

'Shhh!' Rachel hissed at something below the table and stamped on the floor.

Everyone stopped to look at her.

'What's up, love?' Di asked.

Rachel looked up and put on a smile. 'Nothing. It's fine now,' she said going back to her meal in a way that brooked no further discussion on the matter. So everyone else went back to their food and the conversation too.

Di felt her guts turn molten. The possibility that Roslyn

could be right about Rachel sickened and angered her. So she exploded, very unfairly at Roslyn, 'Well, you may remember from your little tarot reading that I am a barrister, so if you have been in cahoots with those Wiccans or whatever they are, I would really recommend that you put a stop to any screwed-up nonsense you've got going on with those other loonies in the woods, or I will not hesitate to apply to court for an injunction to put a stop to all of this…' she waved her hand dismissively at the shop, '…business.'

She stood up and whipped back the curtain, close behind which George had been standing.

He quickly straightened and said, 'Now, no need fer that, yer should tek that back, young lady.'

'NO!' Di cried, and in the thickest Yorkshire brogue, which she was shocked to hear coming from deep within her, and which was not her own voice at all, she added, 'Tha should keep tha neb out of my business and give over meddling wi'things tha doesn't understand.'

She stormed out of the shop and pushed her way unsteadily down the crowded street. But like the unwise mother in the fairy story, in her anger and haste, she hadn't stopped long enough to find out the witch's spell to stop the magic pot from overflowing.

CHAPTER 23
THE VISITATION

Di had hoped that her threat of court action would be enough. She hoped the message would get through to Len from Roslyn, and they would all stop any more of this nonsense before she had to do anything official.

Back home in Goose Barn, with her foot up on the sofa wrapped in a bag of frozen peas, she called Mike in Sweden.

'Darling, when are you coming back?' she blurted before he'd had a chance to say hello.

'You know the training is a couple of weeks.'

'But can't you come back this weekend? It's only an hour or so on the plane.'

'It's more like two and a half.'

'So you don't want to come back?'

'Of course I do, but I thought you were going to come out here?'

'I would, but…'

'Don't you want to come and see me?' Mike said, pantomiming hurt.

'Stop it!' Di pouted. 'I've hurt my leg. My ankle actually. Travelling very far is not really an option for me right now.'

'What?' Mike was concerned now. 'How? What have you done?'

She thought for a moment about how to approach the subject, then said, 'I thought I heard… I went down the hole under the glass panel in the living room.'

'What glass panel?'

'The one under the dining table.'

'The one you covered up with the rug and everything?'

'Yes.'

'Christ. What happened? Did the floor give way?'

'No, I went down there on purpose. I moved the table and the rug and opened the panel. I… I wanted to see what was down there.'

'Nothing's down there. Len blocked it up, didn't he?'

'Well, that's what he said, but it turns out he didn't. There's about a six or seven foot drop under there. Hence my swollen ankle.'

'Jesus Christ. Did you…? How did you get out?'

The sound of the rod being dragged across the stone floor, the sizzling of a fire and the burning of flesh, the screams – all flashed through her mind. 'Where there's a will there's a way,' she said with a mirthless giggle, eyeing the dining table which now had two suitcases full of books piled on top of it – the heaviest thing she could think of moving by herself. She would have put the washing machine on top of it if were possible.

'We'll have to get that sealed up completely,' Mike said. 'What if Rachel had gone exploring down there?'

The thought of Rachel made Di catch her breath. What *if* Rachel had gone exploring down there? She was an inquisitive girl. Look how she questioned the runes and the pentagrams on the houses in the village, and how she couldn't resist examining the altar in the woods, despite being told to leave it alone. Di recalled then how, as they stood by the altar, Rachel had whispered to Chloe:

'He hates this.'

'Who hates this?' Chloe had asked.

'The man in the basement.'

'The man in the basement?'

'Yes. It makes him very angry. That's why he won't shut up.'

Di shuddered at this recollection. 'Come back this week-end, will you?' Di said urgently down the phone.

'I'll try,' Mike said with a sigh, 'but we finish late on Friday and start early on Monday. I'm not sure it'll be worth it.'

'Worth it?' Di snapped, 'Seeing me is not worth it?' She realised that she sounded almost hysterical.

'Darling! Calm down. What's wrong?'

She couldn't tell him about the things she'd seen, or thought she'd seen, in the basement. Either way, he'd think she was going crazy. She was worried he'd think she was the kind of women who are all sweetness and light, until the ring is on the finger and then they show their true psycho colours.

So she said, 'Rachel's coming this weekend. We have to get the basement sorted before she comes. Like you said, what if she goes poking around down there?'

'Just tell her not to.'

'And what did you do, when someone told you not to do something as a child?'

Mike laughed. 'Good point. Look, I'll check with the course supervisor. See if I can get a day off or something.'

'Can you do that?' Di asked, both hopeful and concerned about the effect that would have on his performance record with a new employer.

'I'll see. Can't promise anything. But I'll tell them my beautiful new wife needs nursing.'

Di smiled. 'Thanks.'

'I better sleep. I haven't studied so hard in years.'

'OK. Love you,' she said softly and waited for him to echo her sentiment, but she realised that the line had gone dead.

She hung up the phone cursing the international telecommunication lines, and tried her best to settle down to read her brief on a difficult case she was researching. After a good few hours or so, she found her mind drifting and couldn't concentrate, so she switched on the radio to keep her company. She grabbed some chocolate from the fridge and the pile of photos which had been taken at the wedding. There were all the ingredients to make her smile in the absence of Mike, – music, chocolate and good memories. She sifted through the photos, trying to decide which would go in the large frame in which she was planning to display them. The elderly chaps, Jeffrey and Ralph with arms around each other's shoulders – that was definitely going in. Her and Mike kissing – centre stage of course. Chloe, Rachel and Bella looked utterly beautiful – and Bella was even smiling, so that was definitely going in. The boys flanking Dorothea in her doorway, sentries to the queen on her throne. Even she had made an effort that day and had worn a clean-ish flowery dress and a smart beige cardigan, albeit her knees were covered in Di's warm throw. Ollie with his tongue in Stephen's ear – brilliant! Rachel regaling Anna with a story – the jacuzzi overflowing no doubt. Di dutifully saying cheese while Ralph looked on annoyed about something – that won't go in.

Di's scalp tightened.

She examined the photo further. It wasn't Ralph's face over her shoulder after all. It was another even older man. He had similar white hair around the ears, a lipless mouth, and similar heavy eyebrows over deep-set eyes. But it definitely wasn't Ralph. This man had longer hair, and he looked crooked and cruel. Di remembered now that Ralph was sitting next to Anna when Anna took this picture, just after Len had muttered what sounded like a threat to her. Ralph was behind the camera. And she knew of no other white-haired man at the party other than Jeffrey, and this was definitely not him. It was the black cravat and old-fashioned coat that brought it home to her. This was the same man she'd seen on the TV screen. Her eyes darted at the telly now, which sat inert and dark in the corner of the room. She felt the need to look over her shoulder, but there was no one there, of course. Just as she knew that if she had looked over her shoulder the moment that photo had been taken, there would have been no one there too.

CHAPTER 24

THE CROWS

Di was overwhelmed when Rachel arrived on Friday night with their beloved dog, Charlie; overwhelmed because she was so glad of the company, and yet so worried for her daughter being in the house. At work all through the previous week, Di had lost herself in cases where logic and evidence prevailed. She had stayed in her Barrister's Chambers late every evening preparing a skeleton argument and other written work and prep for cases that could easily have been done at home.

'What's with the suitcases?' Rachel asked, spotting the unusual new addition to the décor in the dining area as soon as she'd walked in and extricated herself from Di's enveloping hug. 'Going somewhere?'

'No, no. They're full of books. I just need to decide where to put them.'

Rachel looked suspiciously at the bookcase which was full last time she was here. 'Don't they belong in the bookcase?'

'Um… yeah. Well, they did, but I was wondering if they might be better somewhere else. I'm mulling it over. Anyway. Don't go near there. We can have dinner on our laps in front of the telly.'

'Yes!' Rachel said with a little fist pump.

They spent the evening snuggled up with Charlie on the sofa, watching the new VHS movies Rachel had brought with her, and stuffing themselves with popcorn. Halfway through the second film, Rachel had started to doze.

'Come on, darling. Up to bed now,' Di said gently.

'No,' Rachel whined. 'When the film's over.'

'You've slept through most of it. Watch it tomorrow when you can actually enjoy it.'

'Mmm,' she moaned. 'But I'm comfortable *here*.'

'You won't be by the morning. Come on. I can't lift you anymore.'

Rachel dragged herself off the sofa and lolloped upstairs with Di shepherding her along. When Di was satisfied that Rachel was comfortably tucked up, she turned off the light and went out onto the landing.

Then her heart almost stopped.

There was an enormous black crow sitting on the arched window's ledge glaring at her. Human and bird stared at each other for what seemed like minutes, before Di ran at the window flailing her arms about to scare it away. But it didn't budge, and she found herself face to face with it, her hands pressed up against the window with only a few millimetres of glass between her and it.

This close, she could see there were actually white feathers among the blackness of its chest and on its head. It had scaly claws, as if infected, making its feet look white too. The crow was joined by two others. As they flapped in and folded their huge indigo wings across their backs, Di flinched. Each landed so close that she could examine them too. One had feathers which shimmered more blue than black, and the other had flecks of auburn on its head and around its beak.

She reached slowly for the handle and lifted the catch. She then opened the window violently which shoved the three crows off their perch and sent them squawking off into the evening sky towards the Victorian church tower.

Di quickly shut the window, her breath loud and rapid and her heart beat heavy in her chest. She checked on Rachel once more and then hurried up to her own room, quickly undressed and got into bed under the imagined safety of the duvet. Once again, as she attempted to sleep, she thought of the time she and Susan called up the spirits of her great grandparents, blue spheres, the perfume of lily of the valley, and she remembered the sequel to the events from her teenage years - as though someone or something was reminding her of a past she had tried so assiduously to forget......

CHAPTER 25

THE MESSAGE

T he week after the blue sphere incident in the attic, Susan and Di went back to the Spiritualist church next door to see if anyone had an explanation for it. The church didn't look much like a normal church to Di. It had no tower, no spire, no ancient stonework, no gargoyles, no great stained-glass windows, nor a gigantic vaulted ceiling inside, which always made Di imagine she was in the belly of a great whale like Jonah from the Bible. This church looked completely out of place among the millstone grit houses of Saddleworth. It was a large red brick Victorian mausoleum, with dark rectangular windows and a black unwelcoming door. The interior was more like the church hall of a Methodist church that she had occasionally visited in North Wales with her grandmother. Chairs, not pews, were lined up under a white ceiling from which strip-lights hung, - no altar, candles or incense. This church was busy though, mainly with elderly women, but with one or two younger visitors who had probably come to find solace by hoping to commune with their nearest and dearest who had passed away.

Susan and Di slipped in at the back and listened to the service, which sounded very much like a Christian service to

Di's young ears. There were the usual hymns and prayers, but the man who led it was not in robes and a dog collar, just a sensible jumper and trousers with a seam ironed in the front.

After a couple of hymns and some prayers, the man introduced a special guest speaker and Di's attention was piqued. The woman who came to the front of the seated congregation looked like a 'hippy' version of her granny, dressed in an Indian cotton Kaftan and be-decked with several strands of colourful beads. She had a wonderfully soothing voice and claimed she spoke to spirit guides, who gave her messages for some of the congregation. When they thought they had received a message from their deceased loved ones, some of the people pressed their hands together with gratitude; some simply sat solemnly and quietly, while some nodded and smiled with understanding.

'And you, dear,' she said pointing to the back of the room.

Di looked over her shoulder and realised that there was no one there. The old woman was pointing at *her*. Susan gave her an excited poke and jiggled in her seat as the woman went on:

'What's your name, my love?'

'Diane,' she whispered.

'Louder dear so we can all hear you!' the man who had led the service addressed her.

'Diane,' she said as loudly as she could, still very self-conscious and very nervous.

'Diane, of course. Diane. That's what they were trying to tell me. The spirits.'

Di flared her nostrils, not convinced that that was really true.

'Don't worry, my dear,' the woman said as she understood Di's expression as fear. 'There's nothing to worry about. You know something about the spirit world already, don't you?'

Di shrugged.

'I am being told…yes, yes, I've got that, thank you…..you are a budding young medium.'

A murmur went through the audience with a smattering of applause.

'Would you share with us what you saw recently?' the woman coaxed Di. 'Or was it something you heard?'

Susan nudged Di. Di shook her head and looked at her feet again.

'We saw a ball of light,' Susan piped up, much to Di's embarrassment. Always the most confident student in their class at school, she went on, 'It was pale blue, like ice. And it smelt of sickly perfume of flowers. It came when Di got her great granddad's and great grandma's things out of the desk.' Susan stopped. 'What happened then my dear?' prompted the medium. Di found her voice at last, 'It floated round the room then disappeared into the back of the bureau. Can you tell us what it was?'

The medium hesitated for a moment. 'Or maybe *who* it was? It very much sounds to me that it was a message for you from someone near and dear that has passed over,' the medium replied gently. The congregation murmured with heightened interest. The medium hesitated again for a moment before continuing, 'Now, my dears, this sort of sign, it has been known to be a message from a loved one that someone close to you is going to join our spirit friends and pass to the other side.'

Di's eyes darted up to the front of the room again. She felt a sense of dread come over her, feeling a cold trickle down her scalp. 'But, dear, there is nothing to fear at all,' the medium said directly to Di. 'Nothing is certain in this life, and death is only a passing over to another life. A better life', she smiled. 'All we do know for sure is that when our time comes, it is ordained, and we will be with our loved ones again, in a beautiful place. So, you see, my dear? No need to worry. No need to worry at all.'

CHAPTER 26

TWO MORE UNWELCOME VISITORS

Her eyes snapped open. She breathed deeply and allowed the dream of her childhood to dissipate into the ether. But it was still dark. She supposed she hadn't been asleep for very long. She looked at the alarm clock. It was 02:22. She sighed. She hoped this didn't mean she'd have trouble getting back to sleep. She examined her senses for a moment. Did she need to go to the toilet? Is that why she woke? No. No need to get up. She closed her eyes again and told herself to get some sleep. She lay that way for a minute, maybe two, before she thought she felt something, some*one* in the room. Her eyes sprang open again and she looked towards the open doorway.

Charlie? She thought. Unlikely, she told herself. She never ventured this far upstairs.

As her eyes strained into the darkness and moved upwards from the floor she thought… no, she was sure that she saw a faint dark shape of a tall man standing there, silhouetted in the door frame against the pale light. He looked as if he was wearing a heavy dark coat with his collar turned up and upon his head, and a large hat with a wide brim. This tall, dark shadow walked… or rather more like glided noiselessly across the room towards her and stopped at the foot of the bed.

Her skin was clammy now. She was petrified, feeling a deep sense of dread. She stayed stock still, not even daring to breathe. The figure turned around, then she felt the mattress tilt as the figure sat on the end of the bed. She felt it shift and spread itself along her body. She felt the weight of it, as it lay itself upon her. She felt such an awful sense of revulsion, she felt cold and terror struck – it was as if this evil thing was sucking the soul out from her body. She summoned up all her strength and started to pray.

'Dear God,' she said inwardly, 'save me. Save me from this evil. I pray in the name of all that is Holy to remove this thing, this person or whatever it is from my house.' Then in desperation, 'Jesus, please help me!' at which point, she lost consciousness.

As she came back to her senses, Di felt its breath on her face. She heard it speak.

'Die,' it whispered. 'Die! Di? You awake, wifey?'

In a split second she realised that it was Mike! She shoved him off her, whereupon he fell with a thud on the floor. She gasped and caught her breath like someone saved from drowning. She slammed her hand around on the nightstand until she found the reading lamp switch, and whacked it on.

'Oh my God! Mike!' she squealed.

'Surprise!' he said wryly, nursing a bruised elbow from the fall.

'Are you trying to frighten me to death?' she said scolding him whilst diving on top of him to hug him at the same time.

'Bloody hell,' Mike said as she held onto him so tightly he could barely breathe. 'I'll have to go to A&E in a minute.'

'A&E?' Di began laughing uncontrollably, 'I'll give you A and bloody E. Why didn't you tell me you were coming?'

'It was all last minute. I didn't even know for sure that I could get permission to come home until this afternoon, and then I doubted I could get a flight. Are you pleased to see me?' he grinned.

'Apart from a near coronary. Of course I am,' she said attaching herself to him like a koala on a tree. 'Don't you ever go away again, OK?'

'Um… I'm only here for the weekend, you know. I have to go back Sunday afternoon,' he said clambering to his feet as she continued to cling to him.

'Can I get undressed?' he laughed.

She laughed out loud at her own overzealous display of affection and staggered back to the bed.

'How's the foot?' he asked as he chucked his clothes on the floor in the corner. This usually irritated Di, but right now he could do whatever he liked.

'A bit better,' she said.

'Need a nurse?' he asked with theatrical sympathy.

She nodded coyly and he cradled her foot on his hands and kissed it. And she was pleased to see he didn't stop there. He kissed her all over and they made love with a passion of such intensity they both fell asleep in each other's arms almost instantly after.

CHAPTER 27

RACHEL

I t was a thud that woke Di sometime later. Unmistakable. She hadn't imagined or dreamt it this time.

It wasn't even Mike mucking about. It reminded her of the sound the removal man had made when he dropped something in Rachel's room the day she moved in.

Rachel!

Di was wide awake now, her maternal instincts roaring as she fumbled out of the bedroom in the darkness to the stairs. She flicked on the lights in the stairwell and they instantly turned themselves off.

She cursed and with a sense of deja vu, she stumbled down the stairs, her foot and the lack of light conspiring to slow her down. When she reached the landing, she slapped her hand on another light switch. This time the light worked and scattered the three crows who were sitting on the window ledge - again. But Di had no time to worry about them. She threw Rachel's door open and felt as if she was dropping from the highest rollercoaster in the world. Her pupils dilated and her mouth stretched as if a huge g-force was acting upon it. The lights in Rachel's room were flicking on and off over and over again, as if someone was playing with the switches. As Di stood unable to move at the doorway, in the strobing lights, she was stunned and horrified to see Rachel being yanked out of bed by her hair by an invisible force. Di tried to reach her, but was unable to move. Strangely, Rachel appeared to remain asleep. She hit the floor with what would have been painful. This woke Rachel up with a start, and she immediately grabbed at her head to keep her hair from being pulled out by the roots. Whatever this invisible thing was, it had hold of her and was dragging her across the floor.

Di, desperate to reach her child, struggled with all her might against the force that was stopping her from entering the room. After what seemed like an eternity, she suddenly found the invisible power release her and she could move. She darted into the room, whilst at the same time shouting for Mike and trying to grab Rachel. Rachel was sliding around the polished wooden floorboards by means of the unseen force. The moment Di managed put her hands on her daughter, she felt whatever was dragging her around had let go.

Weirdly, Rachel had not made a sound. She had not cried out for help, although her pretty little face was deathly white and smeared with tears. And now she was looking up from the floor, her face screwed up as if anxiously listening to someone ranting at her. She shook her head a couple of times. She nodded. She flinched.

'Rachel?' Di said.

But Rachel's red-rimmed eyes were fixed above her. She was hardly recognisable.

'Rachel! Rachel! Wake up!' Di shouted. .

And this seemed to do the trick. The lights stopped flickering and stayed on. Rachel responded and allowed her mum to help her up and usher her from the room, hugging her all the while.

'Oh my God, sweetheart. Are you OK?' Di said when they reached the landing.

Rachel nodded.

'What happened?'

Rachel shrugged and pressed her face into her mother's shoulder.

'Did you see something? What was it?'

Rachel wiped at her face, giving out a faint moan and a large sob.

'Did you…? Was it…?' Di hated herself for even saying it, for admitting it was a possibility: 'Was it the man in the basement?'

Rachel's tearful eyes met her mother's for the first time, and Di knew the answer was yes, but her daughter was not prepared to say.

'I am so tired Mum, I just want to go back to bed,' Rachel said going to the door of her bedroom.

Di stopped her. 'You can't go back in there! We'll go and stay at a hotel or something,' she said floundering, 'while we… while we figure out what to do.'

'It's OK Mum,' Rachel said with an innocent authority that stopped Di in her tracks. 'He won't come back tonight.'

'How do you know, how?' Di asked desperately, trying not to shake the answer out of her daughter.

'I don't really know.' She yawned heavily and sobbed again. 'But I really want to sleep, Mum. I am SO tired.'

'Just come and sleep in my bed then, at least,' Di pleaded.

'It's fine,' Rachel insisted shaking her head. 'I want *my* bed. Really I do,' she said looking at her mother with eyes that reassured Di in a way she couldn't explain as the colour slowly returned to her face.

After a little more hesitation, Di took Rachel back into her room and tucked her up in bed with trembling hands.

'If anything else happens. Anything at all. You call me. You scream your head off, OK?'

'Course I will'. Rachel smiled and nodded and rolled over to sleep. Di watched her beautiful angelic-faced daughter for a few moments, then after scanning the room for God knows what, she crept out and hurried upstairs to Mike.

'Mike, Mike,' she said in his ear 'Didn't you hear me shout you?'

'Mmm?' he said barely awake. 'No I didn't hear anything. What's up?'

'Wake up darling. I need to tell you something.'

'Mmm, OK,' he said clearly not listening.

'No,' she said shaking him and starting to feel genuinely annoyed with him, 'I need you to be awake. I need you to listen to what I'm saying.'

Mike lifted his head, opened one eye and looked at the alarm clock over Di's shoulder before slamming his head back down on the pillow. 'Then why don't you wait till the morning when normal people are awake?'

'*Mike*,' she said, her tone forceful enough to make both his eyes open now.

'What is it?'

'This house. I thought it was Len and his mates mucking about at first, trying to force us out… and… and well, I think it's them still, it is their fault, but it's not a joke… it's… I mean, whatever they've conjured up. Whatever it was has just pulled Rachel out of bed for God's sake.'

'Woah, woah, woah,' Mike said sitting up. 'What are you talking about? Len is doing what?'

'He and Big Will and Rick and the Nuddies? They're all witches.'

Mike raised his eyebrows and opened his eyes wide.

'I've seen them. Remember that altar in the woods?'

After frowning at Di for a long moment, Mike nodded.

'I went back in the middle of the night and they were all dancing around it naked, or at least most of them.'

'So they're all nudists?' Mike said with a half-smile.

'No!' Di said impatiently. 'They're witches. Wiccans apparently. I went back to that shop in town. With the tarot reader - and I think she's in on it too.'

'In on what?'

'Well I believe that they're conjuring up spirits to drive us out of this house.'

Mike shook his head slowly, the words he wanted to say ballooning in his mouth behind pursed lips. Eventually they came out in a huge puff of frustrated air. 'Spirits? What the hell are you talking about, Di?'

'The electric problems. The microwave, the TV, the lights. It's not dodgy wiring, it's THEM! When I went down to the basement--'

'When you fell down there,' Mike said.

'Yes, I... there are things down there. Instruments of torture. Blood.'

Mike examined Di's face with great concern now. 'Did you hit your head when you fell?' he asked with utter seriousness.

'No. There are entities here, and they're really angry. I hear voices.'

She saw Mike wilt and she realised for the first time how she sounded. *I hear voices.* She sounded like she was suffering from a serious mental health illness.

'No,' she insisted, 'not like that. There's one man in particular. I saw his face on TV.'

'On the news?'

'No when the TV was off. When Josh and Andy were trying to get it to work that day.'

Mike looked disappointed in her and it really pissed her off.

'Look!' she said determined to prove what she was saying was true. She reached into the drawer in the nightstand and pulled out the wedding photos. She quickly rifled through the photographs, until she found the one Anna had taken of her and she thrust it at Mike.

'There! That's the same bloke. Did you invite or see anyone that looked like that at our party? No.'

'What bloke?' Mike said studying the photo.

Di leaned over him to point out the obvious.

But there was no one but Di in the photo!

At breakfast the air was thick with unspoken words. Di had so much more to tell Mike about what she had seen and heard; about Dorothea and about the three crows, but the words stuck in her throat when she saw the critical and disappointed words that loitered behind Mike's eyes.

'Get some sleep!' he had said when she'd shown him the photo. 'We'll discuss it in the morning.'

But they hadn't discussed anything. Instead they had brooded and slammed the fridge door and snapped the kettle shut with force, expressing their frustration with each other wordlessly. When Rachel came down to join them, it delayed the inevitable showdown even further. Di hovered around her daughter protectively, asking her if she was all right so many times that even Rachel began to be irritated by her too. So she backed off. She let Rachel watch TV all morning and then draw and paint in the afternoon.

'Not on there though,' she said as Rachel went to deposit her paper and pencils on the dining table, her usual workspace. 'Do it on the coffee table.'

'Why? She can do it on the dining table,' Mike said, his feet already up on the coffee table as he watched a football match on the telly. 'Why are those suitcases there anyway?'

'They're full of books,' Rachel informed him.

'I'm not sure where to put them yet,' Di grumbled.

She saw Mike glance at the bookshelf, just as Rachel had. The sarcasm in his look irked her.

'Coffee table please.' Di said firmly and went off to the kitchen to wash up noisily.

She heard Mike exhale loudly and get up. His voice was

on her shoulder in an instant hissing into her ear, 'Why the hell can't we just move the suitcases?'

'I don't want to move them,' she said almost scrubbing the Teflon from the frying pan.

'But the books were in the bookcase before!'

'And they're not now.'

'Why? Did the poltergeist move them?'

She glared at him to confirm from his expression that that was a snipe.

'I can't believe you think I'm making this up.'

'I can't believe you're taking this so seriously. You of all people.'

'What's that supposed to mean?'

'It means I'm the one who's more likely to believe in ghosts than you. The lights I've seen up above the clouds when I'm flying. The UFOs. You always have a rational explanation for them. You always convince me that they can't be aliens. And of course you're right. So why can't you see that you might have dreamt some of these things? Or been so tired that you imagined them? Or have still got to get used to being in a new house?'

'Because I've considered all those things myself. And I've had to rule them all out. Go and speak to Rachel!' she said hoping it wouldn't come to this. The last thing she wanted to do was make Rachel relive last night, but she was desperate for Mike to believe her. 'Ask her what happened last night!'

'When she was sleeping, you mean?'

'But *I* wasn't sleeping,' she said whacking the pan on the draining board. I was there too. We both couldn't have dreamt the same thing.'

She focused on the washing up, waiting for his reply. But there was none. Just a sigh. Then:

'I'm going for a walk,' he muttered, leaving Di sloshing around the washing up water, to disguise the sound of her weeping, as Rachel worked diligently on her latest work of art.

As her tears subsided and in the quiet of the room, a deep painful memory from her past intruded into her mind and pierced her heart.

She then retired to the bedroom to take time out to think. She wished her father was alive to talk to. He didn't like the idea of her 'messing with the occult' but she wasn't. They, it or whatever was messing with *her*, and she needed a sensible shoulder to lean on. Her father had been a solid, kind and rational man who would listen and he would know she was not crazy. But he wasn't here. Tears came into her eyes as she remembered…..

CHAPTER 28

THE SUMMER OF 1975

I t was the summer of 1971. Susan had secured them both a job in Devon working as chambermaids, along with Di's cousin, Verity, to earn some money over the school vacation. She had worked at a hotel in Ilfracombe with another friend the previous year, and she told Di it was the best summer she had ever had.

'Earning good money and going to the beach on our days off, brilliant. As for the good-looking boys – there's too many to mention!' she had grinned.

So off they went all the way to the southwest of England. Di was full of excitement and a little apprehension of course, but when they arrived at the austere monstrosity of a hotel overlooking the beach, Di simply could not settle. She wasn't afraid of working as a chambermaid, as they still called it then; in fact, making beds and cleaning rooms gave her the opportunity to focus on something else apart from the strange sense of doom which always mushroomed in her mind during her time off. It was an expensive hotel. Each morning, she would wake at 5am, dress in her blue and white chequered uniform and tie on her little white apron. She took the lift to the 6th floor, reaching her corridor by 5.30am. A huge milk churn had already been delivered to her tiny kitchen. On the top of the milk was a layer of thick cream about 4 or 5 inches thick. She would take a tea cup and skim off half a cup full and drink it, persuading herself that it was to keep up her energy until breakfast. The cream was very cold and absolutely delicious. She started her morning's work by mixing the cream thoroughly into the milk, then making tea or coffee and setting it all out neatly on silver trays for all the residents who had ordered it. There was a list of their room numbers pinned to a notice board. She then carried each tray carefully down the corridor, knocked on the door of each room, and when they answered, she would set it down on their table in their bedrooms. Mostly they were still in bed, some were up and in their dressing gowns, reading the papers or sat at the dressing table, putting on make-up, or brushing their hair. Sometimes they were only half dressed. No-one seemed to mind the tiny chambermaid coming into their rooms, whatever their state of attire.

After that, the chambermaids were treated to a full English breakfast in the 'dungeons' of the hotel. After half an hour's break, she was back upstairs, taking out the fresh laundry from a large cupboard ready to change beds and towels, in every room which was done every single day except Sundays. Sundays were usually free. She vacuumed the corridor, and as each resident left their rooms for breakfast, she would quickly change their beds, clear away the tea trays and clean the rooms. No easy matter – it was all sheets and blankets in those days. It was very hard work, but to a 17 year old with plenty of energy, it was not difficult. Her only struggle was accomplishing the envelope corners of the bottom sheets on the beds, which had to be re-done on several occasions after the rooms had been inspected by the manager.

The work was all completed by 1.30pm when the chambermaids were treated to lunch. The girls were entitled to return at 7pm for dinner, and were served what was left over from the guests - and it was always delicious. It would have been easy to put on huge amounts of weight, had it not been for their hard manual labour.

On the girl's free afternoons, they would go to the beach, swim and sunbathe or, if it was raining, they would take the bus to explore the surrounding area. At night they would pop into the bars, (no-one then ever asked their ages), and later on to a disco, or down to the beach for a barbecue. It should have been an idyllic time for the three of them, but Di still felt uneasy. She couldn't explain it; she was not particularly homesick, but there was an impending sense of doom which sapped her energy.

One evening, about 3 weeks into her summer job, she had gone to a disco in town with the other girls. Susan and Verity were in their element, gyrating on the dance floor and chatting to some local lads they had met previously. Di just couldn't find the energy to dance or even join in the chatter and laughter.

'I'm going back,' she shouted in Susan's ear over the music.

'Oh no! Why?' Susan bawled.

'I feel a bit rough. I think I might be coming down with something,' she sniffed as if to demonstrate. 'I can't afford to go off sick.'

'But it's not even nine o'clock yet.'

'I know, but if I go now I'll be better for Saturday.'

Susan thought about this for a moment – they had a big day planned for Saturday afternoon. Then Susan spotted the lad she had fancied for a while. He was talking to the DJ. 'OK,' she said distractedly. 'Take care!' She hugged her friend briefly and went off hurriedly to speak to the dark haired gangly teenage lad, who was now grinning at her from across the room.

Di was in bed by nine. She felt exhausted, her chest tight

and her heart heavy, but despite the discomfort she fell asleep quickly.

The phone ringing woke her. She looked at the alarm clock; it was only 9:20pm. She'd only been asleep for a few minutes. It was her father on the line.

'Diane? Diane, love, can you hear me?' He sounded drained of all energy, but urgent.

'Yes, Dad. What's the matter?' she asked, threading her finger tightly through the coils of the telephone wire.

'I'm so sorry, love, but I have to leave you now.'

'What do you mean? You just called.'

'No, Di. I mean I have to leave you, all of you for good. I'm so sorry,' he said.

That sense of doom she had felt since arriving at the hotel started to sharpen into focus, - and suddenly, she knew that this was what it had all been about. 'No, Dad. You can't please don't go, don't go.' The tears flowed instantly down her face.

'I have to, love. I have no choice.'

'Yes you do, yes you do, Dad, you do have a choice. Please!'

He sighed heavily down the phone. 'It's time, Diane. I can't tell you how sorry I am...'

'No, no, please, don't go. Not yet.'

'I love you, Diane. You look after yourself, all right.'

'Dad, nooooo!' she wailed.

'Goodbye, love. Bye.'

He hung up.

And she woke up.

Her pillow was soaked with tears. She looked at the alarm clock. It was only 9:25pm. She exhaled loudly. A dream. Thank God. She turned the pillow over and threw her head back on it, enjoying the coolness until she slept again.

In the morning she woke up feeling fresh. No sign of her

illness. It was as though the rain had fallen and refreshed the earth after a long dry hot spell. She hopped out of bed, got dressed and went to work with a skip. She started her chores with gusto and finished her floor in record time. All she needed to do now was take the dirty bed clothes to the laundry room.

As she came down the corridor pushing her trolley full of linen, she saw two familiar faces coming towards her. It took a while for her to register that they were two of her closest and oldest friends from back home. She had never expected to see them in this environment so far from Saddleworth.

'Hey, what are you two doing here?! Amazing to see you girls, I can't believe it!' she beamed. This was the cherry on the cake of what she felt was going to be a great day.

'Di,' Sarah said, her face drooping under the weight of the news she had to deliver.

Di's smile quickly faded and her face began to mirror her friend's.

'It's your dad,' she said, but she sobbed and couldn't go on.

Tanya took over. 'Di, I'm so sorry to tell you, but your dad, he had a heart attack last night.'

'Oh my God,' Di placed her hand in shock over her mouth. 'Is he OK? Is he in the hospital?'

All manner of exclamations and questions played on Di's lips, but she couldn't articulate all of them. Her friends shook their heads, sadly, slowly.

'He didn't make it. He died at home before the ambulance arrived'.

Di's face was as white as a sheet in shock, and she sank to her knees. Her friend caught her by the elbow in time and put her arm around her.

'What *time was this*?' Di asked inexplicably.

'About nine o'clock?' She looked to Sarah for confirmation.

'Nine. Nine fifteen, nine twentyish,' Sarah confirmed.

Di then fell to the floor, a dead weight. It was as if the floor of the hotel was collapsing beneath her. Her friends picked her up and helped her to her room. They packed up her things and soon they were all driving back up the motorway to West Yorkshire, going home. But home was supposed to be the place that never changed. The place that she could go back to after the trials and tribulations of her young life, and always find solace. And now home was broken. So how could she go through this life with any sense of security? All those times she cried about boys who'd dumped her - that was nothing. She knew what heartbreak really was now. Everything was a mess. Nothing made sense. Oh, Dad, why did you have to leave us? We love you and will miss you so much.

By the time they reached the moors it was dark and the full moon was illuminating the fields with silver. It looked so cold out there, as though they were snow-covered in the dead of winter. But it was the height of summer. She had the car window down, her face in the wind, trying to blow this turmoil from her mind. She looked up. The moon reminded her of the pale blue sphere she and Susan had conjured up just a few months before.

'It was a sign from the afterlife,' the medium had explained further after the service in the church. *'Now, it can often mean, that someone in the family is going to die. But there is no need to worry at all,'* the medium repeated to Di. *'Nothing is certain in this life. When we are called, we must follow.'* Why, oh why did it have to be my dad who was called? We still need him so much. Death is hell for the people who are left behind, who love you so, so much.

Di stuck her head further out the car window so that the wind roared through her head competing with the rage inside her. She was furious at the medium for telling her the light was a sign, yet telling her nothing more useful to avoid this disaster. If she had known the details, if she had known who was going to die, Di might have been able to stop it. But most of all she was furious at herself for conjuring up that damned sphere in the first place.

'Nothing is certain in this life.'

Well, she was going to make sure that from now on everything was certain. That everything made sense. From now on, plain and simple evidence would be her by-word. Her sense of security. Not the unknown or the inexplicable. And from that very moment she began the process of suppressing all memories and knowledge of the realms beyond our understanding, beyond substance, beyond blind faith and beyond proof. Little did she realise that her spiritual sensitivity, or 'third eye' that she had known she had from as far back as she could remember, would be harder, much harder to close than she would have liked.

CHAPTER 29

SEEKING ANSWERS IN THE CROSS

Back to the present. After a long, soothing bathe in the jacuzzi, Di came out onto the landing to hear that Mike had returned. She could hear him talking to Rachel downstairs. She crept, wrapped in her towel, to the top of the stairwell and listened.

'He grabbed me by the hair and started shouting at me.'

'What was he saying to you?' Mike asked gently.

'I didn't understand *everything*. His voice sounded strange. As if he was using really old-fashioned words. But he wanted to be left alone. He wanted me to tell someone to leave him alone, to leave him in peace.'

'Who?'

'I don't know. He thought I already knew.'

'And you were asleep when this happened?'

Di strained to listen to Rachel's answer. None came. Perhaps it was a shake of the head. Or a nod.

'Do you think you might have dreamt it?'

Di clenched her jaw in frustration.

Another silent answer.

'Do you know what?' Mike said softly. 'I think you probably did. Because things like that don't really happen, do

189

they? Only in ghost stories. And I don't want you to worry. We all have bad dreams sometimes. Your mum had some too. Just like yours. But they're just our imaginations running away with us. You know that, don't you?'

'Mmm.'

Di felt betrayed. Not by Rachel. But by Mike for using the kind of leading questions that would never be tolerated in a court of law. She almost laughed out loud.

A court of law. Listen to me, she thought, *resorting to legalese. How ironic!*

She took herself to bed and after a little time spent with Rachel, she stayed there for the rest of the evening. When Mike came up and got into bed behind her, he wrapped an arm around her. But she shrugged it off. She felt angry, lonely and betrayed.

The next day he left earlier than she expected him to, but he said it was the only plane he could take to get back to Stockholm on time. She drove him to the airport in virtual silence and later dropped Rachel off at her father's in the evening before returning once again to an empty house – she hoped.

She had never felt so desolate, so devoid of joy. Her tears bubbled up as she drove home, and she wept silent tears.

She couldn't bear being in the house alone. Every creak, every click. She didn't know how she would sleep tonight… unless she was drunk.

The pub.

A place she could go to get out of the house and a place where she could consume enough alcohol to give her the Dutch courage to come back to sleep.

Although it was still light, she grabbed the torch from the cupboard so she wouldn't be caught out again on the way back. It was small enough to slip into her raincoat, an essential addition to her outfit since the drizzle seemed as unceasing, as ever. Her ankle was much better, but on her way out she felt the need to grab Mike's walking stick, in order to steady her on the cobbles and avoid any more injury. And it made her feel safer.

As she rounded the corner onto Church Street she looked up the stairs to The Cross Inn and the sight of Big Will and Fiona talking in the doorway stopped her in her tracks.

They noticed her and stopped talking; the two disabled locals leaning on their sticks looking down the steps to the incomer, the outsider leaning on her stick.

Snap, a voice in Di's head said. It was Dorothea's.

The three of them stared at each other for some achingly stretched out seconds. This was Di's chance to go and tell these fools to back off. Threaten them with the law in case they hadn't got the message from Roslyn. At least, that was her intention. That was before she believed that they were *really* conjuring up evil and spirits. Now she was too scared to approach them. What would they do, and what entities would they invoke if she confronted them now? Her thighs were trembling so much she thought it might be visible through her jeans. She tore her eyes from theirs and carried on walking up the road to the only other pub in the village, The White Lion. She entered the black and white ancient pub and ordered a pint of Guinness then found a dark corner in which to hide and felt the Guinness begin to soothe her. Suddenly a familiar voice addressed her;

'Weir's tha better 'alf this evenin'?'

Di looked up to confirm that the words came from behind the thick impenetrable goatee of Robert, the tour guide. In one hand he held the golfing umbrella, which had on the first day they had met, (and why wouldn't he? It always rained in Heptonstall). In the other hand he held a pint of Guinness. He propped the umbrella against the corner of the wall, and without waiting for an invitation, he sat down next to her so they were both facing into the room. Their backs were against the wall, speaking like two spies on a park bench, pretending not to know each other.

'He'… working,' Di said, not wanting to explain further.

'Working, eh?'

'Mmm.'

'On a Sundi neight?' Robert sipped on his stout.

Di threw a glance at him and found herself inexplicably repulsed by the way his goatee caught the foam on his pint. 'Yes, he's a pilot. He doesn't work regular hours. Not everybody does.'

'I s'pose not, no.' And after an awkward silence he added. 'And what about you? Working termorrer?'

'Yes. My hours are a little more regular. Sometimes.' She sipped her pint too. 'And how's your work these days? And why are you here anyway? I thought The Cross was your local?'

'I'm 'avin' a bit o' a change. Aye, my work is very definitely irregular,' he said with a sniff. 'Not sin' many tourists these days.'

'Thank God,' Di muttered. But when Robert looked at her askance she added, 'No, I don't mean thank God you have no source of income. I mean, thank God we'll have no tourists hanging about our house.'

'By 'eck, they do love a good ghost story though, do these Japanese tourists.'

Di felt uneasy. What was this leading up to? 'A ghost story?' she said quietly. 'I thought they just came to see where Ted Hughes lived and Sylvia Plath's grave.'

'Indeed. As you know, they are very famous poets …. But they are….' he hesitated.

'Are what?'

'Sylvia and Ted's story is also a *ghost* story,' he said, in a voice intending to sound mysterious.

'How so?' Di said scanning the room to check whether any of the witches were present. No, thankfully.

'Well, all that stuff about her committin' suicide cos she was a bit on th' sensitive side. and 'cos she was wronged by Ted Yews who couldn't keep 'is hands off other women.'

'The stuff you tell the tourists?' Di asked, recalling the tour she and Mike took.

Di saw him nod. 'It does her a disservice. It's not the 'ole story.'

'Then why do you say it?'

'I don't think the Japanese tourists understand half of worr I'm sayin on account of me accent. And they don't need to. They meight already know th' truth anyways.'

It was all coming back to Di now. The moment on that tour when Robert had muttered in her ear, *'There's many a dark secret about this place.'*

'So what is the truth?' Di said.

'About Sylvia?' He sipped his pint then went on, 'Well, be *my* mind, truth is, they lived 'ere and in th' vicinity and met wi' some things that destroyed their relationship fer good.'

Di held her breath.

'Women always get shitty end o'stick, don't they?'

Di couldn't argue with that right now.

'Stormy luminous senses and a violent, almost demonic spirit. That's what they say 'bout Sylvia. As if it were 'er fault. As if she was th' one causing trouble, when in fact it was just that she, like many wimmin, were mooer receptive to th' spirit world than we blokes. She wern't alwus tormented by 'er mental 'ealth issues. At least, not completely. Be my mind, she were tormented by th' spirits that 'aunts this place. What *I* think is that she and Ted didn't have a tempestuous marriage *just* because of 'is philandering. *I* think 'ee went off philanderin' 'cos ee didn't understand why she were going off 'er 'ed. He didn't believe her when she teld him what were really 'appenin'.'

This felt like a horrible omen. Di felt as if there were dark forces about her, and she felt numb with cold, as though she was standing alone on the highest point of the moors with the winter wind whistling through her. She tried to drink her Guinness to cover her distress, but her hand shook so much, she only managed a quick sip before having to return the glass to the security of the table top.

'Is this what you would have told me if I had come to The Cross that day after our tour with you?' she asked weakly.

He didn't answer, but simply echoed his opening gambit. 'Where's tha husband this evenin'?'

Di wanted to cry, but she held it together. She would have thought Robert was merely peddling his usual tourist tat, had he not just drawn the most frightening and clearly intentional parallel between her relationship with Mike and Sylvia's with Ted. She needed to know more. He seemed to have some answers and from her recollection, she had only seen him with one of the witches, but he was not one of them. The memory was hazy, but she could never forget the essence of it. It was on the steps of The Cross. The evening they had met Fiona and Terry:

'I'll invite who I like, thank you!' Fiona had said. And, mysteriously, she had also said *'He won't harm them.'*

This exchange took on a whole new complexion now. What on earth was she referring to? Di wondered again.

'What do you make of Fiona and Terry?' she said to him, turning her head in an effort to see Robert's eyes behind those thick glasses of his.

'What does *tha* make o' them?' He threw the question back at her.

'I think they're doing some very bad things. And I think you know that. What did you say to Fiona that night outside The Cross, when she was taking me and Mike to her house?'

She saw Robert swallow, though he hadn't taken a sip of Guinness. Then he said, 'I told them… I told them that they shouldn't be doin' what they're doin'.'

'And what are they doing, Robert?' Di said. 'You tell me right now, what are they doing?'

She was still looking at him, but he wasn't looking at her. His eyes were fixed dead ahead, his goatee quivering, his skinny hands wringing together as he noticed the person standing by the fireplace glaring at him.

Len.

Robert downed the remainder of his pint and stood up, grabbing his umbrella as if he might need to protect himself with it at any moment. 'I 'ave to go. Tek care, lass.' He rushed out.

'Wait,' Di said getting up to follow him. Then, realising she'd left her coat and her walking stick, she quickly turned back to grab them and went outside into the dusk too.

But Robert was gone.

She turned back to the pub and saw Len silhouetted in the doorway. So she hurried off down the street. When she came near The Cross she saw Big Will and Rick standing outside, as if they were waiting for her. She immediately came to a halt, her heart racing. She looked to her right and saw Fiona and Terry outside their house, as if they were waiting for her too. She looked over her shoulder. Len was strolling down the street behind her.

She gripped her walking stick tightly and lifted it from the floor, brandishing it like a truncheon. She looked around for passers-by, but there was no one. This was the busiest Church Street had been since the removal men had smashed her neighbour's guttering. She could hear voices in The Cross, laughing and joking, but they seemed a world away. Her chest was heaving. Her vision blurred with tears.

She stood petrified in the middle of this human penta-gram now blinking her tears away. She heard a crow cawing somewhere above. And after what seemed like an hour to Di, Terry approached her and said quietly, mysteriously, 'We need to talk, Diane.'

195

Di took a step back, away from him and looked towards the pub. Voices still emanated from inside. The voices of people who could save her. She took a deep breath, screwed up her face and screamed at the top of her lungs, 'Get away from me!'

Di felt a hand on her shoulder. She swung round in panic about to wallop whoever had a costed her with her stick. Before she brought is crashing down, she heard a familiar voice;

'You all right, my darling?'

She saw with relief she saw Ollie's glowing face smiling at her. Di felt relief wash over her. 'Oh, Ollie, thank God it's you!' she almost fell into his arms.

'You look like you've seen a ghost,' Stephen said, stroking her shoulder and threading his arm through hers.

Di looked around. There was no sign of the five witches, only a jet-black cat sitting on the step of Terry and Fi's cottage, its eyes glowing amber in the streetlight. She instinctively looked up. She was strangely unsurprised to see three crows there on a telegraph wire over the street, staring down at her. She heard an owl hoot, but couldn't see where it was coming from. She wondered if she had ever seen the five humans in the street to begin with.

'Come and have a drink with us,' Ollie said taking her other arm. 'That'll sort you out.'

She didn't resist. And they marched her into The Cross, flanking her, like a couple of security officials.

CHAPTER 30
THE SÉANCE

She stumbled through her work the next day with one hell of a hangover. Fortunately she was working from home on papers and was not expected in court. Stephen and Ollie had plied her with Guinness until closing time then escorted her home, ensuring she was safely tucked in. Throughout her working day, snippets of their conversations came back to her, but never did she recall them asking her what was wrong or why she was screaming in the middle of the street. They just seemed to know that she had sorrows to drown, and they seemed to be on a mission to distract her from them.

When her eyes were too sore and brain too tired to work anymore, she flaked out on the sofa for a while. She was so very weary, but she couldn't fully relax. She was restless. Her mind kept wandering to Dorothea. She felt the need to go next door. She would have liked to say it was to make sure her neighbour was OK, but she was mostly propelled there by the thought that Dorothea may be able to tell her more.

'Of course I heard something, you silly girl. And I still do. Hear them all the bloody time,' she had yelled at Di the last time she saw her.

And if she heard the voices all the time, then surely she should know a lot more about them than Di did. So levering herself from the comfort of the sofa, she went out into the cobbled yard, through the picket gate and knocked on Dorothea's door. 'Fuck off, I'm busy!' Dorothea bellowed at first. Then; 'For goodness sake, come in then if you must!' as Di knocked more insistently.

'Oh. It's you,' Dorothea sneered, sitting on her throne as she usually was. Tights and knickers round her knees.

Di drew a breath then said, 'Dorothea, I am so sorry for upsetting you. I didn't consider your feelings enough. I was too caught up in my own worries.'

'Hmm,' Dorothea pursed her lips. 'Oh well, since you've apologised so gracefully, you're forgiven. They are very serious worries actually, so I really can't blame you.'

The two women stared at each other for a moment, then Dorothea allowed a smile to bloom on her face. Di returned it.

'Well?' Dorothea said.

Di cocked her head, unsure of what Dorothea was asking.

'Go put the kettle on, there's a good girl, and then you can tell me all about it.' This was the kindest Di had ever heard from Dorothea.

Unusually, Di made a tea for herself this time. Almost as much sugar as Dorothea. She needed it to keep the remains of her hangover at bay.

Within minutes, Dorothea was settled, pants back up, with her fortified tea as usual and Di was perched on the rickety chair by the table stacked with papers. Dorothea then looked at her, her eyebrows raised, a rare, receptive look on her face.

'So you went to the Black Cauldron in town?' she asked.

'Yes. But I got angry with them. Told them to keep out of my business. Threatened them with legal action,' Di shook her head.

'I suppose you realise the law doesn't really hold any weight in the realms we're dealing with?'

Di nodded. Of course, she knew that, though she had toyed making out a case of harassment couldn't she? But what court in the land would believe her? In a word, none.

'I know, I appreciate that. I was just shocked and angry.'

Dorothea smiled with great sympathy for her.

'Did Roslyn explain the altar to you?'

'She told me about the Wiccan faith, the emphasis on nature and women...' Di trailed off.

'And?'

'She said that Rachel could also perceive what I had.'

'Your little one?' Dorothea said with a furrowed brow.

Di nodded into her tea as she drank. 'That's what made me really angry. Because it made sense - and that made me scared for her. Especially because I now think she has inherited my third eye and spiritual sensitivity. I thought that I had managed to push to the back of my mind the issues I had with it as a child. After my father died, I decided to firmly shut it away. For good, or so I thought. I believed that I was responsible for my father's death, you see'.

'Now, now, that's nonsense my dear. Many of us are aware of our gifts as young girls. But sometimes we refuse to admit it,' Dorothea said knowingly. 'But one thing I am certain of is that you having 'the gift' would not have caused or brought about his death. Not at all'.

Di was so grateful to hear these words of reassurance from Dorothea, who was not herself normally blessed with the gift of kindness. She felt her face flush as she explained her recent experiences. 'Something dragged Rachel out of bed the other night. I wouldn't have believed it if I hadn't been there to see it for myself. Apparently it spoke to her. Shouted at her. But I couldn't hear it. She told Mike that it told her to leave it alone. Or tell someone else to leave it alone.'

Dorothea nodded. 'Hobnob?' she said offering the packet. Never before had Di been so in need of one. She devoured it as Dorothea asked, 'And what does Mike make of it all?'

'He thinks I'm bonkers. He thinks Rachel and I are dreaming it all. We argued about it.'

'Men!' Dorothea sighed.

'I saw the face of an old man on the screen of our TV. And the same face was in a photo with me at our wedding party. And burnt into a magazine. He's the one that attacked Rachel, I'm sure of it. I have a feeling he's the one that was torturing someone and threatened me in the cellar.'

'He's not a happy chap, is he?' Dorothea said as she chewed on her biscuit.

'Have you heard him too?'

Dorothea nodded. 'I think he's responsible for the screams. Rumour has it that he's hurt, tortured many people in the past…and much of it happened in The Goose Inn, of which your house, mine and Jeffrey's were a part'.

Di sat up, anxious.

So Dorothea clarified, '…when he was of this earth, I mean.'

Di leaned forward so she could say the words quietly: 'Do you think we're in danger from him now?'

Dorothea shrugged and munched. They were both quiet for a moment until Di recalled something from the shop.

'Roslyn said the name David was relevant. She said that might be his name. Or one of them, as if there were more.'

'Oh, my guess is that there's more than one all right.'

'Who are they?' Di asked plaintively.

Dorothea thought for a moment. She chased a crumb around her yellowing teeth with her tongue. She sipped on her tea cocktail. Then sighed deeply and announced, 'Shall we try to find out?'

Di nodded full of apprehension and Dorothea beckoned her over.

'Bring up your chair.'

Di did as she was told and sat directly opposite her neighbour's commode. The whiff of urine was thankfully not as strong as was often the case. Dorothea was yet to relieve herself in Di's presence this evening. Di had become rather inured to the pervading smell by now. Dorothea took Di's hands between her chubby fingers. It reminded her of the way she and Susan had sat on the floor of her bedroom all those years ago trying to summon the spirits of her great grandparents.

'Do we need to have something that belongs to them? Something they've touched to make them come?' she whispered.

'What do you have in mind?' Dorothea asked.

Di thought for a moment. 'The chains and rods in the basement?'

'And would you like to pop down there and get them?' Dorothea said with a wry smile.

Di smiled coyly back and shook her head.

'Don't worry, my dear. They seem to have no trouble appearing when it suits them. And I'm pretty sure they've touched all of this, when they were alive.'

'All of what?'

'This house, your house. It seems that they think it all still belongs to them. Turn that light off, would you?'

Although Di got up to dutifully turn off the only light that was on in the house, she first said, 'Do we have to?'

'They're like bloody mosquitoes,' Dorothea replied. 'They are more likely to come buzzing around when it's dark. That's why they mess with the electrics all the time. Light is a problem for the likes of these spirits. If it wasn't, they would have gone toward the celestial light ages ago and passed over for good. But light those little candles first will you, dear?' Dorothea pointed a filthy nail at a couple of black coloured candles on the table in small glass candle holders, and the box of matches that sat next to them. 'A little Wiccan magic protection is called for. Unfortunately I don't have any sage.'

'What do you mean?' Di said watching her hand own

tremble as she lit the candle. 'I thought you said Wicca was codswallop.'

'Well, I do have a tendency to be a little hasty in my criticism sometimes. Have you noticed?' she said with a warm wink. 'The black will protect us from all the negativity if we focus on it. We could use some sage smudge sticks, if I had any, which would be even better.' Di had no idea what she was talking about. 'But how will the candles help?'

'Ever blown out candles on your birthday?'

Di nodded as she flicked off the electric light.

'And then what did you do?'

'Made a wish?' Di said tentatively as she took her seat again.

'Exactly. Although we won't be so much wishing, but visualising, in order to manifest our safety. Now, hands.'

Di held her hands again and they sat in silence for a moment. The only sound was the rain drumming its watery fingers on the roof and windows. The only movement came from the shadows which the candle made dance on the walls. Dorothea closed her eyes. Di hoped it wasn't a prerequisite for summoning the spirits, because she couldn't bring herself to do the same. She studied her elderly friend's podgy, heavily wrinkled face with puffy bags under each eye as she muttered something unintelligible, invoking the entities, Di presumed. Fingers of fear ran up Di's spine each time the dancing shadows caught her attention, and she thought someone else had entered the room. She watched the shadows play on Dorothea's pumpkin face making her wrinkles look deeper than ever and carving out the hollows above her eyes.

Then Dorothea said, 'Visualise peace, harmony and protection for us dear.

After a few more seconds she opened one eye. 'Shy little buggers tonight, aren't they?'

Di nearly laughed with relief. She desperately wanted answers, but she feared this method of getting them.

'Sod's law,' Dorothea continued. 'The bastards won't shut up when I'm trying to read, but when we actually ask them to come, where the fuck are they?'

The horrific scream which silenced her seemed to emerge from the kitchen, rushing across the living room and passing right through Dorothea, whose face registered the violation and whose hands gripped Di's tightly. The sound not only hurt Di's ears, she felt as though she saw the sound change the shape of everything it passed through. Di threw herself back in her chair as the scream reached her, and then it seemed to change its course up to the ceiling and instantly dissipate.

The candles flickered violently and for a moment Di feared they would be blown out. She held her breath until the room returned to normal.

'Are you OK?' she asked her friend.

'Yes,' Dorothea gasped, but the strong smell of fresh urine belied her words. 'I think we might have lift off.'

The sudden clang of metal against metal made them both jump. Di knew the sound. She had heard it before in the basement of Goose Barn. The sound of iron rods being tossed to the ground. And then the room suddenly felt very hot. The sound of coals sizzling came from somewhere in the shadows. A man's voice cracked and groaned. It was the sound of someone who was exhausted from pain.

'No more, no more!' he pleaded, rising to a cry of pain.

Chains rattled. Rods clanged.

'No,' he moaned.

Hisssssss.

And then the faceless voice screamed with an agony that brought tears silently streaming from Di's eyes. She looked at Dorothea whose expression was a cocktail of terror and exhilaration. 'Fucking hell!' she exclaimed.

'Help!' wailed the man.

'No one's comin' t' 'elp thee,' another voice said. Also that of a man. But this voice was rougher, the accent thicker.

Di had heard this voice and these words before. In her basement. Then, she had thought the words were directed at her, but now she realised that she was listening to a dialogue from long ago, between victim and torturer, that seemed to have been somehow recorded in the walls of these buildings.

'Thass what tha gets for messing with the 'Artley's.'

Those words she'd also heard before. And that name sounded familiar now. 'I've heard that name before,' Di whispered.

The women had to raise their voices now, as the rain began to pound like fists on the house and the clanging and screams continued to rage around them.

'Hartley?' Dorothea said. 'Yes, yes. Me too.'

Di recalled Robert's tour of the village and his words about the churchyard:

'Mebbi Count Dracula himsell o' most likely evil David 'Artley visits on dark neyts.'

'David,' Di said breathlessly. 'Roslyn said David was the name of one of them. It must be David Hartley.'

Dorothea steeled herself and shouted out, 'David Hartley. David Hartley, show yourself!'

Silence.

Eerily, the rain stopped.

The screaming stopped.

The clanging of metal stopped.

It was as if Dorothea's words had silenced that which was frightening them, - or were they waiting to hear more? The women looked warily about the room. Still not letting go of each other's hands, but loosening their grip slightly now.

Then Di saw it move beneath the table. Saw its eyes flash. She was about to jump up as she heard it growl, but when

Dorothea said, 'Oh, do be quiet, Brutus,' she remembered the old collie that always languished there.

'Oh my God,' Di exhaled. 'I forgot about your—'

The words stuck in her throat as she saw over Dorothea's shoulder a man, perhaps in his thirties or forties, encased in a metal cage. His body was rotting and the stench of it filled the air. The atmosphere became cacophonous again. The rain, the clanging, the screams. The cawing of a bird scraped at Di's ears, and she felt powerful wings brush her hair as a large black crow manifested from nowhere and landed onto the top of the cage, and then onto the man's head. It began pecking at one of his eyes. Its sharp beak stabbed and stabbed at it over and over again until it plucked out the viscous mess and swallowed it, its feathers dripping with the man's blood. Di slapped her hand over her mouth in an effort to stop herself from vomiting.

Dorothea saw the horror on Di's face and shifted sideways on her commode so she could see behind her. 'David! David!' she called out. 'Is that you?'

The rotting face began to twist and snarl, the remaining eye rolling around in an effort to focus. And then it cried out, 'Jim! Jim! How could tha? How could tha do this to me?'

The crow flew at the women and they both ducked, fearing for their own eyes. But it flew over them and they watched as it impossibly melded with the other shadows playing on the wall.

They looked back at the caged man, but he and the cage were gone. An old man was standing there instead, and Di recognised him instantly. He was the man from the TV, the man from the photo, the man who attacked her daughter. But this time he was wielding an iron rod, one end glowing red hot.

'Who *are* you?' Di yelled at him, desperate to know, but wracked with fear.

'Leave. My. Brother. Alone!' he roared.

205

He threw himself forward at her, but Di saw no more as the candle went out and, after a terrible yelp and crashing, and a final 'fuck me!' from Dorothea, all was silent again.

Her blood was punching its way through her ears. She scrambled across the floor on her hands and knees towards the table, desperate to find the matches and relight the candles, not just so she could see what the hell had happened, but also because Dorothea had told her it was there to protect them from negativity – and if there was one thing Di could be sure of in this chaos, it was that these entities were dripping with negativity.

'Dorothea? Dorothea?' she called out as she slapped her hands around on the table top. 'Dorothea? Are you OK?'

She couldn't find the matches and she heard no response from her neighbour. She cursed, scrambling to the wall to search for the light switch. She found it quickly but it didn't work. She wasn't surprised, but it did nothing to allay her fear. She felt for the front door. Found the handle.

'Where does tha think tha going?' came the old man's voice over her shoulder.

She gasped. Her legs, seizing with fear, gave way, and she sank to the floor.

CHAPTER 31
REVENGE

Where do you think you're going?' a voice repeated. But the accent was different this time. The voice was that of a younger man. Wonderfully familiar.

'Josh?' Her voice trembled tentatively. 'Is that you?' she said into the darkness.

The voice laughed impishly. And Di recalled the time she and Bella had run from the woods back home only to bump into two shadowy figures demanding, '*Where do you think you're going?*'

It had been Josh and Andy mucking about then, and if they were again, she was going to give him such a talking to.

'Josh? Josh?' she said frantically.

She was about to call out again when the candle miraculously reignited itself and Di flinched at the shadows resuming their dance around the walls.

And there was Josh. But not standing there laughing, having a joke. He was in the cage now, hanging from the ceiling. His flesh was rotting and that damned crow was perched on his head poking out his eye.

'NO!' Di screamed, her body wanting to propel itself

forward to save her son and flee from the cottage all at once. The result of these fiercely opposing forces was stasis.

'Diane?' Dorothea moaned and Di saw that the commode has been overturned and Dorothea was face down on the floor.

When she looked back to her son, there was nothing there. Just the wallpaper peeling from the wall as there had always been. She was first filled with relief, then followed by anger at being toyed with like this by these awful entities.

'Leave my family alone!' she cried out.

'Leave *my* family alone!' the old man's voice bawled in her ear.

There was a knock on the cottage door then, and Di reached for the handle desperately needing rescue for them both. The moment she gripped it she smelt her own flesh burning. The handle was red hot. She yelped and fell to the floor again as the knocking continued.

'Tha don't mess with my family and get to tell th' tale,' the old man's disembodied voice raged, as the photos of Queen Elizabeth and Churchill unhooked themselves from the wall and frisbeed across the room at Di's head. She ducked and they smashed on the door, raining glass on her.

Di snaked along the floor to Dorothea and covered both their heads as old ornaments from the mantlepiece were flung about the room and the mountains of papers on the table top began to swirl like a blizzard, the edges making paper cuts in Di's hands. The old chair Di had been sitting on took off rocket-like and shattered on the ceiling, and Dorothea's over-turned commode span about the place spraying any content still in the bowl around the room. Di heard crockery smashing in the kitchen, electric cables whipping at the air. She looked up through the stinging snow storm of paper and saw a shimmering pale blue globe hovering in the kitchen doorway, just like the one she had seen in her bedroom with Susan when she was young. Her heart collapsed into her guts. Please. No! Not again. Was someone else close to her about to die?

She couldn't bear the thought. Or was it just this evil spirit toying with her yet again?

The globe mesmerised her as it glided slowly into the room, quelling the maelstrom of paper as it went as a sun melted winter snow. The papers fell to the floor, and everything stopped crashing around. Di felt a bizarre sense of peace, almost contentment for a moment. The light it emitted was so welcome after the darkness and shadows of the last few minutes? Hours? For however long she had been in this room.

The sphere hung in the air and it neared Dorothea. Di could smell the same scent as before filling the room. Di hugged her neighbour close in some vain effort to protect her from it, although she had the distinct feeling that this was not itself an evil force. Then, without a sound, it sank to the carpet and disappeared into it like melting ice.

The room was silent, except for Di's heavy breathing and a whimpering from the old collie, with groans of pain from Dorothea. She looked around from her position on the floor, and felt that whatever had been here was gone. For now.

She turned to Dorothea. 'Are you OK?'

Dorothea moaned again, 'Brutus' she croaked.

Di quickly looked under the table and was surprised to see Brutus in the same position as usual looking at her with one eye open, whimpering a little as if he was irritated to have been disturbed by whatever had just happened. Di could have almost laughed at the sight, but when the knocking at the door came again, she jerked as if she had been defibrillated.

She got up and rushed over to the front door. As she went to grab the handle she felt the severe pain in her palm from her last attempt, so she pulled her sleeve down to provide some protection, but she was thankful to feel that the handle was cool metal as she opened the door this time.

'Everything all right?' Jeffrey asked. 'I thought she was just having one of her tantrums again, but this seemed to go on for a bit...'

'Oh, thank you, thank you!' Di said ushering Jeffrey inside. 'Can you help me?'

'Good God!' Jeffrey declared as he saw Dorothea prone.

Di righted the commode and grimaced as she saw and smelt that its contents were all over the carpet and Dorothea. 'We have to try to get her up.'

They both tried to shift her, but not only was she a *lump* as Jeffrey said, but she cried out in such pain that they backed off immediately.

'We should leave her,' Jeffrey said. 'We could be doing more harm than good.'

'I'll call an ambulance,' Di said looking for the phone.

'She really went for it this time, didn't she?' Jeffery sighed looking around the room.

Part of Di wanted to put him straight, but part of her was glad he seemed to have no idea what had really happened. When she found the phone, the line was dead and she felt sick with the thought that the poltergeists were responsible.

'Hasn't paid the bill again, has she?' Jeffery tutted. 'Don't worry, I'll call from my house.' And he hurried out, leaving Di cradling her neighbour and shouldering the heavy weight of guilt - that she was responsible for bringing all this carnage upon dear old Dorothea. She once again felt she was cursed. 'Now you know why I haven't bloody decorated since the sixties,' Dorothea croaked.

Di followed the ambulance to the hospital and had her burnt hand bandaged in A&E. Apart from the time she spent there, she stayed by Dorothea's side. She had had a number of x rays and then admitted to a ward.

It had taken all night before Dorothea was finally settled into a hospital bed. Di was afraid to return home, so has caught some sleep in an arm chair by her side. The next morning, after Dorothea had been made comfortable and had been administered more morphine for the pain, they had some time alone before her operation.

'You mean, this happened to you before?' Di asked, quietly glancing around the hospital ward to make sure no one was listening.

Hospitals made Di feel queasier than supermarkets did. She couldn't wait to get out of here, but she didn't want to leave Dorothea alone either.

'Well, not nearly so violently as last night, but…' Dorothea nodded. She didn't have the strength to say too much.

'I'm so sorry,' Di said gently squeezing her hand. 'It's all my fault.'

'No, no, don't be... It's *their* fault. These blasted poltergeists.' Dorothea winced.

'Are you OK? Should I get a doctor?'

Dorothea shook her head and they sat in silence for a moment. She had broken her hip in the fall, and Di had heard the doctor and nurses talking to each other as if this was a death sentence for the likes of Dorothea. Di was furious at David Hartley, whoever he was, and the spirits in attendance with him. She was angry with the witches conjuring them up, but she was most angry with herself.

'You'll be up and about in no time,' she lied.

'That's what I said to Alice when she was on her way out,' Dorothea smiled weakly.

Di dropped her eyes in shame and found herself looking hopelessly at the catheter tube coming out from the sheets to the bag on the side of the bed.

'We had some good times. Alice and I,' Dorothea whispered. 'We used to get the bus into town every Friday night and get absolutely sozzled. We would talk and laugh. Talk about the world and our dreams and our fears. Or just have a bloody good gossip.'

Di smiled at Dorothea's memories.

'And then we'd get the bus back to the village. And it doesn't go direct, you know. All around the bloody houses. So we'd both be dying for a pee halfway. The only thing to do was to ring the bell and the bus would stop. And we'd get off, pull down our drawers in the road in front of the bus and pee there, otherwise the driver would have driven off without us.'

Di was enchanted with the story. 'Really?' she squeaked, laughing.

Dorothea nodded with just her eyes, which sparkled with the memory. 'And there were a couple of occasions when we finally got to the village, we'd lose our way in the dark. We staggered past the farm where one of us ended up in the slurry pit.'

'Oh no!' Di said, both disgusted and amused.

'And whichever one was not covered in shit… or which- ever one was covered in less shit I should say, they would run a bath in the kitchen for the other.' Dorothea's eyes were moist with the memory. 'I will never forget the gentle touch of her hand. It was better than any booze I've ever had. And you know, I've had quite a lot,' she tittered. 'Her touch was the most intoxicating thing I have ever felt.' She gave out a deep, sad sigh. I'd give up everything, even the demon drink, to have her back with me. I'll be joining her soon enough though, and it will be a blessed relief.'

Di fought back the tears. 'Please don't say that. *We* would miss you', but Di knew it just wasn't the same thing at all.

Dorothea said, 'bless you, Di, that's very kind of you. Talking of booze. Be a good girl and bring me in some vodka next time, will you?'

'The doctors won't allow *that*!' Di said, feigning being

horrified, knowing Dorothea was trying to schmooze her. 'I'm sure you'll get better more quickly if you don't drink.'

Dorothea fixed Di with a look of profound earnestness. 'I won't survive this place at all if you don't bring me my *proper* medication.'

CHAPTER 32

TROUBLE IN TH'
LOCAL SHOP

B ack home, Di hid herself from the fine drizzle – the ghost of rain – and from the residents of Heptonstall under a large golfing umbrella. She stood in the graveyard of the ruined church staring down at one of the slabs there. She had retraced the steps she had taken on her wedding day, from the house she now struggled to call home - towards the church where not so long ago she married the man from whom she felt so distant from right now. And she had stopped here over the grave of David Hartley, which glistened in the rain giving it the appearance of being freshly laid.

David Hartley
1770

The slab was full of the details of other members of his family who were interred here with him – their death dates and ages, but David's own details were sparse and unclear. After many long grey minutes pondering the grave, Di spoke to him, hoping her words would find him beyond the grave.

'David, I ask with all my heart that you and your family would leave us in peace. God knows, I hope and pray we will all find it soon, she pleaded earnestly.'

She paused for a few moments, almost expecting him to answer, but all was quiet, apart from a single cawing from a crow somewhere nearby. She paused a minute longer, took a deep breath and walked on to the Victorian church graveyard, and once more found the grave of Sylvia Plath.

'No wonder you took your own life,' Di muttered. In her own misery, she could almost sense for herself the beautiful poet's loss and torment. But the epitaph beneath Sylvia's name, seemed to leap up and speak to her.

EVEN AMIDST FIERCE FLAMES
THE GOLDEN LOTUS CAN BE PLANTED

Di read this over and over, like a mantra. It flickered in her eyes and thoughts, and as it did so, a sense of hope slowly emerged in her beating chest.

The memory of the white-hot steel that was the source of so much excruciating pain meted out by the Cragg Vale Coiners to their hapless victims intruded into her thoughts. Yet, after enough repetition of the mantra, the unwelcome and horrifying thoughts began to subside as the beautiful notion of a lotus flower growing from the embers of such fire took hold. She took great courage from this, and then carried on her way across the grass and gravestones, up the cobbled lane out of the village to Slack Top Farm. The legend of the Phoenix rising from the ashes came to mind – and Di was fully determined that the spirits of the dead could and would be laid to rest in peace, come what may. She did not yet know how, but she would find a way.

· · ·

She had agonised all day over the idea of smuggling booze into the hospital for Dorothea, and when she finally decided that it was the right thing to do – partly because Dorothea had been so clear that it was her lifeline, and partly because Di couldn't have handled the look of disappointment -if not the expletives- that the old woman would throw her way if she didn't, but there was nowhere to buy it in the village, save for the farm shop at Slack Top. Di trudged her way up there once more.

The farm house was as black and forbidding as ever, so Di tried not to look at it and hurried to the shop behind the house in the farmyard. The light in the little latticed window was incongruously welcoming, but Di was under no illusions, as she knew the kind of reception the shopkeeper was going to give on occasion. Nevertheless she went inside through the stable door and the brass bell loudly announced her arrival – a surreptitious entrance was unfortunately out of the question. She headed straight for the counter – she didn't need anything else but the booze. As she did so, the shopkeeper slowly rose from behind it, as if the bell had summoned her from the bowels of the earth.

'What can I do tha for today?' she droned, glaring at Di through her cat-eye glasses.

'That bottle of vodka please,' Di said firmly, despite her unease, pointing behind the counter.

'Dotty Dorothea got you fetching and carrying fer 'er again, has she?'

Di wasn't in the mood for being sniped at. 'And what makes you think it's for her?'

'Well, it is, i'n't it?' the woman's red eyes bulged.

Di shrank a little, but muttered defiantly, 'I'll probably drink most of it.'

'Ah,' the shopkeeper's lips toyed with the idea of smiling. 'Trouble at 'ome?'

'Not really any of your business,' Di smiled away the affront. 'Now can I take the vodka please?'

'I wouldn't be happy living next t' 'er neither.'

'Look here,' Di snapped. 'Dorothea has fallen and broken her hip. She's in the hospital, which I'm surprised you didn't know, since you seem to find it so hard to keep your nose out of everyone else's business—'

Suddenly the brass bell rang loudly, making Di nearly jump out of her skin. Before she had time to turn around to see who had joined them, she jumped even more as the shop-keeper yelled, 'Get out!' The woman swelled with anger and her eyes bulged even more, if that were possible.

Di wilted, fearing she had gone too far and was concerned for Dorothea if she wasn't able to get the booze she came here for. 'I… I didn't mean to…'

'Get out o'my shop!' the woman said again - and now Di realised that those red rimmed eyes were not glaring at her, but over her head at someone behind.

Di turned, to see who it was.

It was Rick. He smiled at Di, and would have looked very handsome, if it hadn't been for his brown nicotine-stained teeth.

Di gripped her umbrella.

'Are tha deaf?' the shopkeeper screeched.

'Give me a moment!' Rick said to her. 'I don't want trou-ble.' Then he turned his gaze to Di. 'We need to talk, Di,' he said gruffly but softly.

Di's skin crawled. She was speechless. Her mouth was too dry to say anything.

The shopkeeper sighed heavily. 'Reight. Perhaps tha'll listen to this, then.'

There was a heavy clunk behind the counter and two loud clicks. When Rick's jaw dropped and he put his hands up defen-sively, Di turned again to the counter to see what had changed.

This crazed shopkeeper was wielding a huge shotgun. Di instinctively ducked and moved aside, but the gun was trained on Rick, not her.

'No need for that! Come on! I just need to talk t'incomer. Nowt to do wi' thee.'

''Course it's to do wimme, you fool.' She took aim.

'OK, OK!' Rick said loudly and quickly. 'I'm going. I'm going.' He backed off, tripping over a box of baked beans waiting to be emptied onto the shelves.

Despite her fear, Di was quite enjoying his misfortune, and felt a sense of power, standing next to this gun toting old woman, as Rick hurried out of the shop, with an 'OK, OK, you win. This time.' the bell clanged as if it were mocking him.

'They're trouble that lot,' she growled at Di without taking her eye from the gun's sight, as if she expected Rick to come back at any moment.

'That lot?' Di said.

'Him and his little gang. *You* know. But don't let 'em get to you,' she said putting the gun down at last. ''Ere! Come wi' me, I'll drive you home. No doubt they'll be loiterin' out there waiting for you.' She pulled a green Barbour over her pink housecoat.

Di was shocked at the sudden change in the woman's attitude. She seemed all mumsy and friendly now, and Di wasn't about to turn down her offer. The shopkeeper gently shooed Di from the shop and locked the door.

'This way!' she said, striding and splashing across the yard in her wellies to the Land Rover at the side of the house.

They drove down the road in silence, apart from the rough engine of the land rover and a strange humming coming from the old woman, which sounded more like a strangled cat. Di couldn't work out if it was a sound of contentment, or anticipation of more trouble. The shopkeeper threw the big vehicle around like a young racing driver. She rumbled through the village and turned down the lane to Di's house, barely slowing down to do so as she barrelled over the cobbles.

'There,' she said, slamming on the brakes and throwing Di forward.

'Thanks,' Di said. Regardless of the dubious driving, she really was grateful. 'Thank you so much.'

'Don't forget this!' she said pulling a bottle of vodka from her coat.

Di had indeed forgotten all about the booze in the midst of the drama. 'Oh, yes. Yes of course.' She shook her head. 'Thanks for that too,' she said fishing in her pocket for her purse.

'Don't worry about it. On th' house.'

'No,' Di protested.

But the shopkeeper insisted. 'A present for you and Dotty. Tell her I'm sorry to hear about 'er accident. No one wished for *that* t'appen.'

Di studied the woman's face. Her turn of phrase made Di wonder what she *had* wished to happen, but she responded to the thawing in the woman's icy exterior. 'OK. Thanks again. And… I'm sorry, I didn't catch your name. I'm Di,' she said holding out her hand.

'Jenny,' the woman said shaking the proffered hand with hers, which felt strikingly hairy to Di. 'Jenny Hartley.'

Hartley.

Di released her grip and inhaled sharply.

'Hartley?' she said as calmly as she could. 'No relation of David Hartley by any chance, are you? The one who died in 1770. He's buried in the old church yard. Do you know anything about—?'

The woman's maternal demeanour disappeared as quickly as it had arrived. 'Time for you to go.' She said darkly, and her eyes flashed yellow and menacingly in the light from the dashboard. It sounded like a threat.

'But… I…' Di began.

'Get. Out. Of. My. Car!'

The woman was clearly unhinged. Blowing hot and cold in extremes. Before she whipped out another weapon from somewhere, Di thought it best to do as she was told and she jumped down from the vehicle, slamming the door firmly and hurrying inside.

CHAPTER 33

THE CRAGG VALE COINERS

Dorothea perked up no end when Di slipped the small bottle of vodka beneath her hospital sheets.

'OOOO! You are good to me,' she smiled and her eyes lit up.

'Don't let anyone know you've got it. I could get in a lot of trouble,' Di said unable to suppress her smile too.

'Well, get us both a cup of tea then!' Dorothea winked.

And so Di did just that and she surreptitiously made the usual cocktail for her friend.

'I nearly got my head blown off getting that for you, you know,' Di said with a degree of histrionics, partly to entertain her elderly friend.

'Oh, goodness, how so?' Dorothea said supping zealously on her drink.

'Turns out the shopkeeper at Slack Top Farm is a Hartley.'

'Jenny?'

Di nodded. 'Did you know?'

Dorothea shook her head. 'No. Strange to say, I never knew her surname.'

'She must be related to David.'

'A great, great, great, great granddaughter or something perhaps?'

'She wasn't at all happy when I asked her about him. In fact she went pretty bonkers. But she seems to have a problem with the Wiccans too. Rick came into the shop and she pulled a shotgun on him.'

'Really?' Dorothea was enthralled at this.

'Hence, me thinking I was about to get my head blown off.'

Dorothea, swilling her tea around her mouth, swallowed and said, 'Is it any wonder she has a problem with the Wiccans, if she knows they're conjuring up her dead ancestors? I mean, would you want someone digging up your relative's spirits, so to speak? She said this without a hint of irony, which was not lost on Di.

As Di drove home she felt a little lighter, knowing that Dorothea seemed to be getting a bit better, or at least she was not in as much pain. She got stuck for a mile or so behind a bus in town, and she smiled as it reminded her of Dorothea and Alice getting off to squat for a pee in front of a bus back in the day. As she drove through Heptonstall, she passed the lane next to The Cross Inn, which led to Northgate Farm where she spotted the slurry pit near the junction. This might be where the couple had had some unfortunate accidents in their time. She smiled again at the thought of a much younger and fitter Dorothea, in 'companionship' as it was then described, with her alive, yet simultaneously she felt a pang of grief on her friend's behalf for the life and the love she had lost.

When she parked the car she saw that the lights were on at home, and her heart started galloping. She'd been so preoccupied with Dorothea this week that she had almost forgotten what day it was.

'You're back,' she said bursting with relief as she saw Mike slumped on the sofa watching TV.

'I am,' he smiled. 'You sound surprised.'

'I am. Pleasantly surprised,' she added and threw herself next to him, wrapping herself around him. 'I missed you so much.'

'Me too. I was disappointed when I arrived and you weren't here.'

She sighed. 'Sorry. I was at the hospital.'

'Hospital?' Mike sat up. 'What's wrong with your hand?' he said looking at her bandage. In the wars again?

'No, no. Well, yes, I have hurt myself. But I was visiting Dorothea.'

'Dotty Dorothea?'

Di nodded.

'Why? What's wrong with her?'

Di took the remote control from the coffee table and turned down the volume on the TV a little so she didn't have to raise her voice. 'She fell and broke her hip.'

Mike winced. 'Ouch, that's terrible. Especially at her age.'

'Yes. Indeed. And I'm afraid I'm to blame… sort of.'

'Why?' Mike frowned.

'Well,' Di sighed, 'I went to see if she knew anything about the voices and the things I'd been seeing in the house.' She felt Mike shrink from her a little, but she crashed on. 'And so we did a kind of séance thing.'

Mike said nothing. His face hardened.

'And it worked, Mike, it really worked. The place went wild. Things flying about the room. Horrific apparitions - and that old man. Something to do with the Hartley family. Whatever Len and his cronies have conjured up, it's not happy at all. Look!' She pulled aside the bandage and showed him the singed skin on her palm which had now crusted over. 'They made the front door handle turn red hot - and they threw Dorothea off her commode, poor woman. That's how she broke her hip.'

She stopped for breath and looked at Mike. He was

chewing his lip, his eyes closed as if he was considering something of great importance. Then he huffed loudly.

'Mike, are you listening?'

'Are you serious - why are you talking like this?' He shook his head.

'Do you think I'm making it up? Ask Dorothea for God's sake. Come with me to the hospital tomorrow and ask her what happened. She'll tell you. I'm not... why would I?' Di was desperate for Mike to believe her.

Mike picked up the remote, turned the TV back up again, slumped back onto the sofa and folded his arms, locking Di out.

'Don't do this, Mike! Talk to me! I'm not insane. Nor was Sylvia Plath,' she blurted.

Mike threw her a quick questioning frown, clearly wondering what Sylvia Plath had to do with anything, and then returned to scowling at the TV.

She knew how she sounded. But she couldn't let it go. 'Come with me to see Dorothea tomorrow morning. Please, Mike.'

'Rachel's coming tomorrow morning. Remember? Your daughter?' Mike grumbled.

Di felt her face flush with guilt. With all that had happened, she had forgotten.

'But you feel free to go and see your Mystic Meg. It's probably safer if I look after Rachel anyway.'

If this was designed to hurt her, it did. Di hurried upstairs and locked herself in the bathroom, opening the taps to full so the thundering water would hide her sobbing. She slept in Rachel's bedroom that night. She couldn't bear to be around Mike if he refused to be supportive, if he insisted in treating her like a pariah.

When Rachel arrived the next day, Di had a full program of activities devised so she could take her daughter out of the house and away from him and the village all day.

'Are you coming?' Rachel asked Mike as they put on their shoes and Charlie scampered around them, excited at the prospect of a walk.

Mike looked to Di for the answer.

'No,' she said, 'Mike can't come. He has to…..do some things around the house.'

Mike grumbled something under his breath and went back to stacking the dishwasher.

'What was that?' Di said in his ear.

'We'll talk when you get back,' he muttered.

'Oh, we'll talk, will we?' Di huffed. 'That would make a nice change.'

Charlie whimpered and went back to her bed when she realised she wasn't going anywhere.

Di and Rachel went to Haworth, a village very much like Heptonstall, but much more touristy, courtesy of the Bronte sisters. They visited the Brontë Parsonage and Rachel was enchanted by the costumes the women wore in the nineteenth century, while Di was distracted by exhibits about *Wuthering Heights* and the madness of Catherine.

'Was it madness?' Di said to herself. 'Or just the label men attributed to the women they don't understand?'

In the afternoon upon their return, they stopped at a museum within an old mill, between the villages of Mytholm-royd and Hebden Bridge. Di wanted to show Rachel the exhibits about the history of the woollen industry which was once the mainstay of the area.

'Look, Mum!' Rachel said tugging Di towards the first exhibit, which read:

Until the nineteenth century Hebden Bridge was much smaller and more insignificant than Heptonstall.

'It must have been tiny,' Rachel beamed, 'to be smaller than our village.'

They read on:

Whereas Heptonstall had been a flourishing cloth-making centre for centuries, Hebden Bridge was little more than a bridging point over Hebden Water for packhorses en route to Heptonstall via the Buttress (an incredibly steep stone-paved track). But following the industrial revolution, everything changed. Hebden Bridge expanded rapidly and the Calder Valley became a hub for large water-powered and steam-powered textile factories.

Di was pleased that Rachel was enthralled by local history. After they had absorbed all they could from this exhibit, they went onto the next, which was about Ted Hughes. Di didn't loiter here, annoyed that it didn't tell the whole truth about the poet's 'tormented wife,' - at least according to Robert.

The next exhibit that caught Rachel's eye displayed a life-size waxworks of men in eighteenth century garb apparently embroiled in a fight.

'What are they doing, Mum?' Rachel asked.

'Well, let's read and find out,' Di smiled.

In Cragg Vale in the eighteenth century, most people eked out a bare living by weaving cloth in their little cottages or keeping a few animals to produce milk, butter or eggs to keep themselves fed and alive. Some men sold their labour on farms and in mills, working in appalling conditions and for incredibly long hours. For some it became too much, and so a gang of them got together, determined to improve their lot by counterfeiting gold coins. Their leader was David Hartley.

Di felt faint. She grabbed the railing in front of the exhibit.

'Mum?' Rachel said, noticing her mother's pallor.

'Keep reading,' Di said plastering on a smile.

The gang operated with the connivance of local publicans who took genuine gold coins out of circulation and gave them to Hartley's men. The coins were then clipped or filed so that some of the gold was sheared off making the coins marginally smaller but unnoticeable to the naked eye. The clippings were carefully accumulated and melted down to make new gold coins which were passed back to

226

the publicans to put back into circulation. The counterfeiters' activities were so effective that they came close to wrecking the British economy.

William Dighton, an excise officer, was appointed to investigate the matter, and one of the coiners, James Broadbent, betrayed the gang and informed Dighton of their activities.

Di was transported back Dorothea's cottage and the hanged corpse which had called out *'Jim! Jim! How could tha? How could tha do this to me?'*

'Jim. James. James Broadbent,' she whispered as Rachel read on:

David Hartley was hanged in April 1770 and his body was buried in an old graveyard in Heptonstall. He was forty years old.

She read on; it seems that he had been sentenced to death at the York Assizes, hanged by the neck, and then placed in a cage for the crows to gorge upon.

Di had no doubt now that the middle-aged man hanging in the cage in Dorothea's living room was David Hartley.

Hartley's brother Isaac offered £100 to anyone who could kill Dighton, and the excise officer was soon ambushed and shot in the head. Isaac also made sure that any informers were rounded up and murdered for their betrayal, often in the basement of local pubs. The tortures he designed for them involved flaming coals and inserting red hot pokers into their rear ends.

Di examined the waxworks again. The scene made perfect sense now. She was trembling as she took in a life size visual of the horrific soundscape she had heard in the basement of her own house.

Isaac Hartley was never brought to trial due to lack of evidence. He died an old man of 78 in 1815, one of the few principals among the Cragg Vale Coiners to escape the hand of justice.

'The old man,' Di whispered. 'It's Isaac.'

She recalled how he had bawled at her to leave his family alone, and she had a bizarre pang of sympathy for this man that must have seen his own brother hanged in such a horrific way. Perhaps that explained Isaac's terrible violence to those who informed on his brother and his accomplices.

'Mum, look!' Rachel was saying. 'That's why we have ridges on the edges of coins these days so you can tell if the edges have been shaved off.'

'Ha!' Di said distractedly. 'I never knew that.'

CHAPTER 34

THE FURTHER VISITATION

Mike wasn't in when they came home. There was no sign of him, and no note saying where he might be.

After Rachel went to bed, Di sat on the sofa with the TV on in the background for company, mulling over the things she'd discovered that day in the museum. She wondered if the Wiccans were even aware of who they had conjured up, and the pain and torment the Hartleys had brought on themselves and others. She eyed the dining table and imagined the cellar beneath the hole in the floor. She recalled how publicans were an instrumental cog in the machine for the Cragg Vale Coiners, and how Isaac had used the cellars of pubs to carry out his murders.

Goose Barn.

Of course, she said. This used to be a pub. This house, Dorothea's, even Jeffrey's. All part of The Goose Inn, as the estate agent had told them on that very first time they had ever heard about this place. Why hadn't they done more research? Even the surveyor's report had not reported on the well or the old room below. He obviously hadn't been told about it and the cellar room wasn't on the plans of the house either. Everyone had been fooled by Len's dishonesty about having it blocked up.

The phone rang and she jumped. After composing herself, she went across to the telephone table and answered it.

'Hello?'

'Darling, it's Ollie. I'm at the pub. Just checking you were in. We're bringing Mike back. He's somewhat tipsy, I'm afraid.'

'Oh,' Di said, relieved he was OK. 'No problem. But when you say tipsy…?'

'I mean pissed as a fart, darling. See you in a mo.' And he hung up.

And indeed he was. Babbling incoherently and hanging off Stephen and Ollie as they stumbled through the door.

'Sorry, Di,' Stephen said rather red faced. 'We were having a quiet drink and he came in looking a bit lonely, so we invited him over to play dominos with us. Before long we were more than a few rounds in.' Ollie joined in, 'by this time he was professing his undying love for us.'

'Good lads, they are,' Mike slurred. 'Good boys. Got the right idea they have.'

'And what's that, Mikey?' Ollie said grinning, with a twinkle in his eye.

'Being with a bloke. Not a woman. Too much trouble.'

'Ooh,' Ollie grinned. 'We might have a convert here.'

'Shush!' Stephen said and apologised to Di yet again. 'Where do you want him?'

'Upstairs if you don't mind,' Di sighed.

Stephen nodded, 'Come on, Mike. Up to bed.'

'No, no. Sofa,' Mike grumbled.

'No, no. Bed!' Ollie insisted and used his powerful arms to hoist Mike up the stairs, with Stephen flapping about a few stairs below ready to catch them if they fell backwards.

When Mike was safely on the bed and Ollie and Stephen had left, Di took off Mike's shoes and undid his belt, as he went on yet again about gay people having the *right idea*. She knew it was designed to wind her up. It didn't.

'It wasn't that long ago you were fretting about going to dinner with a couple of gays and getting offended at lesbians kissing in the woods,' Di reminded him, as she whipped his trousers off somewhat roughly. 'How things change!'

She threw the trousers on a chair and a pocket full of coins came tumbling onto the floor. She huffed and went to pick them up, examining the ridges on the edge of each of them. She thought about David and Isaac Hartley. She thought about Dorothea and the poltergeists. She thought about the pale blue sphere in her attic bedroom when she was young, reappearing twice since they moved here. She thought about the twenty odd years she'd spent immersed in a world of evidence and proof.

'Yes. How things change,' she whispered, crawling into bed beside her husband.

Her eyes snapped open at 02:22, according to the alarm clock beside the bed. She peered into the darkness of the room, and to her abject horror she saw a familiar shape standing there. She could see once again the heavy dark coat with the collar turned up, and the large hat with a wide brim. Somehow, he seemed to have become more opaque than he was previously, more real. This tall, dark shadow glided noiselessly across the room towards her. Once again, it stopped and turned at the foot of the bed, then sat down.

Di's skin crawled, ice cold, but this time she felt slightly less afraid, and angrier than she expected. Yet still she was paralysed, as once again, the overpowering sense of evil was palpable. She felt the mattress tilt as the figure sat on the end of the bed. She could sense it shift and spread itself along her body. She felt the dead weight of it as it lay itself upon her. She felt again that awful sense of darkness and revulsion.

This time she prayed as if she were casting a spell of her own, visualising the light from Dorothea's black candles as she did so.

Within less than a minute, the weight lifted and the figure was gone, simply disappearing into thin air.

She lay there stock still, hardly daring to breathe - as an effigy on a tomb, frozen, before the silence was rent by a heaving gasp, and Mike's body convulsed. 'Arghh!' he cried out.

'Mike? Mike, are you OK?' Di asked urgently.

He sat bolt upright. Eyes so wide, she could see the whites glinting in what little light seeped around the blinds. His breathing was fast and loud.

'Did you see it too?' she asked.

He slammed on the bedside light and looked at her with real fear in his eyes.

'A man in a heavy coat and a wide brimmed hat. He lay on you, didn't he? You felt it.'

'How do you know?' Mike said, his eyes darting around the room. 'It was a dream, wasn't it?'

'No it wasn't - and don't lie to yourself Mike. I wasn't asleep, and nor were you.'

'I was pissed,' he said rubbing at his eyes. 'My mind was…' He couldn't articulate.

'Well I wasn't drunk. And I saw and felt the same thing as you.'

He took a deep breath and then let it out as if it were a lungful of smoke. 'That felt so *real*. It was horrible. I couldn't breathe, it was actually lying on top of me. I could feel it.'

'That's because it *was* real, Mike. This is what I've been trying to tell you. I think that was one of the Hartleys - I think it was probably David or Isaac Hartley's spirit.'

'Who?'

Di donned on her dressing gown and made them both a hot milky chocolate, partly so that Mike could clear his befuddled mind. They sat side by side in bed, sipping the comforting drink, as she told him everything she had learnt at the museum. Mike's brow furrowed creating crags so deep in his forehead that she never thought possible. His lips moved as he mouthed unintelligible things to himself, and his eyes darted around the room distractedly. Then, without warning, he plonked his cup on his bedside table, jumped out of bed and out of the room.

'Mike? Mike, what are you doing?'

Di followed him downstairs and immediately the lights started flickering. When they reached the landing Mike stopped at looked up at the bulbs in the ceiling. And then he looked at Di as if he was waiting for her to say, 'Told you so.'

Despite her concern for Mike, she said nothing as he darted down the next set of stairs to the living room, where he threw the suitcases of books from the dining table and yanked it across the floor, dragging the rug with it until the glass panel was exposed.

Di was afraid, but also strangely exhilarated at the possibility that Mike was starting to understand. But she was afraid of what he might awaken. He opened the panel and turned on the light which began to flicker like the rest of the lights throughout the house, so he went to the kitchen and grabbed the torch from the drawer.

'Be careful!' Di whispered. 'Use the handles!' she said urgently pointing them out in the side of the well.

Still without a word he lowered himself carefully down into the cellar. Di heard his feet thud on the stone flagged floor below, though he landed with more grace than she had. She peered down into the well, but the strobing effect of the lights started up again and the flickering left her feeling nauseous.

'Mike?' she hissed.

Nothing.

For a minute. Maybe more.

233

Then, 'Jesus Christ,' he breathed.

She heard the chains and handcuffs rattle against the ground. He must have found them. They must have really been there. She heard the rods clanging. And then the screams came. Roaring through the basement and up the well like an icy wind that went straight through her.

This time, Mike heard it all. 'Fuck!' he yelled and suddenly his hands were grabbing at the handles in the well, struggling to get a grip - because his palms were covered in blood. They kept slipping, and he would disappear into the darkness again, while the terrible screams as before kept on and on.

'Mike! Mike!' Di said lying prone on the living room floor and hanging her head and arms into the well. 'Grab me!'

His hands shot up from the darkness again and this time he managed to get a grip on Di. 'I've got you,' she called out, but in those unusually lucid moments that come in times of utter catastrophe, she knew deep down that those hands were not the hands of her husband. He had caressed her and held her so many times before, she would know his touch anywhere. Yet she couldn't suppress her instinct to yank on those hands and save whoever was attached to them.

The trouble was, no one was attached to them. And to her utmost revulsion, Di found herself holding nothing but the charred appendages of a body that had been consumed by fire.

CHAPTER 35
DESPERATION SETS IN

Di let out a blood curdling scream at the sight of the charred hands and dropped them back into the well. She felt sick to her stomach.

'Mike!' she called out wrestling with her instinct to run away and her desire to help him.

'Jesus!' The expletive had never sounded so devout in Mike's mouth, as his hands grabbed at the handles again and then reached out above the well. 'Di?'

After a millisecond's hesitation whilst she examined those hands for authenticity, she grabbed at them and helped Mike out. She closed the panel after him, and they both pulled the rug and dining table back over it, holding onto it as if it were a lifeboat in a raging storm.

Silence reigned again. Only the sound of their heaving breaths was heard, as they looked at each other across the table. Mike was very shocked and was shaking.

After what seemed like an age, Mike hissed angrily, 'You think Len is responsible for this?'

Di nodded. 'Yes I do. And Terry and Fiona, and Rick and Big Will.'

She watched as Mike examined his own hands, now free

of blood. He was completely bemused. Then, Di watched as his jaw tightened defiantly. 'Right!' he said slapping his hands on the table. 'Get dressed! We're going to sort this out.'

Up in the bedroom, although she was throwing on her clothes as quickly as Mike, she was urging him to think twice before rushing around to Terry and Fiona's house. 'They're dangerous. Look what they've done already! Shouldn't we go to the police?' she said weakly, knowing the answer.

'And what would the police say?' Mike replied. 'They'd lock us up as loonies.'

And so, a minute later Mike was hurrying downstairs with Di hot on his heels.

'What about Rachel?' Di hissed in a last-ditch attempt to get out of going witch hunting tonight. Mike stopped on the landing and looked at her. 'We can't leave her here on her own,' she whispered.

Mike thought for a moment, then said, 'You stay with her. I'll be fine.' And he marched off.

Di stood there helpless for a moment, caught between a rock and a hard place. Every maternal bone in her body told her to stay and watch over her daughter, yet her head told her that Mike would be more vulnerable, if he were faced on his own with the necromancers he was now looking to challenge. She recalled how calm and collected, how fearless Rachel had been after Isaac had dragged her out of bed, and that was when she knew she had to go after Mike.

A moment later, she was on Church Street where Mike was already pounding on the door of Terry and Fi's cottage.

'Come out! I know you're in there,' he shouted.

Di watched as lights came on in other cottages in the street. Her own concern not to make a scene at this time worried her, but she could not leave Mike in this state.

The front door of the cottage next door was yanked open and an elderly man, whose face looked as stony as the millstone grit his house was made from, barked, 'Do you mind? It's the middle of the bloody night.'

'No I don't mind,' Mike said ready for a fight.

'Well, you're wasting your time,' the man said. 'They're away for the weekend.'

Mike suddenly stopped beating down the door and looked embarrassed. 'Oh.'

The neighbour closed his door muttering something about incomers. Di and Mike stood on the doorstep for a moment wondering what to do now.

Eventually Mike grumbled, 'Where does Len live?'

'I don't know.'

'Big Will? Rick?'

Di shrugged. 'And we're not going to find out at this hour, are we?' she said eyeing the curtains that were twitching in nearby cottages. 'We'll ask around in the morning.' She put her arm around Mike, knowing first-hand how bemused, frightened and angry he must be. 'Let's get back to Rachel and try and get some sleep,' she said leading him back to Goose Yard. But he ground to a halt before the house, and he looked at it with great apprehension.

'It'll be OK,' Di said feeling much braver and greatly relieved now that she had Mike on her side. 'We'll look after each other, right?'

He examined the house for a long moment more, then nodded and they went inside.

More than once that night, Di woke up to find Mike standing by the skylight looking frantically out into the gloom. Each time, she had to close the blind and coax him back to bed as he swore to her that someone had been watching them through the window.

They both woke late in the morning, feeling more tired than when they had gone to bed, but they put on a show of normality for Rachel, who was none the wiser about last night's antics. Whilst Mike made her breakfast, Di called Ollie and Stephen.

'We were wondering if you wouldn't mind looking after Rachel for an hour or two this morning,' Di said down the phone.

'Well, darling, usually I'd run a mile where children are concerned, but seeing as it's Rachel, and of course she's adorable, that's absolutely fine darling,' Ollie said.

Di explained as much as she felt was appropriate to Rachel, who was more than enthusiastic at the idea of spending time with Ollie and Stephen. They got on famously, in spite of the couple's pretended dislike of 'ankle-biters', as they often referred to them.

'Everything, all right?' Stephen mouthed to Di when he answered the door and Rachel hurried inside to find Ollie.

'Yeah… no… yes… I mean….' Di listened to Ollie and Rachel chatting animatedly in the kitchen, then thought it safe to add, 'Well, we're having some issues with the house and we need to track down Len. You don't happen to know where he lives these days, do you?'

Di noticed a cloud pass over Stephen's face. 'What issues with the house? Something we can help with?'

'Erm…' Di stuttered. 'I mean… no, we really need to talk to Len. It's difficult to explain, but let's just say we're not happy with him, or the house at all.'

'Oh,' Stephen looked a little nervous to Di now, but it could have just been her cagey words making him uncomfortable. 'Well, actually, I think we might have an address for him. Why don't you come in and I'll see if I can dig it out.'

'Great,' Di said stepping inside.

'Go through to the kitchen,' Stephen smiled a little too broadly. 'Ollie would love to see you.' As Di started to go through, he stopped her with a question that seemed a little incongruous. 'Where's Mike?'

'At home,' she stated, then felt the need to add, 'waiting for me to get back, so we can go out.'

'Ah,' Stephen said, ushering her through to the kitchen.

'There she is!' Ollie jumped up from the kitchen table where he'd been reading a magazine with Rachel, and threw his muscular arms around Di. 'How's it going, darling?'

'Not bad,' she sighed.

'Oh dear.' Ollie pouted. 'That's doesn't sound good,' he pulled her away a little to look into her eyes closely, concern etched on his face.

Di threw a glance at Rachel. 'No, no, I didn't mean… I'm really good actually.'

'Oh! You Brits,' Ollie flapped his hands at her. 'Everything's always *not bad*, *can't complain*. So unemotional. So on the fence, as you say. Smile, laugh, party, for God's sake! Or scream with rage! Either way, let it all out, won't you.'

Di laughed with Ollie, but her smile quickly faded as she heard Stephen muttering in the living room and she realised he was on the phone. 'Right *now*,' she heard him say urgently as her eyes met Ollie's, and he seemed to be watching her like a hawk.

'What are you reading?' she said to Rachel, in a bid to break the awkwardness of the moment.

'She's been reading about your namesake, Princess Di,' Ollie cut in, plonking himself back down next to Rachel. 'Terrible accident that happened to her, don't you think? A real tragedy.'

'Some are saying it wasn't an accident,' Di said looking over his shoulder at the double page spread.

'You don't believe in all that conspiracy stuff, do you?' Ollie said absorbed in the pictures of the princess looking dazzling.

'You'd be surprised what I believe,' Di muttered wryly as Stephen poked his head around the door.

'Babe?' he said to Ollie.

Ollie looked up and Stephen gave his partner a coded look.

'Ooh!' Ollie said jumping up. 'Come on, Rachel! I got something *amazing* to show you in the garden.' And before Di even registered what was happening they were gone and Stephen was crossing the kitchen, locking the back door behind them.

He saw Di frown at the action and he said with genuine remorse, 'Sorry, my darling.'

Di had no idea what this meant, but her body seemed to guess, and it flooded itself with adrenaline. She took a few quick steps back to the living room, then she saw Big Will filling the front door frame like a boulder in front of a tomb.

She turned back into the kitchen and called out, 'Rachel!' but she was silenced by Stephen raising his finger.

'Darling. No need to worry her. She's quite safe.'

'What the fu… What *is* this?' Di said glaring at Stephen.

There was a knock on the back door. Di could see through the frosted glass that it wasn't Ollie or Rachel. Stephen unlocked the door and Di prepared to run through it, until she felt the huge weight of Big Will's hand on her shoulder and she could do nothing but watch as Stephen let Len inside.

'At last,' Len said through his red beard, as a fox might having cornered a hen.

CHAPTER 36
REVELATIONS

D i could barely control her own legs as Big Will steered her into the living room and sat her down on the sofa. Her heart was racing, her eyes were like saucers, her mouth a desert.

Big Will plonked himself next to her and Len pulled an armchair across the room, so he could sit directly opposite her. He leaned in so close she could smell his breath, a cocktail of stale beer and his roll-ups.

'Get the lass some watter!' Len bellowed to Stephen, who hurried off to the kitchen. 'Must have been a trying time for yer, ey?' he smiled.

She glared back.

Stephen brought the drink promptly, and as he held out the glass to her she swatted it away in anger and it fell to the carpet spilling its contents.

'What do you want?' Di said, hating the way her voice sounded so frail.

Len opened his mouth to speak, but was stopped by a knock on the door. 'Jesus,' he huffed as Stephen let Rick in. 'Better late than never!' he growled.

'Sorry,' Rick stropped as he loitered by the door. 'I came as quick as I could.'

'The lass is out of her mind with worry,' Len tutted. 'Time is of the essence 'ere.'

'Well, go on then!' Rick said, shifting about on the door mat.

'I will!' Len said.

'Good,' Rick snapped back.

'Boys, boys!' Stephen chided them.

Len cleared his throat and looked with his piercing blue eyes into Di's. 'We hear from Roslyn from Tod that you…' Di was surprised to see him blush. 'That you might have seen us in the woods… ritualising.'

'Is that what you call it?' Di sneered.

'Yes, but you might have got wrong end o'stick, lass.'

'Oh, and how did I do that?' Di said with a brave sarcasm. 'A bloody voodoo doll of me hanging in the trees - and you lot conjuring up the Hartleys to scare me off. Why did you even sell the house if you didn't want anyone else to live there, you bloody fool? Do you know what you've done? What you've unleashed? And how you've potentially damaged my relationship with my new husband?

'No, no, Diane, *we* h'ant done anythin',' Rick piped up.

'Yeah,' Len glared at him, 'and that's th' bloody problem.'

'Well, it's not *my* fault,' Rick grumbled.

'Isn't it?' Len said. 'If you were as committed to this as th' rest of us, we meight 'a' been strong enough t'achieve our goal.'

'Don't worry,' Di said. 'You can have your bloody house back. We'll be moving out at the first opportunity. Now let me and my daughter go. If I'm not home in five minutes, Mike'll come looking for me and then you'll be in trouble.'

Big Will let out a little derisive laugh and Di realised that, despite his masculinity, Mike would have a real struggle against this lot.

'We don't want yer to move out, my good lady,' Len said. 'We want yer ter stay.'

Di cocked her head, incredulous.

'It's Isaac and th' rest we're tryin' to get rid of. We're tryin' ter keep yer safe.' Len could see Di was bemused, so he elaborated. 'It's not a voodoo doll, what you saw in th'trees. It's called a poppet.'

It was a bizarrely benign sounding name to Di, so it caught her attention, and she focused on the explanations more keenly than she had before.

'A poppet is…' Len seemed to struggle to explain it, but he did his best.

'Lass,' he began, 'it's just an effigy of a person who in't there with th' Wiccans. It is a substitute fer a person. It's fer a wish, er a prayer, or a spell if yer like, ter focus on th' poppet so that th' person receives the blessin's or protection that th' Wiccans want to bestow on it. It's called Sympathetic Magic. It's based on th' principle of like attracting like. It's a bit scientific yer know – particles in the universe can affect each other, 'owever far apart they are. It sounds a bit far-fetched, tha knows, but people have been usin' such magic for thousands of years. We were tryin' to keep th' spirits away from you, not 'urt you.' He looked across as Stephen, who nodded in agreement. If Stephen hadn't done so, Di might not have believed it. She still wasn't wholly convinced, but she could feel her certainty quaking. 'Then why not just tell me what you were doing from day one? And why has this load of nonsense not done anything whatsoever to help so far? In fact, it's probably even made things much worse!'

'We all thought you were a city type. A barrister. A very clever wuman,' Len said. 'We thought yed think we were bonkers. We thought we'd o' scared you.'

'Ha! More than screaming disembodied and rotting spirits, and the ghosts of men that torture them?' Di scoffed.

'Well,' Len blushed again, 'we thought we'd 'av it sorted

before it got that out o'hand. That's why I told you I'd blocked up th' cellar. I didn't think you'd be going down there, snoopin'.'

'Snooping?' Di snapped. 'It's my bloody house. I should be able to go where I want in it. I should be able to feel *safe* in my own home.'

'That's what th' missus said,' Len said mournfully, looking at his hands.

Di glared at him. 'So this was going on before we lived there? Is this why you sold up?'

'It's what drove Glenda away.'

'Right - *and* her bloody toyboy,' Big Will muttered.

'Yeah, well,' Len explained, 'she wasn't too 'appy with all th' goins on in th' house, so when he came along it were th' perfect excuse fer 'er to get out.'

'So you just thought you'd offload the house onto some other poor sods, like us?' Di said tearfully.

'No.' Len put his hand on her arm, but she pulled away. 'Actually, I weren't sure if I had disturbed somat when I started doin' th' renovations. That's when Big Will 'ere told me we should talk to Terry and Fi, coz they know all about Wiccan stuff and that. And they trained us up, like. Recruited us, the three of us,' he indicated to Big Will and Rick. 'We thought we were getting someweir on them nights in th' woods.'

Di blinked the memory out of her mind of them all dancing, virtually naked in the firelight, but as she did so she remembered something that made her doubt them again.

'You,' she said turning to Big Will. 'And Fiona. When you were dancing. You didn't seem to have any difficulty with it. Both of you. So is this,' she said gesturing to the stick by his side, 'just some front for…' She had no idea what it could possibly be a front for.

'No, pet,' Will said. 'It's just, like Len said, like, it's mighty powerful stuff when you get going. It fills you wi' an energy you've never had before. Call it magic, call it intoxication, call it mass hysteria if yer must, but in the moment, like, we feel reborn, leaping around like gazelles. Mind you, I bloody ache the next day, I can tell you.'

Rick sniggered like a naughty school boy. Len and Stephen shared a smile. And even Di felt one tugging at the corner of her mouth.

'So sorry about that,' she said to Stephen pointing to the glass she has swatted earlier and the wet patch on the carpet. 'Could I have another one please?'

CHAPTER 37
Hatching a Plan

'So what do we do now?' Mike said after Di had managed to calm him down. Just as she had predicted, he had come looking for her when she hadn't returned home. Rick had answered the door without thinking it through, and when Mike had seen Di surrounded by three of the witches, completely out of character for such a gentle man, he had lunged into Stephen's house and had Rick by the throat up against the wall instantly. If it wasn't for Big Will, Di doubted that Mike would have ever let go. The champion wrestler and sumo of a man had restrained Mike with a bear hug, while Di talked him down and explained as quickly as she could what Stephen and the Wiccans had explained to her.

'Where's Rachel?' Mike demanded, still quite suspicious of this rogue's gallery as he paced around the room.

'In the garden with Ollie,' Stephen had answered quickly. 'Come and look!' He'd led Mike through to the kitchen to prove she was safe. Di and Mike had watched her through the window putting a daisy chain on Ollie's head. For once the weather was warm and pleasant and it made a pretty scene. 'We didn't want to scare her.'

246

'Well, she bloody well has been scared getting dragged around the bedroom by her hair,' Mike had growled.

'They always go t'females in th'ouse first,' Len had sighed joining them in the kitchen. 'Females are more in tune wit' th'matters o' the spirit world.'

'Let me make you a cuppa,' Stephen offered, encouraging Mike to sit at the kitchen table.

Mike had asked for something a little stronger instead, and soon they were all sitting around the table, sipping on Jack Daniels.

'So what do we do now?'

'Well, Fiona knows best,' Len said, 'but me guts 'r' tellin' me we need to all go down to th' altar and try again.'

'What good will that do?' Mike asked. 'It hasn't worked so far.'

'Why aye man,' Big Will said, 'but now we have you lot for real. We don't have to rely on poppets anymore.'

'That's right,' Len said, 'If you come and do it with us, you two as well as Rachel, th' spells should be much mooer powerful.'

'No, no, no, you leave Rachel out if it,' Mike stated protectively. 'She can stay here with you and Ollie,' he said to Stephen. 'We're not dragging her into this. Messing with the occult in front of her, putting all sorts of weird thoughts in her head.' He looked to Di to second his motion, but she was surprisingly mute.

''Fraid she 'as to come,' Len said. 'She's part of this a'ready. She's part of that 'ome. And she's a girl. Like I said, females, especially young 'uns are more in touch with these things. And the mooer female energy we 'ave around that altar the better it'll be, trust me.'

Mike looked to his wife. 'Di?'

'I have a feeling she already knows more about these spirits than I do,' Di sighed. 'And she doesn't seem to be much disturbed by it all either.'

Mike scowled uncertainly.

'If it's going to help,' Di announced, 'then I would very reluctantly agree for her to come. But it's her choice at the end of the day. If she says no, then that's it.'

The Wiccans agreed with Di's assertion, and they all looked out of the kitchen window as she went down the garden to talk to Rachel. When they saw Rachel nod without hesitation, they all let out a whoop.

'Fine,' Mike grumbled as Di came back inside with Ollie and Rachel.

'That's settled then. We meet at the altar at midnight. Bring your crystals, lads!' Len said clapping his hands together decisively.

Mike raised an eyebrow. 'Your what?'

'Crystals. You bring some if you can an'all. Roslyn'll sell you the reight ones. Great for clearing th' negative energy and creatin' a feelin' o' peace. Kyanite, selenite, obsidian, hematite and desert rose are th' best. I keep a piece of kyanite on me windowsill under the full moon to charge it up every month. Ask Roslyn. She should have some ready to go.' Len turned to Rick and Will and said, 'We should make an offering to the Great Goddess too. Something more significant this time. We need 'er onside.'

The two men nodded and promptly left the house.

'See you later then,' Len said, heading after them.

'Hang on!' Mike said.

'Aye?'

'Um…' Mike stuttered. 'W-w-we… um… we don't have to do this naked, do we?'

Len fixed him with his twinkly eyes for a while, then said, 'You do…'

Mike wilted.

But Len hadn't finished. 'You do whatever you feel comfortable doing, lad. A' right?' he winked. 'We're Wiccans, not nutters.'

CHAPTER 38

THE BLOODY RITUAL

D i and Rachel spent the remainder of the day, which predictably had turned grey and wet, at home with Charlie on the sofa, watching family movies and eating unhealthy snacks, while Mike went to the Black Cauldron with a short list shopping for crystals. Di wanted to make Rachel as relaxed as possible, trying to distract her from the imminent nocturnal events – although, Di might have needed the distraction a lot more than Rachel. But she remained as calm and enigmatic as ever, except for the moment when she sat up and looked at the dining table.

'What is it?' Di asked gently.

'I feel like they know,' Rachel said in a matter-of-factly.

'Who? What?'

'Isaac and David if that's their names. They know what we're going to do tonight. And I also somehow feel that someone's going to try and stop us.'

'Someone?' Di asked, trying to sound as calm as Rachel. 'Not him?'

Rachel shook her head. 'Someone still *alive*.'

'Do you know who?' Di pressed.

But Rachel shrugged, 'No, I don't really know for certain,

Mum, sorry. I just *sense* it'. She slumped back on the sofa immersing herself in *Beauty and the Beast* as if she had been talking about the weather.

Di woke Rachel up at 11:30pm. She had fallen asleep on the sofa, and Di was glad that her daughter had more than a few hours of sleep. She wished she had had some too, but she was far too apprehensive to rest. After coming back from Roslyn's shop with three simple necklaces threaded with beads of kyanite that shimmered in the light like a peacock's tail, Mike had a simple supper grazing on cheese and biscuits and several pickled onions, after which he then dozed off in the armchair. But now he was wide awake, putting on his hiking boots and zipping himself into a warm jacket.

'Not going naked then?' Di said feeling the need for some gallows humour.

'No,' Mike said. 'I thought I'd give it a miss. You?'

'Not me!' Di smiled.

Rachel sniggered as she put on her coat and Charlie jumped up and down, hoping she was going out too.

'No, Charlie, you're staying here.' Charlie, tail between her legs, walked back moodily and slumped into her basket.

'Bugger.'

'What?'

'The torch.'

'Where is it?'

Mike looked with dismay at the dining table. 'I dropped it down there when…'

'Oh,' Di said, knowing neither of them had any intention of going down there now, or probably ever again.

So, in their walking boots and wrapped up in their anoraks, and with nothing but the half-moon to light their way, they set off, Mike with walking stick in hand. And, although the grown-ups tried their best to look calm for their young charge, the scudding clouds of condensation coming from their mouths in the cool night air, betrayed just how nervous they both were.

Before they entered the wood, Mike stopped and looked at his watch. 'It's not twelve yet. Are we too early?'

Di could forgive him if this was an attempt at procrastination, but she couldn't help but say, 'Can you be too early for the exorcism of evil spirits from your home?'

'Mmm,' Mike conceded with a crooked smile and into the woods they went.

'I don't think they *are* completely evil,' Rachel said as they all trod carefully over the dank ground.

'What was that, darling?' Di asked.

'The spirits. They're not really bad and evil. I don't think. Just sad and angry.'

Di and Mike looked at each other for a moment, marvelling at the wisdom of this child.

'Out of the mouth of babes,' Di muttered.

Mike smiled. 'I hope you're right, Rach,' he said. 'But even so, we have to help them leave our home, don't we? Otherwise we can't stay there with all that going on.'

Rachel nodded her understanding, and they carried on towards the sound of gently running water.

The river was an opalescent carpet, leading them through the forest toward the bridge. As they neared the location of the altar, there was no sign of any of the Wiccans. Di helped Rachel down the muddy bank as Mike lingered at the top, looking around.

'Told you we were too early,' he whispered.

'Oh God,' came Di's voice from the riverside. 'Mike! Mike!'

Mike launched himself down the bank as he heard Rachel begin to cry. At the bottom he saw Di smothering Rachel's face in her coat to stop her from seeing the altar. But she had clearly seen it already.

'Get her out of here!' she said, handing her to Mike.

'What is it?' Mike said taking Rachel by the hand and focusing on the altar under the tree where the moonlight fell on Brutus, Dorothea's dog. He was hung by the neck, his legs splayed out, his paws nailed to the boughs and his belly sliced open so his guts cascaded slowly over the altar top. 'Oh, no, poor Brutus!' The last time she had seen Brutus was when earlier that day she had popped round next door to feed him and take him for a short walk with Charlie into the nearby field. Whoever had done this must have broken into Dorothea's house to steal him.

'Sick bastards,' Di hissed, her eyes full of tears.

'Who would do this?' Mike said.

'Do you remember there was mention earlier of an offering?' Di recalled.

'What?' Mike said.

Di ushered Rachel up the bank as she elaborated. 'The last thing Len told Big Will and Rick to do was make an offering to the Great Goddess. Something more significant, he said.'

'Yeah?' Mike said. Then, as the implication dawned on him, 'No way. What fucked up shit is this? *They* did this? After all they said to persuade us that they were on our side? He raged into the darkness. 'I knew this was too good to be true. They're fucking psychos the lot of them. We sucked up all their shit, and now they've got us to come to a dark forest in the middle of nowhere in the middle of the night. How stupid can we be!'

'Poor, poor Brutus,' sobbed Rachel. 'Dorothea will be so sad and lonely without him'

'Try not to think about that now Rachel,' Di said as calmly and reassuringly as she could. As the three of them sat in silence gathering their thoughts, when a sudden howl echoed through the woods.

This was not the howl of an animal, but a human sounding like one. Di thought that she heard it once before;

the first time she had seen the coven of Wiccans dancing right here by the altar, when she had run for her life.

'Di! Mike! Doon here!' then as they didn't move, 'Quick, quick man, dee as yer telt afore it's too late!'

They turned to see Big Will brandishing something, the shape of a club, some kind of cudgel. But they didn't wait to find out exactly what it was. As Terry and Rick appeared from behind him, Mike and Di ran, pulling Rachel along with them. Rachel cried out, as Mike yanked her along but quickly disengaged herself.

'I can run myself,' she insisted and bolted off ahead of the parents.

'Wait for us!' Di shouted. 'Don't get lost! We have to stick together.'

'Eeee… Gerrem back 'ere!' Len's eternally exasperated voice was unmistakable to Di.

'It's not my fault,' she heard Rick shout back at him, his jarring tone indicating that he was running after them.

'Terry!' Len shouted.

'I'll catch up wi' 'em,' Terry called out and Di heard the sound of feet slapping the muddy ground in pursuit of her and her family.

Just as before, panic and darkness conspired to stop Di from finding her way back out of the wood.

'This way!' Mike yelled.

'NO!' Di insisted, looking up through the trees. 'There!' she said pointing to the spire of the Victorian church silhouetted against the moon. 'It's where we should have gone in the first place.'

Mike didn't argue, and the three of them headed towards the edge of the wood by Northgate Farm, but before they reached the relative safety of the farmer's fields they were arrested by that howl again, this time only meters away. They all skidded to a halt, and Mike pushed Di and Rachel down to the ground where they could see without being seen.

As they peered over the dark dry-stone wall, they spied a bonfire burning in a clearing, with a tall thin figure dancing manically around it. It might have been the colours that the flames cast, but to Di everything about the figure seemed red. Red hair, red eyes, red coat, but it was the glasses that did it. The red cat-eye shaped glasses which glinted in the fire light.

'Bloody hell. It's Jenny Hartley,' Di whispered.

'Who?' Mike asked.

'You know - from Slack Top Farm shop.'

The shopkeeper raved at the moon. The howling coming from her, although at this proximity, to Di, it sounded more like the unearthly scream of a fighting tom cat.

'Come! ……Come! ……' Jenny wailed at the sky. 'Come back to meeeeee! Don't leave me here alone. Come home to me, my family!'

'Let's keep going,' Mike whispered, though he was rooted to the spot by the grotesque sight of the woman wobbling awkwardly around the fire, holding up her hands which appeared to be dripping with blood. However, he was only rooted to the spot until she turned in their direction. She appeared to spot them snooping at her crazed antics.

'Yooooo! ' she maniacally screamed.

Di knew that look. Those bulging eyes had done the same thing in the shop when she had pulled out her shotgun. However, once again, she was mistaken. Jenny's glare was, in fact, trained over the top of the trio's heads at Rick who had come up behind them.

When Di saw Rick with Terry hot on his heels, she urged them all to run, hoping Jenny's animosity toward the Wiccans would keep them all occupied, while Di and her family headed as fast as they could to the church. But in their haste, they all crashed through the tree line and leapt over a railing into what they assumed was a field.

But they were not where they thought they were. It was a stinking slurry pit! It had not been seen previously, as it was hidden with a sheet of tarpaulin behind the wall. They had all landed on top of the tarpaulin, but their combined weight had caused it to collapse. The muck underneath was warm with effervescent rotting cow dung from the farm, from goodness knows how many years of dairy and meat farming.

At the moment she fell into the pit, Di thought she heard Jenny howl and Rick and Terry shout, but it was difficult to tell, as she and Mike and Rachel all cried out, finding themselves chest deep in the primeval soup of revolting animal faecal matter. Di grabbed at Rachel, who was short enough to be fully submerged in the sludge. The stench was overwhelming, and they all gasped for breath whilst at the same time trying to keep their mouths right shut.

'It's OK, it's OK,' Mike said, gagging and retching. 'Take my hand!'

Rachel clung to Di's neck, as her mum clasped the hand of her husband and he led them to the edge of the pit. They waded slowly through the mire, and Di once again had the unwelcome sensation of being in a nightmare - of trying to run but her legs were unable move fast enough. They heard Jenny shrieking, 'Stop them! Stop them! Help me, Isaac! David!'

'Gerr off, you mad bitch!' Rick's voice yelled from the woods.

'Help me, Isaac! David! I need you. NOW!' Jenny Hartley's voice screeched.

And then, almost as if in response to her invocation, the bog around Di's feet began to bubble. She felt some kind of debris bumping at her legs as it floated up from the depths. She looked down, squinting in the gloom, and when it finally broke the surface she saw to her horror in the fleeting moonlight, the withered remains of somebody.

Somebodies.

Skulls and bones broke the surface around them, the skulls grinning horribly in the gloom, some still with putrid flesh hanging from them, some even with ragged clothes stuck to their wet rotting forms. All just floated there inanimate, as if the slurry pit had been made on the site of a burial ground in times past.

Robert's words flashed through Di's mind as she thrashed about to escape this shoal of the dead, as she tried not to retch in revulsion.

'They are lying here beneath our feet. There's so many buried 'ere, they are piled up five or six deep.' But these were not bodies buried in the churchyard, in consecrated ground. So who in hell were they? Di did not have time to think beyond this.

Rachel tucked her head in her mother's chest as Mike and Di beat their way to some railings on the far side of the pit and pulled themselves out. When they all collapsed onto the grass on the other side of the railings, they heard Jenny scream hysterically as if in terrible pain over and over again, just like the tortured soul had in the basement of Goose Barn. It propelled Di and Mike back to their feet. Di saw Terry crash through the tree line and stop himself on the railings of the slurry pit.

'Di!' Terry bellowed. Or was that, 'Die!'?

She didn't wait to find out. Mike scooped up Rachel and they ran on down the lane back to Church Street where they slipped and stumbled over the wet cobbles to the ruins of St Thomas à Becket. Through the graveyard they hurried toward the Victorian church.

'This way!' Di said as Mike headed for the church door.

'Where are you going?' Mike was confused, clearly assuming they were seeking sanctuary from evil on hallowed ground, in the manner of a classic horror movie.

'The vicarage,' Di said impatiently.

She led the way to the vicar's residence and hammered on the door. There were no lights on, which wasn't surprising for midnight; the vicar was no doubt asleep, so she hammered some more, until the bedroom window above their heads illuminated. It felt like a lighthouse in a storm to Di.

She opened the letter box and called out, 'Reverend Sykes. Reverend Sykes! Please help us, oh please God help us!'

She saw the slippered feet of the old vicar descending the stairs and so she snapped the letterbox shut and straightened up. After a lock or two had been undone, the door opened. The vicar looked as austere and drawn as he had on the day he had married Mike and Di, but in their current state of agitation, his presence made them both take a step back, as his white gaunt face resembled one of the corpses they had just encountered in the slurry pit.

'What on earth is the matter?' he asked trying to sound compassionate and authoritarian at the same time, but mostly sounding annoyed at being woken abruptly. He then saw the horrible mess they were in. 'Dear God, what happened to you?' he said taking in both their filthy appearance and awful rancid smell of rotting cow dung.

'We're so sorry to wake you, but this is an *emergency*,' Di said glancing over her shoulder to make sure none of the Wiccans had caught up with them. 'Can you come to our house now? Please? We are being plagued by evil…' she looked at Rachel. '…*angry* spirits. People have been hurt. We genuinely fear for our safety. Our house needs exorcising. Can you do it, please, please?' She begged.

The vicar stammered for a moment, his mouth opening and shutting soundlessly.

'It really cannot wait. I am really really sorry to disturb you, but you have to come NOW!' Di grabbed at his dressing gown. 'It's just across the other side of Church Street, in Goose Yard, behind Goose Fold -.you know, Goose Barn, remember?'

'Yes, yes, all right, but I must dress.'

'There's no time for that!' Di insisted, not letting go of his robe.

257

'Well, I can't do an exorcism without a crucifix and some holy water. Let me bring those at least,' he said whipping his dressing gown from Di's muck-laden hand.

'Hurry please!' she said as the poor Reverend lumbered back inside. Di looked over her shoulder again, then at Mike. He was speechless, bemused. He knew how to deal with aggressors in the physical world, but in the realm they were dealing with now, Di could see he felt somewhat impotent and out of his depth, but she had to try. She put a reassuring hand on his arm and one on Rachel's shoulder. Rachel just blinked up at her as if she was waking from a deep sleep.

The vicar then emerged, with a cassock over his pyjamas and a large silver crucifix over his head. In his hand he held a plastic four-litre milk container, stuck with a white label over the Tesco sign with HOLY WATER printed on it in comic sans font. It wasn't quite the ornate chalice Di expected in which such a liquid should be contained, but she didn't really have time to quibble over such minor details. If it was good enough for the vicar then it was good enough for her.

They rushed around to the house, the Vicar keeping up, despite his age, on his long crane-like legs. There saw no sign of Jenny or the Wiccans.

When they came into the yard, to their horror it looked as though a disco without the usual beat of music was carrying on inside. The lights were flickering on and off - and the voices of the tortured and torturing were audible from inside.

'Charlie!' Rachel cried as she heard the little dog barking, whining and frantically scratching from inside the front door.

'Dear God,' muttered Reverend Sykes, as he tightened his grip on the milk container.

Mike went to the door and unlocked it. He looked back at Di and she nodded. When he opened the door, it was almost ripped from his grasp. He had to hold it firmly to stop it from being smashed against the wall. It was as if a hurricane was blowing from inside.

'Come inside!' the vicar shouted.

Di and Mike were not sure if their presence was needed for the exorcism, or if the vicar just wanted some company, but they did as they were told and went in with Rachel.

Charlie rushed out of the house and was instantly by Rachel's side barking at the house protectively. They all trooped in cautiously. Mike closed the door behind him to stop the glass from being smashed to pieces. Di, her fingers gripping Rachel's shoulders, spotted the glass panel in the floor clearly, as the dining table had been shoved across the room, the rug thrown into the corner and the light beneath it pulsated like a heartbeat.

'There!' Di shouted over the roar of the wind and the screams. 'That seems to be the source of it.'

The vicar opened his bottle and began sprinkling the holy water from side to side as he slowly approached the panel, reciting incantations and calling upon God the Father, Jesus and the Holy Spirit for protection. As he did so, the light beneath it began to pulsate faster and faster, not unlike Di's own heart. And when the first drops of Reverend Sykes's holy water touched the glass panel, it shot up into the room with a loud explosion, shattering into a million pieces and showering them all, leaving many tiny bloody lacerations in their exposed faces. Di had pulled Rachel to her and covered her head with her arms.

The vicar had covered his own balding pate with his hand, which was now bleeding. When the raining glass had ceased falling, he declared, '*In the name of God the Father, Jesus Christ His Son and The Power of The Holy Spirit, and by the blessings of Michael the Archangel, the Blessed Apostles Peter and Paul and all the Saints, and powerful in the holy authority of our ministry, we confidently command and repulse the acts and deceits of the devil and his dark angels cohorts.*'

The clanging of metal from within the basement was frantic, and Di recognised the voice of Isaac cursing profusely as the vicar went on.

'God arises; his enemies are scattered and those who hate Him flee before Him. As smoke is driven away so are they driven; as wax melts before the fire, so shall the wicked perish at the presence of God.'

Di watched in awe as he stood over the well and threw handfuls of holy water into it. The screams coming from below were more blood curdling than ever, as if his water burnt more ferociously than the hot pokers in the bowels of the Hartleys' enemies.

'In the name of Jesus, we drive you from us, whoever you may be…We command you to leave this place and go back to whence you came!'

Yes, yes, thought Di, *we drive you from us.*

'Unclean spirits, all satanic powers, all infernal invaders, all wicked legions, assemblies and sects,' the Vicar roared. *'You do not belong here. Go back to whence you came!'* he repeated the command authoritatively.

And the room fell silent.

The lights remained on.

Even Charlie was quiet, though shivering in fear between Mike's legs. Rachel peeped out of her mother's arm pit with one eye.

Di looked at the Vicar looming over the hole, and she was reminded of the image of Len, the very first time they had left this house after the initial viewing. Back then, light had been beaming up from the glass-covered well, and from the yard Di had seen the silhouette of Len standing over it, looking down into the depths below. Listening. Waiting.

'Mum?' Rachel's voice, squeaked. 'Are they gone?'

'Reverend?' Di asked.

The vicar looked over his shoulder at her and smiled, just as a pair of blood-soaked hands swiftly darted from the well, grabbed his ankles and yanked him into the basement.

CHAPTER 39

A FIGHT TO THE DEATH

The roaring of wind, of once-human voices and Charlie's barking filled the house once again, as the vicar was pulled into the depths of the house, cracking his delicate cheek on the living room floor as he was toppled.

Rachel let out a yelp and Di pulled her close. Rachel instinctively buried her head in her mother's shoulder and moaned, 'Oh, not again, PLEASE!'

'Reverend!' Mike called out into the depths of the well.

There was no answer from the vicar and they all knew he wasn't going to come out again of his own accord. Mike jumped down into the well. Di cried out 'No!'

Mike found the vicar lying white faced on the stone flagged floor. He checked his pulse, he was alive, thank God, just knocked unconscious, but he had no time at present to call an ambulance, so he would have to lie there for now. In any event it would take some hefty guys and a stretcher to lift him out. He found the metal handles easily this time and heaved himself back into the living room to join Di's side.

The bottle of holy water was glugging its contents onto the

floor in a puddle where it had landed inches from the edge of the well. Mike looked at Di, then at the plastic milk container.

'Mike?' Di shouted against the storm, concerned for his safety.

Mike steeled himself, then went to retrieve the container.

He had only made one step across the room, when Di felt a large bulky presence behind, which lumbered past her and enveloped Mike.

'No!' Di yelled as Big Will wrestled Mike to the floor. Mike yelled as Big Will shouted in his ear, 'stop ya shooting and bawling man!' Len snaked his arm around Di's shoulder. 'Get off me!' she screamed, but he held her in a vice-like grip.

Charlie didn't know which intruder to go for first, and so only succeeded in running in a circle between Big Will and Len.

Mike put up a valiant struggle, but Big Will had to do nothing but be 'Big Will' and he just lay on top of Mike restricting his movement.

'I'll kill you,' Mike spluttered with what little breath he could take from the air. To which Big Will responded, 'na point in bein in a gan propa radge, calm doon man.'

Terry was there too, and so was Rick. Di watched help-lessly as they poured something around the floor from the jerry cans they had brought.

Then Fiona suddenly appeared, taking Rachel away from her. Di called out to her, but a strong, mysterious howling wind came from nowhere and carried her voice away. She was transfixed to the spot, and could only watch as Fi, her hands on Rachel's trembling shoulders, seemed to give her instructions. Rachel nodded, looking more relaxed with every moment. Fiona delved in a small cloth shoulder bag and her fingers emerged covered in some kind of soot. She smeared it on her cheeks and offered the bag to Rachel. Rachel did the same and with a nod from Fi, she brought the bag over to her mother.

'It's OK, Mum,' she shouted. 'Do what I do.'

She held the bag up to Di and urged her to smear her face with the ash too. Di studied her daughter for an infinite second, and saw in her face an utter faith in the people Di had been convinced were out to destroy her.

'They're here to help,' Rachel said. 'It was Jenny that killed Brutus.'

And with no better alternative, Di was persuaded by the serenity of Rachel's expression. She jabbed her fingers into the bag and put on her war paint. The smell was unmistakable to any half decent cook. It was Sage. Fiona then lit some dried bundles of the herb and handed one to each of them. The little family trio copied the initiated, as they started to walk around the well, in a circle, waving the sage smudge sticks so that the smoke started to fill the room. When they had completed a full turn, they threw their smoking sage into the hole. There came a deep throated growl from beneath their feet, which grew louder and louder. Rachel covered her ears, and Charlie whimpered in the farthest corner she could find.

Fiona, Len, Rick and Terry started bellowing in unison against the tempest, '*I beseech the Great Goddess of the universe to bless this home and fill it with light and love. Negativity and darkness are not welcome here. This is a positive sanctuary.*'

'Tha must say it with us! All of you,' Len cried out at a bewildered Mike and Di.

'*I beseech the Great Goddess and all the powers of the universe to bless this home and fill it with light and love. Negativity and darkness are not welcome here. This is a positive sanctuary,*' the Wiccans chanted as they encircled the well again, Rick, Terry and Will who had at last released Mike, emptying their jerry cans into it.

Rachel joined in now. '*I beseech the universe to bless this home and fill it with light and love. Negativity and darkness are not welcome here. This is a positive sanctuary.*'

She took Di's hand and led her toward the circle. As Di

crunched across the floor she looked down and realised that Terry and Rick had poured salt mixed with dried sage everywhere. She looked at Mike. He had been freed by Big Will but was mute with shock, as if he couldn't quite contemplate what was going in in his own living room.

'I beseech the Great Goddess and all the powers of the universe to bless this home and fill it with light and love. Negativity and darkness are not welcome here. This is a positive sanctuary.'

'Say it, Mike! It's OK. Say it with us!' she called out trying to look as calm as her daughter.

Big Will released him from his grip with a gesture that told him Di was right; he didn't need to fear the Wiccans now. The men both got to their feet and slowly, like the new boy in school trying to pick up the words to the Lord's Prayer from the older kids, Mike gradually joined in.

'I… verse to bless… and fill it with light and love … are not welcome here …is a … sanctuary. I… the universe to bless this home and fill it with light and love. Negativity and darkness are not welcome here. This is a positive sanctuary.'

Over and over the eight of them chanted, gathering in a circle around the well which sent lewd and vile curses spewing upwards in a blast furnace wind, trying to drive them back. Big Will went to the door and brought what Di recognised as the cudgels she'd seen him carrying in the woods. But in the flickering light of the living room now, she saw they were bottles of wine and cider, which he offered up to the Great Goddess, just as Len had told him to.

Fiona led a change in the chanting now. *'So it is said, so it shall be.'*

'So it is said, so it shall be,' they all said taking each other's hands.

Di felt something akin to electricity flowing through them all, but not in a shocking way; it was more of a pulse, massaging, soothing, empowering.

'So it is said, so it shall be,' she said with more conviction

than she had ever said anything in her life. 'So it is said, so it shall be,' she cried out.

'*So it is said, so it shall be!*' they all roared the chant together. The sheer power of positive energy was overwhelming.

And at this, it seemed as if every window in the house exploded outwards. A tsunami of air and wailing erupted from the basement, rushing like an inverted waterfall over the eight humans and one dog, taking their breath away, before it hurled itself through every opening in the walls and out into the night.

Silence reigned for several minutes, as the Wiccans and the incomers looked to each other to confirm what they hoped to be true. Even Charlie was silent. She raised her little head hopefully and then gave out what sounded like a grateful little yelp. Rachel stirred first to run to her, eager to give her a comforting cuddle. 'Poor Charlie, you must have been so scared,' she cooed.

Gradually, one by one, upon witnessing the brave young girl giving cuddles and reassurance to the little dog, the adults flinched, recovering slowly from what they had just encountered. They then heard an old man's voice coming from the yard.

'Good God!' Jeffrey exclaimed entering the house through the front door and gingerly picking his way through the broken glass, examining the carnage. 'Not again! 'What's been happening here? And I thought Dorothea was a noisy messy neighbour!'

'Is anyone there? Can someone help me?' The vicar's trembling voice was heard from the depths. 'Oh heavens, I forgot all about him. It's Reverend Sykes. We're coming, hang on!' They all scrambled towards the hole in the floor to help out the poor vicar. Di turned to Jeffrey and said, 'Call an ambulance again please Jeffrey. Then let's just get out of here.'

A gruff Geordie voice piped up, 'Is everybody areet? I'm

proper paggered an' in sore need of a snout - an' atter all this, I'm clamming fer some bait'. To this, everyone laughed in spite of the horrors they had just endured.

CHAPTER 40
PEACE REIGNS

A nd you trust them?' Dorothea said, tapping Di's hand companionably where it lay on her hospital bed as she gulped down her usual cocktail.

Di nodded into her own virgin tea. 'Mmm,' she swallowed. 'Yes, the house has been perfect ever since. You can feel it. The whole atmosphere is completely different. They're gone. I'm sure of it. But we have been invited to stay with Stephen and Ollie until the house is sorted out. Nearly all the windows have to be replaced. Thankfully, the barn door remained intact.'

'And how's poor Reverend Sykes?' Dorothea grimaced expecting the worst.

'He's downstairs actually, in the ward below you. Doing pretty well. He took a nasty blow to his cheekbone and has suffered a concussion, but the doctors say he's going to be fine.'

Dorothea shook her head and took another gulp of her 'medicine'.

'And Jenny?'

Di's face clouded over. 'She's not doing so well. In actual

fact, I'm sorry to tell you that she died that night. It was horrible.'

'Oh no. How?'

'Rick and Terry swear that when they left her she was still OK. Raving mad, but OK. Seems that she was the one who invoked Isaac and David all along. In fact, that's what she was doing when we stumbled upon her the night of the exorcism. Terry said she always had problems, mentally, I mean. Apparently, she was childless and was determined not to let the Hartley bloodline end with her. In her warped way she thought bringing back her ancestors would solve that issue and give her some companionship in her adage.'

'Poor deluded soul,' Dorothea muttered. 'But how did she die?'

'Her body was found the next day in that bonfire she'd made. Only a stump of her arms and her hands remained apparently.'

'Oh, good grief, how awful.' Dorothea shivered and took a large draught of her tea. 'And it was she who took the life of poor Brutus?'

Di nodded. 'Len is sure of it. I'm so sorry. I should have taken him next door with me to keep Charlie company. I should have looked after him better.'

'Don't be silly, my dear. He wouldn't have liked having that boisterous terrier around him. In any event, he was more incontinent than me! It wasn't your fault. Brutus's quality of life was pretty poor anyway, bless his canine soul. No sight, no smell, deaf as a post, arthritis in his back legs. Not much of a life for a dog. He *was* 16 years old and he had a jolly good life in his younger years. As long as he didn't suffer.'

Di shook her head to reassure her neighbour. She had carefully left out the details of Brutus's death for Dorothea's sake. 'But,' she said brightly changing the subject somewhat, 'I took the liberty of getting your front door fixed, and we've given the entire place a bit of a spruce up. I hope you don't mind.'

'Mind?' Dorothea sat up like a child receiving a birthday present. 'Why would I mind? Especially if the Hartley's have stopped making a pigsty of the place. Perhaps now I can keep it nice. But I will need a bit of help, especially now with this bloody hip. Not that I could do much before.'

'Don't worry about that. Jeffrey's been in touch with social services…'

'Oh, tell that interfering old queen to keep his nose out of my business!'

'They are going to send someone to give you a hand just a few hours a week. All the other days, me and the girls are going to help you out. It's the least we can do.'

'Oh, not more of your brood?' Dorothea frowned.

'Rachel and…'

'Hey, how're you doing old girl?'

Dorothea turned to see Di's be-gothed stepdaughter smiling at her, nursing a tea from the vending machine.

'…and Bella,' Di finished.

'Less of the old girl, cheeky madam,' Dorothea chided.

'Apologies Dot!' Bella chirped.

'It's Dorothea as you know full well,' she growled, 'and you better get that right if you think you're coming around to my house, you naughty young thing!'

'Sorry,' Bella said with a twinkle in her eye.

'She's come to live with us,' Di told Dorothea. 'She thinks it's the coolest place on the planet since…well, all the goings on. Don't you, darling?'

Bella grinned. 'Yeah, it is pretty wild.'

'Not that we're going to be messing with any *angry* spirits, are we?' Di said sternly to her before turning back to Dorothea. 'Fiona and Terry are teaching her the ways of Wicca. I thought it couldn't do any harm to have another generation trained up.'

Dorothea scowled at Bella, and it reminded Di of the way she had looked at her the first time they had met. That's what made her sure that Bella and Dorothea were going to be the best of friends, at least for the time they had left. Di knew from what the doctors had said, that tragically, the chances of poor Dorothea coming back to her little cottage were pretty negligible, and in her heart of hearts, Dorothea knew it too. In fact, whilst there, she had asked Di to draft her will. She had left all her worldly goods to an animal charity, as she had no close relatives. Not of the living variety anyway.

After she was discharged from the hospital, unfortunately, she had to be placed in a nursing home, as her hip was not healing well. She passed away a few weeks later, peacefully in her sleep to join her beloved Alice. She was greatly missed by her friends, - by Di and all her family, by Len and the rest of the Wiccans, and even by Jeffrey, who had no-one to exchange insults and banter with. In fact, surprisingly, he took it far worse than anyone else, and very sadly, he too passed away within the year.

Meanwhile, they had all visited her and regaled her with gossip from the village, occasionally sneaking a bottle of vodka in for her to keep her merry.

'One for the road?' Dorothea said to Di, her face softening as she pulled out a bottle of vodka from beneath the sheets and topped up her NHS hospital green tea cup.

CHAPTER 41
FINALE

T he sun was shining in Heptonstall and the vastly expanded crowd of tourists were hanging upon every word of their skinny guide. He had mud brown hair tied back in a thick pony tail with a goatee beard. His eyes loomed large behind thick round wire-rimmed glasses, and he used a huge golfing umbrella which he used to point out what he thought might be of interest to the group. As always, he was explaining in his inimitable lyrical way his personal view of the history of Heptonstall. However, this time, with a few additional tweaks. He had already taken them to what was now the infamous slurry pit. It turned out, after some research, that the skeletons that had risen to the surface were the bodies of poor souls who had been buried there en masse in a hurry after they had died of a plague, sometime in the early 1800s. Since their re-discovery by Di, Mike and Rachel, they had been professionally removed and buried with proper respect and dignity in consecrated ground.

The tourists, now thoroughly intrigued, all followed their shepherd poet up the cobbled street, past The Cross Inn where he announced, 'There were as many as six pubs here in times gone by. Now only two remain,' and looking longingly at the Timothy Taylor sign and leading past The Cross, he muttered with a twinkle, 'I could murder a pint. See yer anon - just earnin' me beer money'.

But he didn't stop there. The end of his tour these days had taken a rather different turn as Robert led them off the main street into a cobbled courtyard. *Goose Barn* was written on the wooden double gate. He pushed one side of the gate open and strode inside as if it were for all the world a public right of way. He led the tourists down the cobbles to the wishing well in the middle of the yard. As the tourists assembled, he placed a small piece of bread, half an apple, now going a little brown round the edges, and a little lump of cheese on the floor by the well, as if they were an offering of some kind.

'Now this 'ouse,' he grinned salaciously as he stood up again. 'This 'ouse is the most ghostly of all o' 'em. Can tha 'ear me back there?'

The tourists all nodded keenly.

'Good. Se then, let me begin.' He fixed them all with those magnified eyes of his and commenced his tale. 'They war 'ouse huntin'. Or p'raps th'house war 'untin' them........'

Printed in Great Britain
by Amazon

18367867R00160